*The Hula M...*
*a short-lived*
*appearance to...*
*throwing the...*
*upscale Haei...*

EM WEN1...
Lillian was...
her tailbon...
covered on...
in all his se...
to a downr:...

Camer...
spray tan. F... tall honeycomb glass vase, gagged a couple of times, and hurled into it.

Wally spun around, his eyes wild. "Put that down! That's the Salvadori vase Fernando was given after his sold-out concert in Venice!"

He raced to the side table, spread his arms, and planted himself between the vase and Delacruz. Lillian managed to raise her head to see what was going on.

"Why, that vase looks just like the one I got at Pier One." Her head flopped back onto the pillow.

"Oh, my precious doodoo," Wally cried. "I'm sweating. My head is sweating, I kid you not."

Just then Leo Kekina hurried in from the direction of the kitchen. He glowered at Delacruz as the producer wiped his mouth on a cocktail napkin. Delacruz took one look at the security guard, crumpled the napkin, and tossed it toward the side table.

"Well? Are the police here yet? Did you find something?" he demanded.

"Found something all right. Found my Uncle Bass."

"Where was he? Sleeping it off on a *lanai* lounge?"

Leo shook his head. His expression made Em fear for Delacruz's life.

"I found him near the entrance to the driveway. The gates were still closed. He's *make*."

Delacruz glared at Leo. "Okay, so clue me in. What's ma-kay?"

"Dead."

# Other Books by Jill Marie Landis

## The Tiki Goddess Mysteries

Mai Tai One On

Two to Mango

Three To Get Lei'd

Too Hot Four Hula

Hawaii Five Uh-Oh

## Also by Jill Marie Landis

Glass Beach

# Hawaii Five Uh-Oh

Book 5 The Tiki Goddess Mysteries

by

# Jill Marie Landis

Bell Bridge Books

This is a work of fiction. Names, characters, places and incidents are either the products of the author's imagination or are used fictitiously. Any resemblance to actual persons (living or dead), events or locations is entirely coincidental.

Bell Bridge Books
PO BOX 300921
Memphis, TN 38130
Print ISBN: 978-1-61194-672-7

Bell Bridge Books is an Imprint of BelleBooks, Inc.

Copyright © 2016 by Jill Marie Landis

Published in the United States of America.

We at BelleBooks enjoy hearing from readers.
Visit our websites
BelleBooks.com
BellBridgeBooks.com
ImaJinnBooks.com

10 9 8 7 6 5 4 3 2 1

Cover design: Debra Dixon
Interior design: Hank Smith
Photo/Art credits:
Tiki god (manipulated) © Iuliia Poliudova | Dreamstime.com
Drink (manipulated) © Liusa | Dreamstime.com
Monkey (manipulated) © Dannyphoto80 | Dreamstime.com
Flowers © Alana290 | Dreamstime.com

:Lfhu:01:

# Dedication

To Silver Rose
*Mahalo* for the Title!

To Mel, Darcel, and Rita
You are missed.

# 1

"DID YOU HEAR? Kiki's out of the nuthouse."

Em Johnson, manager of her uncle's Tiki Goddess Bar on the North Shore of Kauai, closed her eyes and took a deep breath. She ignored the mile-long things-to-do list in her hand and turned to her second-in-command, Sophie Chin, who'd shared the startling news as she climbed out of her beat-up Honda.

"What did you say?" Em prayed she'd heard wrong.

"Kiki's out of the hospital." Sophie shrugged.

"Already? I can't believe it."

"Maybe she escaped."

"This is no time for jokes," Em said. "We've got a party starting in twenty minutes, and the last thing I need is for Kiki to show up."

The latest, and by far the biggest catering gig Em had ever booked, was about to begin. In a few minutes wealthy Hollywood A-listers would be mingling beneath a forty-by-eighty party tent on the vast lawn of Fernando's Hideaway, an estate located a couple of miles up the road from the Tiki Goddess in Haena.

"Nope, not kidding. For reals. Kiki's out."

"You don't *really* think she escaped?"

"If she did, she's not hiding. According to the coconut wireless, somebody saw her getting into her car outside the post office a couple of hours ago."

The coconut wireless was faster than high-speed Internet, but like the web, it wasn't always accurate. Her concentration completely blown, Em stared up at the central peak of the white open-sided tent and urged herself to keep it together. A few steps away, a mountainous stack of plastic bins recently emptied of serving utensils, water goblets, table settings, and catering supplies needed to be hauled out of sight.

*So much to do. So little time. Now this.*

Normally, the overly dramatic Kiki Godwin was problematic. A stark raving mad Kiki would be impossible to control.

"She surely won't want to perform tonight." Em stared at the bins again and absently added, "We've got to get this stuff loaded into the van."

Sophie picked up three bins. This week the twenty-three-year-old hipster's tinted, spiked hair sported neon pink tips. Twin rows of silver studs and rings pierced through one eyebrow kept most people from noticing her hair color.

"You know Kiki. Have you ever tried to stop her from doing what she wants?"

"Tonight I've got a thousand and one other things to worry about," Em said.

Even with day-glow pink hair and piercings, Sophie cleaned up well. Em envied her cocoa-colored skin and long limbs, not to mention her athletic figure. She was wearing a little black knit dress that clung to her like a second skin.

"You look great, Soph. Really sexy. I hope you'll be able to work with all the men who are bound to be hitting on you tonight," Em said.

"You don't have to worry. Not interested. I'm still in recovery from The Jerk."

Em didn't know The Jerk, just that he was the guy Sophie broke up with before she moved from Oahu to Kauai a couple years ago.

"I'll get someone to help me haul these bins out of here," Sophie said. "You'd better get cleaned up."

"I'll change and be good to go," Em promised.

Before either of them walked away they surveyed the sea of white tablecloths one more time. The starched linen corners luffed on the trade wind breeze. Wine glasses and water goblets glistened at each place. Low bowls full of tropical flowers were lined up and down the center of each table. Strategically placed tiki torches flickered around the outside perimeter of the tent and were scattered around the garden beyond. On the far wall, Buzzy, an old hippie who worked for Em part time, filled the ice bin below a folding table covered with tropical fabric and transformed into a bar.

"Kiki can't possibly be in shape to hula anyway," Em said.

The last time she'd visited the sixty-six-year-old at Kukuoloko, the local mental rehabilitation facility, Kiki had been anxious and jittery, constantly glancing over her shoulder and rubbing the bald spots on her scalp.

Sophie shrugged. "You know Kiki. She rebounds fast."

"She was in there what? Six weeks?" Em tried to recall.

Sophie thought for a moment. "Yep. To the day. Her insurance musta run out."

"Kiki's hard enough to handle when she's not unhinged. This is definitely *not* what we need tonight. This party is a really big deal for the Goddess."

Em had gone over her schedule, crossed off everything on her to-do list. Until a moment ago, she figured there'd be smooth sailing ahead. She had no contingency plan for the very real threat of the unhinged ringleader of the Hula Maidens showing up and losing it in the middle of the upscale event.

"Considering who the guest of honor is, this party is going to be attended by very, very wealthy mainland *malihini* and also all the part-timers who consider themselves local."

"Yeah, I know the kind. They're here for two weeks every year and want *kama'aina* discounts."

"If things go well tonight, we may get a lot of referrals."

"How about we call Kimo and have him tell Kiki to stay home?"

Kimo Godwin, Kiki's husband, had been the Goddess's chef for nearly twenty years. Not only was he talented, but he was as loyal to Em's Uncle Louie as the day was long. But even Kimo couldn't work miracles. Even now Kiki might be running loose while he was at the restaurant putting the final touches on the entrees soon to be loaded in a van and trucked up the road to the party.

"He's so sweet. Can you imagine him getting Kiki to do *anything*, let alone miss a performance? If she finds out the rest of the Maidens are dancing, there's no way she's not going to show up," Em said.

"They've managed without her leadership for six weeks."

"They definitely haven't been in any trouble since she's been away."

The Hula Maidens, a troupe of senior dancers, were still basking in notoriety due to a short-lived reality show featuring them dancing at the Tiki Goddess Bar. Their appearance tonight had been specially requested by the host, Wally Williams, who was throwing the party to welcome well-known film producer Cameron Delacruz to the upscale Haena neighborhood. Even before she heard Kiki was out of the hospital, Em had had her doubts about involving the Hula Maidens.

"Does that dance floor look uneven to you?" Em couldn't believe she hadn't noticed the tongue-in-groove faux parquet floor wasn't level. "Looks to me like it slopes downhill to the left."

Sophie studied the dance floor and tilted her head. "It's definitely not level. No time to move it. That's about the flattest spot on the lawn.

Besides, it's better the tables are level than the dance floor, don't you think?" She shrugged. "It's not that tilted."

"I guess." The imperfection still bothered Em.

"Don't look so worried," Sophie said. "You're gonna need major Botox to get rid of those frown lines after tonight."

Em pressed her fingers against her brow. Botox? She was only thirty-six.

"How can I not worry? The Maidens attract trouble the way dead fish draw flies."

Sophie looked Em up and down. "You'd better go change before the guests arrive. Where's your dress?"

"In the house. Wally told me to use one of the guest rooms."

Sophie glanced over her shoulder and laughed.

"*House?* Mansion is a better word. That hulk is as big as Macy's in Kukui Grove Center."

"Almost." Em finally smiled before she started jogging across the lawn toward the imposing modern home made mostly of marble, glass, and concrete. There were just enough wood elements and water features to soften the industrial big box quality of the place.

The entire side of the house that faced the garden was filled with sliding glass doors slid open to reveal an expansive kitchen. Em had hired a crew of four for the evening, two young women and two young men recommended by various Maidens and local patrons of the Goddess. She knew the food would be up to any island standard and beyond—the Goddess had been named "Best of Kauai" North Shore Restaurant every year for the past ten years even though service was sporadic at best. Impatient tourists often stormed out, not caring that the food was worth the wait. Nor did they forgive the occasional surliness of the staff when the bar was choked with regulars, and tables were hard to come by.

Em studied her cobbled-together crew. "Motley" was a polite description. In an effort to add a touch of professionalism, she'd asked them all to wear black knit shirts and long black pants. She gave in when they negotiated to wear rubber slippers—flip-flops, as mainlanders called them—instead of closed-toed shoes. The two young men, used to shorts, looked uncomfortable in long pants.

For a moment she hoped the entertainment would make up for the crew's lack of polish, but who was she kidding? Guests were probably expecting an upscale staff in white aprons along with a Polynesian review featuring exotic, sexy young dancers, not a bunch of old, mostly *haole* ladies in *muumuus* flapping their underarm waddles while they tried to stay in step.

"There you are!" Wally Williams, the estate owner, waved to Em. He rushed up to her as she stepped inside the house. "Is everything ready, darling?"

"We're good to go. The bar is all set up. The entrees should be here soon." Em scanned the kitchen. Two of the wait staff were filling pupu platters. "The waiters will circulate pupus as soon as the first guests arrive. I've asked them to be as unobtrusive as possible. The Tiki Tones are setting up on the dance floor. As you suggested, the Maidens are using the pool cabana as their dressing room." With any luck none of the old gals would land in the pool as they made their way to the portable dance floor.

"Did you book that handsome fire dancer? The detective? What's his name? Ryan?"

"Roland. No, unfortunately he's on duty tonight. I booked someone else."

"I hope this one looks as good all oiled up as Runyon."

"Roland. His name is Roland Sharpe."

"How do I look?" Wally executed an awkward pirouette. He was outfitted in a long-sleeved white shirt and white pants with an aqua cummerbund and matching aqua boa.

"Honestly?"

"Of course." His smile slowly deflated. "What?"

"The boa might be a bit much," she said.

"But . . ." His eyes teared up. His lower lip quivered. His right hand shook as he reached up and patted his lacquered bottle-blond hair. He ran his left hand down the boa. "This was one of Fernando's."

Em already guessed as much. Fernando, heir to Liberace's Vegas fame, had been Wally's partner until he'd been hit in the head with a rock and drowned in the koi pond at the front entrance of the house. Wally had inherited the pianist's billion-dollar estate, including the Kauai residence they'd named Fernando's Hideaway. Tonight was the first gala Wally had held here since the memorial celebration after Fernando's untimely death.

Em shivered despite the heat when she recalled they had also catered that fateful affair.

Wally continued to absently pet the aqua boa and stare into space.

"Ignore me," Em told him. "Go with the boa if it makes you happy."

"Why don't you like it?"

"You look hot."

"Hot as in good?" He was suddenly smiling. "Or as in sexy?"

"Oh." Em thought a second and lied. "As in good."

"Great, then I will wear it. Thanks."

"If you'll excuse me, Wally, I really have to change."

He went on as if she hadn't spoken. "Cameron will be here any minute. I told him to arrive twenty minutes before the others so I could give him a tour of the house."

"Hasn't he seen it yet?" Em said.

"He's been too busy moving into his own place. He has a few things tweaked and some painting done. He also installed fancy new security. Anyone as famous as Cameron can't be too careful."

Delacruz had recently purchased the compound that bordered the north side of Wally's property. After an ancient burial site had been discovered on the property, the previous owners had cut and run.

Em started to walk through the house with Wally trailing behind her, still going on about his new neighbor. "He has his own chef in LA. He's got an extensive art collection that includes Picasso, Warhol, and Jackson Pollock. He brought the Pollocks over here, and it's taken two weeks of working with a designer just to figure out where to hang and how to light the pieces."

"He must be planning on spending a lot of time on Kauai," Em mused.

"He told me he heard that people refer to *my* house as the bad karma house even though that old burial ground bordered both our properties. For heaven's sake, do people really think my house has bad karma?"

A man-made stream ran through Wally's huge living area and meandered out to an open-air atrium where it flowed beneath an arched bridge into a pond of exotic koi. The pond featured a faux waterfall, which unfortunately was exactly where Fernando's body had been found. His last act was floating face up surrounded by his pampered pet fish.

"I might have heard something about bad karma, but try not to let it upset you. I'm sure the name will wear off." She sighed. Time was slipping away.

He followed her into the guest room. For a minute she thought Wally was going to keep on chatting while she changed clothes, but just then, Sophie thankfully showed up.

"The guest of honor is here," Sophie said.

"Oh! Oh, my giddy aunt!" Wally ran off, flapping his boa. "Hurry, Em! I want you to meet Cameron before things get too hectic."

"Is everything ready?" Em asked Sophie.

"The Maidens are in the tent arguing over their lineup. It's verging on very ugly in there."

"What's the problem?"

"They'll barely all fit on the portable dance floor. Good news is Kiki isn't anywhere in sight."

"Shoo them away. Tell them to stay inside the pool cabana until show time. Please tell me there's room for all of them in there. Have Pat leave the bar long enough to settle things if she needs to."

"There's plenty of room for them. That *cabana* is bigger than my apartment."

"Good. Maybe they'll stay out of each other's way. I'll be back out in a couple minutes," Em promised.

"Take your time. I can handle for now. Just don't disappear and leave me in charge."

"If only."

# 2

EM QUICKLY SLIPPED into a black dress, ran a brush through her hair, coiled it into a bun, and anchored it on her head. Then she touched up her lipstick and mascara. As she was heading back to the kitchen, she ran into Wally again. He was hurrying toward her with the guest of honor in tow.

"Em, this is Cameron Delacruz." Wally introduced Em to the producer and went on to sing Em's praises and ended with, "They're so busy, I'm just thankful the Goddess was free to cater my little event."

"Do you plan on spending much time here on Kauai?" Em studied Delacruz. In his late forties or early fifties—it was hard to tell with his dyed hair and the cosmetic work he'd already had done—he was not much taller than her own five foot six inches. He appeared to be physically fit beneath his silk Aloha shirt and long linen pants, thanks to a personal trainer, no doubt.

Delacruz shrugged, glancing around before he turned to Em again. "I'm not really sure. Splitting time between Aspen, LA, New York, and St. Bart's, it's hard to say."

"I can see where having that many choices might be a dilemma." Em didn't care if he'd picked up on her sarcasm, not when so many people on Kauai were hard pressed to find any housing at all.

Just then a big Hawaiian *moke* who looked to be in his mid-thirties, dressed in all black, carrying a two-way radio, walked up to Delacruz. His black hair was buzz cut, his tattooed biceps as big around as Em's thighs. He wore a triple X T uniform shirt with MAHALO SECURITY emblazoned across the front and the back. The name Leo was embroidered on the front over his heart.

"Got my guys set up over at your place," he told Delacruz.

The producer nodded. Em stared at the Hawaiian. She didn't recognize him, but that didn't mean anything. He probably wasn't one of the North Shore crowd. The man's deep-set black-eyed gaze continually roamed the house, the grounds, the interior of the tent. He was on high alert even though there were only a handful of people moving around, and they were all Em's staff.

"I hope you don't mind," Delacruz said to Wally. "I feel safer having my own security with me. Leo here will be moving back and forth between our two places. He's got a couple of men stationed at my house. I'm sure by now word is out all over about this party. Who knows? Someone might see the diversion as an opportunity to break in."

Wally was too bedazzled by the man's wealth and celebrity to mind much of anything at this point.

"Of course. I'm just so happy you're letting me host this little affair to welcome you to our island. Now, let me show you my house." Wally tossed one end of the boa over his shoulder and gave Em an off-handed finger wave as he led Delacruz away.

Em headed to the kitchen, but half the wait staff was already out in the tent circulating among the ten or so guests who had arrived. She went outside where Pat Boggs, a.k.a. Sarge, Kiki's second-in-command of the Hula Maidens, was stationed behind the long bar table behind open bottles of five-star red wine, assorted top-shelf bottles of the hard stuff, and mai tai ingredients. Pat wore her hair in a buzz cut and dressed like a guy.

She waved Em over.

"Need anything?" Em asked. The bar looked well stocked and organized, just the way Pat liked things.

Pat rocked back on her heels, hooked her thumbs into her pants pockets, and winked at Em. "Not unless you got a naked gal in your pocket."

"Sorry. Maybe one will show up." Then Em quickly added, "No fraternizing with the guests, remember."

"Fraternizing?"

"You know what I mean."

"What about after the party's over?"

"That's up to you. *After* the party's over."

"Hey, I picked up some gossip about the guest of honor. Mr. Day-la-de-da-cruz." Pat pronounced every syllable in her slow Southern drawl. "What have you heard?"

More guests were filtering in now, ambling toward the tent. In a glance Em made certain the waiters were circulating, smiling, offering pupus, and showing folks the way to the bar before she answered.

Em said, "All I know is that he's a producer, he owns at least five homes in celebrity hot spots, and he collects very, very expensive art. He's afraid this party is going to attract thieves to his place. Go figure. He's got a three-man security team on duty over there. One is to patrol the perimeter. Maybe he's even a bodyguard."

"Yeah? See that guy over there? The short one leaning against the tent pole? The one with the bad toupee? He was already in the bag when he got here, and he's got jabber jaw. He said De-la-cruz had not one but two big movies bomb this year. You heard of *Dead and Dead Again IV*, right?"

"No, but I don't get out much," Em admitted.

"The cast was made up of Delacruz's ex-wife Alanna Grant and a bunch of former action-adventure stars from the eighties. Even with new facelifts and ab implants they looked like hell. Not Alanna, though. She's still young and hot, hot, hot. Anyway, the flick went straight to DVD. Talk about rotten tomatoes. That was *one* of De-la-cruz's bombs this year."

Em glanced toward the cabana. She had more to worry about than Delacruz's box-office disasters.

"Keep an eye on the Maidens. Sophie said they're having lineup issues."

"Oh, *hell*, no. That's bad. That's *real* bad. I'm tendin' bar, n' Kiki's not here to keep 'em under control."

"If you have to, and *only* if things get out of hand, step away from the bar and get them organized and ready to perform."

"You got it."

People had come filtering in, and suddenly there was a line at the bar.

"Better get to work," Em told her. Pat nodded and hurried away.

Em spotted Buzzy. The lanky hippie only had one name as far as anyone knew. He was wandering around the perimeter of the tent looking lost in space. He'd been a fixture at the Goddess for as long as anyone could recall, and Em had hired him to show up and bus tables tonight as well as circulate and keep an eye on things in general. Besides doing electrical and building repairs, he sometimes filled in as a bus boy and waiter. Right now he was headed her way.

"Buzzy?" She tried calling to him without shouting. Apparently in a fog, he kept walking. "Buzzy!" Em said, louder this time.

He turned, blinked, and looked around until he spotted her. He waited near a tiki torch as she walked over to join him.

"Wazzup, Em?"

"Wally's guest of honor, Mr. Delacruz, brought along his own security guard."

"So, you want me to leave?"

Em shook her head. "No, of course not. I just wanted you to know he's supposed to be here if you happen to see him roaming around between the two properties. You can't miss him. He's got a *Mahalo* Security logo on his shirt. I still need you to help clear tables as soon as dinner is over, and I'd like you to keep an eye out and make sure party crashers don't try to sneak in through the hedge or come up from the beach."

He stared at her a few seconds, digesting everything she'd said.

Slowly he nodded. "Cool. Got it. Clear tables. No crashers. Man, that's a lot to remember."

# 3

AFTER AN HOUR during which the guests enjoyed chatting over pupus and cocktails, Em found Wally and told him the buffet spread was ready. Together they joined Cameron Delacruz. Guests had gifted the producer with so many flower *leis* that they were piled around his neck up to his chin. He had a martini glass in one hand and a young buxom brunette on his arm.

Delacruz introduced her to Em as Jasmine Bishop.

"She's an actress," Wally interjected.

Jasmine was three inches taller than the producer with a show-stopping figure. Her breasts were enhanced by surgical magic and well displayed beneath a plunging neckline. Her skin tone was a lovely golden brown, a fortunate mix of undetermined ethnic origins. Her long dark hair curled artfully past her shoulders. Her full lips were apparently locked in a permanent pout.

An abundance of curves around her hips and bootie filled her skintight maxi-halter dress. Jasmine's hand tightened on Delacruz's arm until she finished giving Em a slow once-over. Then, obviously dismissing Em as no threat, the brunette's gaze went blank, and she relaxed her grip.

Em smiled and thought, *as if I care.*

Somehow in the middle of a cocktail party surrounded by friends and island acquaintances, Cameron Delacruz still managed to appear agitated. Either the man didn't know how to relax, or his two recent box-office bombs weighed on his mind twenty-four seven.

"Attention! Attention, everyone!" Wally clinked a fork against a water goblet, and the assembly eventually fell silent. "Welcome one and all. We'll have a toast as soon as everyone is seated. Please head to the buffet table and then find a place to sit. It's open seating."

Em escorted the two men and Delacruz's arm candy to the buffet table and indicated they should go first. Delacruz surveyed the long table covered with mounds of food in steamer trays and on platters.

"A buffet. Quaint. Nothing like dishing up my own dinner," he said.

Jasmine rubbed his shoulder as if soothing a headstrong toddler. She leaned against him until her breasts oozed out of the low-cut black halter dress and cooed, "You go on over to the head table. I'll bring you a plate. I know what you like, baby."

As the woman gave his earlobe a nip with her pearly capped teeth, Em bit back a retort, quickly excused herself, and walked away. Maybe it *was* a buffet, but it was certainly not standard *luau* fare. Kimo and the rest of the staff had knocked themselves out over the last couple of days to make certain everything was perfect after Delacruz's assistant sent her a long list of dietary requirements outlining the special needs of the rich, famous, and not-so-famous guests.

Em tried to explain to Kimo the difference between a vegan and a vegetarian, dairy-free and gluten-free foods, and how people claimed their systems didn't tolerate them to Kimo.

He'd stared back as if she were crazy. "You know what? These gotta be *haole* diseases. Hawaiians cannot afford."

"You think you can manage to come up with something anyway?" Em hoped.

"I'll look on da Net. Find some recipes I can adapt."

"Great."

"Or maybe I'll put one sign on da pulled pork and say it's tofu. How they gonna know the diff? Once they taste it, so *ono*, broke da mouth!"

Earlier Em made certain the kalua pork wasn't labeled tofu.

Once the guests were seated, Wally walked up to the stage and turned on the mic. The Tiki Tones, a trio that provided music most nights at the Goddess, were already there.

Wally surveyed the crowd, took a deep breath, and said, "Test. Testing. I'm Wally Williams, your host. Welcome to Fernando's Hideaway. The place is named after my late partner, Fernando, the famous pianist. I'm sure you all know who he is. *Was.*" Wally mopped a tear off his cheek with one end of the boa.

"I'm sure if Fernando were here tonight he'd join me in welcoming Cameron to Kauai. We're so blessed to have him as a neighbor here on the North Shore. I hope he spends as much time as he can on the island."

Wally raised a wine glass. The guests raised their own drinks.

"To Cameron. Welcome to Kauai!"

After the toast Wally complimented Em and her crew from the Goddess.

"The Tiki Goddess is an institution here on the North Shore," Wally went on. "Em and her Uncle Louie befriended Fernando and I when we moved here, and I wouldn't have gotten through the *ordeal* of his murder without them and the incomparable Hula Maidens. I just adore these women. Why, they're as flamboyant and *ageless* as I am!" He waited for applause that never really came before he quickly went on.

"I hope that all of you will go to the Goddess one of these evenings for the *fantastic* show and the best tropical beverages in Hawaii. Each and every one of Uncle Louie's cocktails has a legend behind it." Wally's voice cracked, and he mopped off his cheeks. "Louie even named one for my dear departed Fernando."

The guests who were still eating ignored him and concentrated on their plates. Silverware clinked, and the low hum of conversation was building to a loud buzz.

"And now," Wally shouted to get their attention, "without further ado, I'd like to welcome the Hula Maidens. A couple of months ago the ladies traveled to Waikiki where they performed at various tiki bars and venues. Tonight they are appearing as a special favor to me. This is a tropical show like no other. A show the likes of which you'll never see at a hotel *luau*. This is the real deal. So sit back, relax, and enjoy the Hula Maidens!"

He gestured toward the pool cabana. Em had been so busy she hadn't even gone to check on the ladies who, for the most part, were never going to see sixty again. She glanced toward the cabana just as Big Estelle Huntington, a heavyset *haole* of formidable height with salt-and-pepper hair, stuck her head out of the open door to see what was going on. Wally waved them on.

"Come on, girls. It's show time," he yelled into the mic.

Big Estelle stepped out of the cabana. One by one the rest of the Maidens hesitantly appeared. With Kiki out of commission they'd been on their own to design their costumes and adornments. Obviously not a good thing.

Fonts of multi-hued feathers appeared to be exploding from their heads.

Instead of their usual colorful *muumuus* that hid a multitude of figure challenges, tonight they were wrapped in simple, understated black *pareaus* or sarongs. Obviously all the focus had gone into the extravagant headgear that looked more suited for a Brazilian carnival than anything remotely Polynesian.

Each of the Maidens carried *kahili-pa`a-lima* or small *kahili*, feathered standards, symbols of the *ali`i* chiefs and royal families, of the islands. The Maidens' *kahili* were small enough to hold in the crook of an arm.

"There they are." Wally finger-waved to the Maidens as they clustered up before they made their way toward the party tent. "While they're getting organized, I'd like to announce that the ladies want you to know they are dedicating tonight's performance to their fallen leader and hula sister, Kiki Godwin. We're all hoping and praying Kiki's back in the fold in no time at all."

Big Estelle separated herself from the knot of women who were apparently suffering from a rare case of stage fright. Usually they were locked in a push and shove for front-row positioning, but not tonight. Maybe it was the presence of so many *malihini* or newcomers—most of whom were ignoring Wally and engaged in their own conversations—or it was the absence of Kiki, their fearless leader. But for whatever reason, the Hula Maidens were taking their own sweet time heading over to the stage.

Finally Precious Cottrell, a diminutive Little Person, the newest member of the group, fell in behind Big Estelle. Suzi Matamura lined up behind Precious. A successful realtor who lived in the neighborhood, Suzi's home was far humbler than Wally's and Cameron's beachfront McMansions. Trish Oakley, a redhead and professional photographer, fell in line next. Of average height, she still towered over Suzi and Precious. Stately Hawaiian Flora Carillo ducked so that her headdress cleared the doorway as she stepped out of the pool cabana. The black *pareau* and the *kahili* tucked into the crook of her elbow made her the most authentically regal-looking member of the lot of them. Last to appear was former Iowan Lillian Smith. She hovered in the doorway, one hand on the headdress, the other clutching her *kahili* to her breast until Flora turned around, grabbed Lil's arm, and pulled her into line. Prone to bursting into tears, Lillian appeared to be on the verge already.

Big Estelle waited until Lillian stopped propping up her headdress and then, shoulders straight and eyes ahead, Estelle led the barefoot Maidens across the wide pool deck and onto the lawn as she headed for the tent. They followed her like obedient ducklings until they reached the edge of the parquet dance floor. Instead of leading the women onto the makeshift stage, Big Estelle eyed the floor and remained frozen in place. No easy feat when the evening temperature hovered at a humid eighty degrees.

Whispering ensued as the Maidens broke rank to argue among themselves. Suzi pointed at the dance floor, indicating Trish should go first. Trish didn't even respond to her hula sister. Instead, she slipped around the edge of the group and tried to hide behind Lillian.

Their hushed whispers escalated. The knot of women tightened on itself as they faced one another arguing about who should walk onto the dance floor first. Then one of them let out a high-pitched yelp, and Precious shoved her way out of the center of the circle with her head-dress tilted to one side of her head. She shoved it back into place and stamped her foot.

Just as Em was about to head across the tent to calm them, out of the corner of her eye she saw Pat Boggs toss down a bar towel. Pat hurried out from behind the bar and marched over to the Maidens. Still on the edge of the circle, Trish saw her first and quickly began to shush the others. They were silent and penitent by the time Pat reached them. Without a word she took hold of Precious's hand and led her out onto the dance floor and placed her front and center.

"Stay there," Pat growled barely loud enough to be heard. By now the guests had fallen silent to watch the unfolding drama.

Pat crooked her finger at the women and said, "Big Estelle, come here." She pointed to a spot on the floor to the far right of Precious. Big Estelle moved like a cruise ship headed for port.

"Don't move," Pat warned. "That's your place."

One by one she signaled to each Maiden until she had them lined up with three in the front row and three behind in the empty spaces.

"Now *stay in your puka!*" Pat commanded.

They stayed. Em sighed with relief. Wally was searching his shirt pocket for something. As he pulled out a folded piece of paper, Em's relief vanished when she noticed Sophie standing directly across the tent from her. She was motioning toward a spot a few feet away from Em.

Em turned and spotted Kiki lurking in the shadows about two yards to her left. Beneath the glow of a flaming tiki torch, the woman's face appeared sallow and wan. A bright spot of blush stood out on each cheek. Her lipstick was such a dark red it looked black in the torchlight. Her hair had been styled and appointed with flowers scattered here and there to hide the bald patches. She was staring at the women lined up on the dance floor.

Worried that Kiki was about to head for the stage, Em quickly slipped along the edge of the tent beyond the poles and torches until she reached Kiki's side. The troupe leader was so focused on the dancers she hadn't heard Em approach.

"Kiki," Em whispered. Then a little louder, "*Psst!* Kiki!"

Kiki immediately threw her arms up to cover her head and staggered backward with a barely audible squeak.

Em grabbed her by the elbow and caught her before she could trip and fall over. Once she was sure Kiki regained her balance, Em let go.

"It's good to see you," Em said. "How are you doing?"

"I've been better." There was a quiver in Kiki's voice.

"You look good."

"You're lying, or you need glasses."

"Seriously, how are you mentally?"

"I'm still trying to put what happened behind me. I don't remember much, and what I do remember still scares the pootootie out of me." Kiki stared toward the stage. Em was prepared to grab her if she took a step in that direction. "Oh my heck," Kiki mumbled.

Em followed Kiki's stare. Wally was beside the band, holding the wrinkled paper in his hands as Pat stomped around on the parquet floor rearranging the women. Apparently Lillian was not happy in the front row. Tears were streaming down her face. Pat looked like she was ready to grab Lillian's *kahili* and bonk her on the head with it.

"You'd think they could line themselves up by now," Kiki grumbled.

"They're used to having you do everything for them."

Precious staggered under the weight of her headdress as Pat moved her a couple inches to the left.

Wally started reading from the paper in his hand, and thankfully, Pat took it as a cue to get off the dance floor.

"The Hula Maidens are dedicating their three dances tonight to their fallen comrade, Kiki Godwin. We all hope Miss Kiki is on the road to recovery!"

Kiki never avoided the spotlight. When she didn't call out or wave to announce her presence, Em took it as a sign of just how much trauma she'd suffered.

"All three dances are about *manu* or birds," Wally added.

"Well, that explains the headgear," Em said.

"They must have plucked every rooster and hen on the island," Kiki said.

"I was afraid they were going to do the Kalua number again." Too late Em recalled that Kalua, a special number that Kiki had choreo-graphed, was one of Kiki's personal favorites.

"The crowd loved it," Kiki defended.

"Until Lillian caught her hair on fire."

"It was a wig. Besides, they aren't carrying oil lamps tonight."

"If we're lucky they'll keep those *kahili* tucked in their arms and won't start whacking each other."

"This first song is *Manu O'o*, a song about the black honey eater who sips from the *lehua* blossoms."

Kiki closed her eyes, reached up, and gently started tapping her forehead along her eyebrows as the Tiki Tones started playing. The Maidens danced carefully, their steps controlled as they adjusted to the uneven dance floor. Oddly enough, they were keeping time to the music and all going the same direction. Pat watched them perform half of the first verse before she hurried back to man the bar.

Em whispered, "You should watch, Kiki. They've been working hard just to make you proud."

"*Humph*," Kiki snorted. She opened her eyes and stopped tapping.

Both Kiki and Em joined the audience as they applauded the Maidens at the end of the first dance.

Wally bounced back up to the front of the gathering and grabbed the mic from Danny again. "This next number is entitled *Manu Kapalulu*. The song was written by Hawaii's last Queen, Lili'uokalani, and it's about a nagging quail."

The Maidens were halfway through their second number when the slight slope proved too much for Flora, and she went down like a burlap bag full of *taro*. Rolling down the floor she wiped out Precious and Suzi in the front row. Precious's headdress flew off and landed in front of Lillian. She screamed as she hit the ground and slid into the pileup.

Big Estelle kept dancing. So did Trish. They were moving in opposite directions on either side of the tangled heap of Hula Maidens. The fallen dancers fought to keep their *pareaus* tied while they pulled themselves out of the pile.

Precious stepped on Suzi's arm as she tried to stand and fell over the realtor again. Suzi yowled. Lillian cried out, "I think I broke my coccyx! Help me! Help me! I can't get up."

Danny and the Tiki Tones stopped playing, but Big Estelle kept dancing with a smile wide as a rainbow pasted on her face. Trish sneaked off the side of the stage and ran back to the cabana.

"What's a coccyx?" Kiki's complexion had gone from sallow to alabaster.

"Tailbone." Em didn't know whether to laugh or cry. Wally was at a loss for words. Like the rest of the crowd he stared in openmouthed awe.

Finally Pat ran over to the stage again and started pulling the Maidens apart. She put her hands under Precious's armpits and hauled her to her feet and set her far enough away to keep her from falling on Suzi again. Precious hoisted her *pareau* up over her breasts, righting the wardrobe malfunction. Next Pat grabbed Suzi and stood her up, then picked up the feather headdresses and tossed them to the dancers. Lillian, unfortunately, was still lying on her back sobbing. She refused to move.

"Don't touch me!" she screeched when Pat leaned over her.

Pat turned to the audience and yelled, "How about a hand for the Hula Maidens? Betcha you folks never seen anything like that in LA! What an ending. I guess you'd call it a grand-fine-alley!" She started frantically clapping and kept it up until there was scattered applause.

Suzi was picking feathers out of Precious's hair. The Little Person looked shaken as the two of them joined hands and staggered off toward the cabana together.

"For this I gave up the nuthouse," Kiki muttered. "What a fiasco."

"Obviously they need you," Em said.

Kiki was rapidly tapping her fingertips against her forehead again. "But I'm not supposed to be in stressful situations. The Maidens are a stressful situation. I should avoid the Maidens. I should not have come. I am calm and peaceful. I am *clams* and *peaceful*. No. No. I am *calm*. Calm and peach fuzz. Common peach fuzz."

"Don't hurt yourself," Em said. Kiki was tapping hard enough to leave bruises. "What are you doing?"

"Tapping therapy. Anti-anxiety. Gotta stay calm. Gotta clap. I mean, I gotta tap. Gotta stay lap. No. Not *lap*. Lamb. *Lamb*. I'm lamb and peaches."

"Come with me, calm and peaceful." Em gently took Kiki's arm and led her toward the house where Kimo was manning the kitchen. By the time they were inside, Kiki was tapping her knuckles against her forehead so hard her eyeballs jiggled up and down.

Kimo took one look at Kiki and stopped plating his famous Upside Down Tropical Fruitcake.

"I got her," he told Em. "You get back out there."

Kiki was knocking on her head so hard it sounded like she was trying to crack a coconut open.

"Have Pat make her an emergency martini," Kimo said as Em was almost out the door.

"Is that a good idea?"

Kimo shrugged. They both looked at Kiki. Now she was hitting herself in the head with the heels of both hands.

"You got a better idea?"

"I'll tell her," Em promised.

She rushed back outside. The Tiki Tones guitarist was playing mellow Hawaiian slack-key. Wally's guests were carrying on as if there hadn't just been a four-alarm flab pileup on the dance floor. Most were still seated around the tables gabbing. Others stood in twos and threes chatting over cocktails. Cameron Delacruz appeared to be in an intense conversation with two other men. Jasmine still clung to his arm.

One of the waiters had taken over for Pat behind the bar. Em signaled for him to double up on the liquor. He mouthed, "Already am."

She looked around for Buzzy but didn't see him anywhere. She hurried over to the dance floor where Pat was hovering over Lillian. The former Iowan was still flat on her back. With her headdress smashed and sticking out beneath her she looked like rooster roadkill.

Pat saw Em and sounded disgusted. "I can't get her to sit up."

"I'm not moving until the paramedics get here," Lil wailed. "Has someone called MyBob? The one night I leave him at home, I break my coccyx!"

"Where are the others?" Em asked Pat.

"Hidin' out in the cabana." She looked down at Lillian. "How're we gonna haul her outta here?"

"I'm not some side of beef, you know," Lillian whined. "I can hear you. Is anyone getting photos for my Facebook friends?"

"Maybe it's best we call the EMTs. She may have broken something," Em said.

"My coccyx, that's what," Lil said. "Did anyone call MyBob? Tell him to bring the camera."

"I'll call him." Em pulled her cell phone out of her bra strap. "Pat, would you please make a martini, a double, and have Buzzy take it into the kitchen?" Em looked around. "Where is he anyway?"

"No idea," Pat said. "I haven't seen him since you opened the buffet line. Kimo needs a drink?"

Em leaned close and whispered, "It's for Kiki. Kimo's keeping an eye on her in the kitchen."

"Kiki's here?" Pat didn't bother to lower her voice. Her eyes bugged out.

"Oh, no! Did she see me fall?" Lillian cried. "She'll be furious."

"It's not all about you, Lillian. It wasn't all your fault anyway. Precious's feathers tripped you up. I've told you ladeez over and over again you have to learn to dance over anything. *An-y-thing.* Even each other."

Em sighed and looked over her shoulder toward the house and hoped Kimo had Kiki calmed down and hidden away somewhere. "How about that martini, Pat?" She leaned close and whispered, "Stay mum about Kiki being out."

"I'm on it." Pat snapped a cell phone photo for Lil before she headed back to the bar, leaving Em stuck with the coccyx crisis.

# 4

EM SCANNED THE tent. The waiters were efficiently clearing tables, but there weren't enough of them, so it was slow going. Buzzy was still MIA. Em figured he must have smoked a fatty and was asleep under a tree somewhere. If they started booking more gigs as large as this one, she'd need to hire more help.

Delacruz was still in deep conversation at the far end of the tent, the buxom brunette starlet hanging on his arm.

Suddenly Wally was there, and he was all aflutter. He immediately fell to his knees beside Lillian, took her hand, and pressed it to his heart. She'd been one of Fernando's biggest fans, and she and Wally had grown close since the pianist's untimely death.

"Oh, Lillian, my dear. How dreadful! What can I do?"

"Take a photo of me for my Facebook fans. Make sure someone has called the paramedics," she whispered. "Please."

Em handed Wally her phone. "Use this," she said. "I'll be right back."

"Where are you going?" Wally panicked.

"I'll be right back."

Em walked away, unwilling to give him any more to worry about as she headed over to where Cameron Delacruz had just been joined by his private security guard. The tall Hawaiian named Leo towered over Delacruz with an angry scowl on his face.

Em reached them and heard the guard say, "I'm telling you, it's not like both of them to disappear. There's a problem. We gotta call KPD."

Delacruz glanced at his watch then concentrated on the foot he was tapping. "What do you mean *problem*? There'd better damn well *not* be a problem at my place."

"Well, neither of my guys is answering his two-way."

Delacruz snorted. "I had my doubts about the old guy. He's probably asleep."

"Dat *old* guy is my uncle, Sebastian Kekina. He's a former cop. He's no problem."

Their voices grew louder. Em noticed guests near them starting to eavesdrop. She gently pulled the two men aside. Jasmine tossed her long dark hair over her shoulder and stared vacantly into the garden. Em discretely signaled Sophie over.

"Let's walk over to your place, Mr. Delacruz." Em turned to the guard Leo. "Put both of your minds at ease. I'm sure everything's all right. Let me take care of a couple of things, and I'll go with you."

When Sophie arrived, Em leaned close enough to whisper, "The fire dancer and his drummer are behind the cabana. Have them get started and tell him to keep twirling as long as he can. We'll pay over-time. Find out if any of the Maidens can get it together enough to dance again. Surely Suzi and Big Estelle could pull something off."

"Will do."

Sophie hurried away. Em headed back to where Wally was still comforting Lillian on the dance floor. She tapped him on the shoulder.

"Wally, you have to get Lillian off the dance floor. The show needs to go on."

"What's happening?" He studied her face for a moment and said, "What's going on? Something is happening."

Em pulled him close and lowered her voice.

"I need you to be calm, Wally. Please, for once in your life, no hysterics."

"But . . ."

"I have to walk over to Mr. Delacruz's house with him and the security guard for a moment."

"Something's happened. I can see it on your face."

"Nothing's happened. I want you to announce the fire dancer." She glanced over the lawn outside the tent where the Tahitian drummer lowered himself to sit cross-legged on the ground. "Please."

Before Wally could protest, the drumming started, and the guests were mesmerized. After the first few beats the fire knife dancer came bounding out from behind the cabana with the whirling ends of the knives ablaze.

"Em Johnson, what is going on?" Wally demanded.

"Hopefully nothing. I'll be right back. If something is up, you'll be the first to know."

Lillian, still prone on the ground, tugged on Wally's pant leg. "Are the paramedics on the way?"

Wally reached down, grabbed Lillian's ankles, and started sliding her across the parquet floor.

# 5

JASMINE HAD OPTED to stay behind and chat with a young couple after Delacruz assured her he'd be right back. It took no time at all for Em, Delacruz, and Leo Kekina to walk across Wally's gardens and through an archway in the hedge between the two estates. When they reached the intricately carved Balinese front door, Delacruz tried the knob, but it didn't turn.

"That's a good sign." He looked relieved as he pulled his cell phone out and tapped in a security code. "Smart house," he said. "I had a state-of-the-art system installed. Looks like everything is fine. The house is still locked."

"My guys still aren't answering yet." Leo shoved his two-way radio onto his belt and shook his head. He frowned so fiercely he had a unibrow. "I better do a walk-through, make sure nobody's in there before I go look for them."

A shiver slid down Em's spine when Delacruz opened the door. Not all that long ago she'd been kidnapped by a deranged realtor, the same one who'd killed Fernando and held her hostage in the safe room in the interior of this very place. Bad karma house, indeed.

If his realtor hadn't disclosed that, it wasn't something she needed to inform Delacruz of at this point.

He opened the door then stood aside and let Leo enter first. Then he walked in, and Em brought up the rear. It was fifteen degrees cooler inside. Despite the ocean breeze, Delacruz kept the house closed up and the air conditioning on.

Sophie's paycheck probably couldn't touch the man's electrical bill.

They were six strides into the main section of the open concept living area when Em noticed two huge stretcher bars on the floor. They'd been tossed near a long bank of plush white sofas. A couple of massive white frames were lying empty in the middle of the room.

Cameron Delacruz grabbed one of the frames and stared at it in horror.

"My Pollocks are gone." His gaze swung slowly around the room as he sank to sit on the edge of the twisted steel and beveled-glass coffee table. "Both of my Pollocks are gone!"

Em stepped around the empty frames, careful not to touch anything.

"Millions in art." Delacruz, head in hands, moaned. He slowly looked up at Em. "As if my life isn't already in the toilet. Now this."

She took in the massive home, the expensive furnishings and accessories and thought, *some toilet.*

"I gotta go find my guys." Leo rushed out of the house.

"So much for a walk-through," Delacruz said.

Em looked around, hoping the thief or thieves weren't hiding somewhere inside the massive house. It wasn't long before Leo Kekina walked in, helping another man almost as huge as Leo, who leaned on him for support. The second man was pressing a rag against the back of his head.

Leo started to lower him to the sofa.

"Stop!" Delacruz shouted. He leapt to his feet. "No blood on the furniture." He pointed to a bar across the room and followed the two men as they walked over to the leather barstools. Leo lowered his employee to a stool.

"You're fired," he told Leo. "If you think you're getting paid for tonight, think again. I'm out millions. *Millions.* I'll sue you. You'll never work on this island again."

The Hawaiians both ignored the producer. The second guard with the name Mo printed on his shirt was hurting. He was obviously hurting too much to care what Delacruz thought. Em hurried over to the bar sink, grabbed a towel, and held it under the faucet. She handed it to Mo. He dropped the bloody towel on the travertine floor.

Em started to open the small mini fridge under the bar and then noticed an icemaker beside it. She filled another towel with ice and handed it to Mo. He nodded appreciatively and dropped the second dirty towel on the floor.

Delacruz looked like his head was about to explode.

"Stop that! Stop dropping bloody towels all over the place."

Em ignored him and asked Mo, "What happened?"

"No idea. Somebody hit me in the head. Didn't see a t'ing." He looked around. "Where's Uncle Bass?"

"You don't know?" Leo asked.

Mo shook his head no and winced. "Never saw him. He was patrolling da other side of da house."

"Patrolling. Ha!" Delacruz planted his hands on his hips. "Off sleeping somewhere is more like it."

"We should call 911," Em said.

"I did already," Leo told her. "Soon as I never heard from Mo."

"You called them *before* you even came in here? I just discovered my paintings were missing," Delacruz shouted. "How do I know you're not in on this and trying to make it look like you're all innocent?"

"Why would I call them if we're in on it? I got a man hurt here. You got some missing stuff. So I called 911." Leo left Mo's side and towered over Delacruz. The shorter man backed up a step. Satisfied, Leo went back to Mo and said, "You gonna be okay? I'm going to look for Uncle Bass."

As Leo walked out, Cameron Delacruz tapped in a number and yelled into his cell phone.

"911? I've been robbed! Where are you people? You should be here by now. Address? I don't know the address. I just bought the place. It's in Haena. It's an estate with the statues of Poseidon and Amphitrite atop two lava-rock pillars at the gate. Near Tunnels. What? What are you saying? Not Tunnels. *Makua?* I don't care what the Hawaiian name of the damn beach is. Just get someone out here. Wiki-wacky or however you say *pronto.*"

When he ended the call, Cameron stalked across the room and kicked an empty picture frame.

"I realize you've just been robbed, Mr. Delacruz, but talking to people like that on this island is going to get you nowhere fast," Em counselled. She imagined the police dispatcher contacting the officers en route and telling them to take their time.

She and Mo exchanged glances. He shrugged and gave her a knowing smile.

Jasmine walked in the door with an empty champagne flute dangling from her right hand.

"Everyone's missing you at the party," she told Delacruz. "You should see the fire twirler. He's great."

"Missing me? Want to know what's missing?" He gestured around the room. *"My Pollocks!"*

Jasmine eyed the empty hooks on the otherwise pristine walls and the two empty frames on the glossy travertine floor.

"Oh, wow."

"*Oh, wow?* That's all you've got? Oh, wow?"

"Sorry, babe." She walked over to his side, cupped his cheek with her hand. He shook her off. "Did you call the police?" she asked.

"Of course. Twice. They aren't here yet."

"Takes a while for help to get all the way out here," Mo said.

Delacruz waved his hands in the air. "I'm glad the house isn't on fire. I'm glad I'm not having a heart attack!"

"Settle down, babe," Jasmine crooned. "You'll have a stroke. Why don't we walk back over to the party and tell everyone what happened? Have a drink. Say good night. There are a couple of guys over there willing to back your next project, remember? Then we'll come right back."

"Leo can let you know when the police get here," Mo said.

"You don't understand what's happened here," Cameron said to Jasmine. "I didn't have the typical tourist swimming dolphins and sunset shit on the wall. I didn't have a bunch of movie posters like you have in your condo, either. Whoever did this got away with a fortune in Jackson Pollock art!"

"You're yelling again, babe."

"Bettah you go back to the *luau*," Mo suggested. "When the police get here, we'll come get you."

"Good idea," Em agreed. "Let's go back."

Jasmine grabbed Delacruz's hand and led him toward the door.

After they were outside, Em paused to speak to Mo.

"Will you be all right? Do you feel like you'll pass out again?"

"I'm okay. Better you get him outta here. Don't worry about me. I'm worried about Uncle Bass. Leo shoulda been back by now."

"That's what I thought," Em said, worried. "Let us know when the police arrive."

# 6

EM HEARD THE party guests hooting and hollering the minute she stepped out of the Delacruz house. She hurried through the gate in the hedge and across Wally's lawn and then the pool deck. At the edge of the party tent she saw the Tahitian drummer beating away on his *to'ere* made of a three-foot hollowed-out log. Staring at nothing, he appeared to have slipped into a trance. The fire dancer was dripping sweat, jumping and cavorting while tossing two long blazing knives in the air. Then he hit the ground, stretched out on his back, and balanced one of the knives across the soles of his feet. The crowd went wild again, the women shrieked, the men whistled and lifted their drinks, toasting the action.

Em glanced at her watch. She'd owe the entertainers big time, but at this point it was worth every penny. At the bar Pat was making mai tais in water pitchers and pouring drinks as fast as she could make them. From the looks of things she'd more than doubled up on the liquor quotient and was going through gallons of rum.

Big Estelle, Suzi, Precious, and Flora were lined up beside the dance floor, watching the fire dancer go through his act while waiting to perform again. Lillian was nowhere to be seen. Em half-expected her to be lying just off the edge of the stage, but apparently Wally had mustered the strength to drag her away. Thankfully Kiki hadn't made another appearance.

Cameron made his way through the crowd, trying without success to speak to people as he snaked around tables and chairs, but most of them were mesmerized by the show. Finally he headed straight to Wally. With mic in hand, Wally stared at the bare-chested drummer and gyrating fire dancer like a kid holding his first shave-ice.

Sophie walked up to Em with a tray full of drinks.

"You look like you could use one of these," Sophie said.

Em glanced at the tray. "I could use all of them."

"What's up?"

Before Em said anything, Cameron Delacruz grabbed the mic from Wally.

"Hey, drum guy. Thanks a lot," he shouted into the mic. "Now knock it off."

The drummer came to, stopped, and looked around. The fire dancer was on his back, feet in the air, balancing the fire knife. He let it fall to the grass. Then he rolled over onto his hands and knees and slowly stood up.

Standing beside Cameron, Wally fluttered his hands as if he'd lost control of them. Jasmine walked over and helped herself to a drink from Sophie's tray. Cameron took a deep breath and scanned the crowd.

"Sorry to do this, folks, but the party's over. My security system was breached. All my Pollocks have been stolen."

There was a collective gasp. Party guests looked at each other and then Delacruz.

"Don't worry. The police are on the way," he shouted into the mic. "So they say."

Those on the edge of the crowd set down their drinks.

Em heard someone say, "What if they're hitting more than one home?"

"With so many of us here, it's open season on all of our places!"

"My kids are home with the nanny," a woman cried.

A tidal wave of panic swept the party. Guests fled the tent, headed toward the entrance.

Within two minutes the tent was deserted. Empty glasses were scattered all over the tables; chairs had been pushed aside.

"So does this mean we're not dancing again?" Suzi asked no one in particular.

The sound of frustrated voices filled the usually still night air. There was a backup at the front drive as two harried valets tried to do the best they could to meet demands.

Wally ran inside the house. Cameron and Jasmine followed.

"I'd better go with them." A lock of hair had escaped Em's ponytail. She brushed it back.

"Is it okay to start cleaning up?" Sophie asked.

"Why not? The crime scene's next door." Em surveyed the post-apocalyptical chaos out at the valet station.

"Don't worry," Sophie said. "I've got this."

"*Mahalo.* It's nice to know I have one person I can count on," Em told her. She looked over at the bar and saw Pat packing things up. "Two actually," Em amended. "Have you seen Buzzy?"

"He wandered through here a little while before you came back, but

I haven't seen him since."

"Remind me not to hire him to work any more parties. He's better off at the Goddess with Louie where he's contained within four walls."

"Got it."

Em went inside and spotted Wally near the bank of wide couches. Lillian was sprawled out on one of them with an ice pack tucked beneath her tailbone. A DVD was running on a huge television screen that nearly covered one wall. There was the late Fernando performing at the piano in all his sequined, boa-wrapped glory. The video added an eerie touch to a downright disastrous evening.

Cameron Delacruz paced behind Wally, ghastly pale beneath his spray tan. He suddenly stopped in front of a long side table, grabbed a tall honeycomb glass vase, gagged a couple of times, and hurled into it.

Wally spun around, his eyes wild. "Put that down! That's the Salvadori vase Fernando was given after his sold-out concert in Venice!"

He raced to the side table, spread his arms, and planted himself between the vase and Delacruz. Lillian managed to raise her head to see what was going on.

"Why, that vase looks just like the one I got at Pier One." Her head flopped back onto the pillow.

"Oh, my precious doodoo," Wally cried. "I'm sweating. My head is sweating, I kid you not."

Just then Leo Kekina hurried in from the direction of the kitchen. He glowered at Delacruz as the producer wiped his mouth on a cocktail napkin. Delacruz took one look at the security guard, crumpled the napkin, and tossed it toward the side table.

"Well? Are the police here yet? Did you find something?" he demanded.

"Found something all right. Found my Uncle Bass."

"Where was he? Sleeping it off on a *lanai* lounge?"

Leo shook his head. His expression made Em fear for Delacruz's life.

"I found him near the entrance to the driveway. The gates were still closed. He's *make*."

Delacruz glared at Leo. "Okay, so clue me in. What's ma-kay?"

"Dead."

# 7

"WHAT?" DELACRUZ WHISPERED.

The last of the color drained from his face along with his anger.

"My uncle is dead in your driveway. Someone was able to get in through your electronic gate and close it behind 'em."

"It's an all-in-one system. State of the art. One code works everything, and only I know the password."

"Then it ain't worth piss," Leo mumbled.

Wally moaned and headed for the couch. Em asked him for her phone as he walked by. He tugged it out of his pocket. She stepped aside, turned her back on the group, and hit Detective Roland Sharpe's number.

When his voice mail came on she whispered into the phone, "Call me. I need you."

As if things weren't bad enough, Em looked up and saw Kiki walking slowly toward her with her arms out for balance and a martini glass clutched in one hand. She set the empty glass down on a glass cube table and smoothed down the front of her *pareau*.

"I'm okay. I'm okay," she told Em.

"You sure?"

Kiki nodded. "What's going on? I saw the stampede for the exit. People are going crazy out there yelling for their cars."

Now was not the time to tell an already fragile Kiki what had happened next door. Em struggled to figure out what to say.

"Something is up," Kiki pressed. "Why else would there be vomit in that vase? Come on and tell. You know I'll find out one way or the other. What do you think I am? A blabbermouth?"

Em shrugged. "Kiki, really. I can't say."

"Okay, so maybe I am a bit talkative. Don't you think it's best I hear it from you and not later when the story has been blown out of proportion?"

"I guess you'll find out anyway," Em agreed. Kiki was right about the story being blown out of proportion. By morning folks would be circulating tales of a mound of dead bodies piled in the Delacruz drive-way, not to mention hundreds of missing paintings.

Em stepped closer to Kiki and lowered her voice. "There's been a break-in and a murder."

"A murder? Here?" Kiki yelled.

"My house is cursed!" Wally threw himself down on the opposite end of the sofa from Lillian and pulled a throw pillow over his face to muffle his screams.

"Not here," Em told Kiki. "Next door, at the Delacruz place."

Kiki went dead silent for so long Em thought she'd lost the ability to speak again, but then she slowly smiled.

"I hate to admit it," she said, "but this might be just what I need to help me snap out of my nervous breakdown."

"What are you talking about?" Em glanced at her cell and wished Roland would call back.

"Don't you see?" Kiki said. "Now I can focus on solving this murder, take my mind off of my, well, off of my own mind."

"Oh, Kiki, I don't think that's the kind of diversion you need. How about quilting, instead?"

Kiki stared at her. "Have you lost your mind?"

Suddenly they all heard a siren wail into the driveway.

"The police are here." Delacruz ran out to the wide entry complete with the koi pond and stream.

Within seconds four handsome EMTs strode into Wally's living room.

Jasmine had just sauntered in through the garden side of the house. "Where do they get these guys? Central casting? They're gorgeous."

The EMTs stared at Lillian and Wally spread out on the couches. Wally managed to drop the pillows and smiled.

"We had a call about a broken coccyx," one of them said.

Lil raised her arm and finger-waved to him. "That would be me," she trilled.

"I'm just feeling a bit faint," Wally said before he covered his face with the pillow again.

"Hey, my uncle is dead next door. You guys need to come over there," Leo said.

"You sure he's dead?" the EMT asked.

"Real dead."

"Then you don't need us. You have to call the police and wait for them to call the coroner."

Leo nodded. "We did." He turned to Em. "I'm going back to stay with my uncle and Mo."

"I'll go with you," Delacruz said. "Jasmine?"

"I'm ready."

"Wally, do you want to come and see what a disaster my place is?" Cameron asked the stylist.

Wally pulled the pillow off his face long enough to yell, "Oh, my stars and garters, no!"

Em turned to Kiki. "Please tell Kimo to oversee the packing and get things organized for the tent guy. He and his crew will be here in the morning to pick up the chairs and take down the tent. Things will go faster if the Maidens help. Tell them I'll comp them free drinks until the end of the week."

Since it was already Thursday she felt fairly certain their tab wouldn't break her uncle, but she couldn't guarantee it.

"Okay." Kiki nodded.

"Don't you clean up, Kiki. You take it easy. Go home and get some rest. The Maidens need you." It was easy to see Kiki's mind was elsewhere. Em remembered what Kiki had just said about the robbery and murder and added, "It's too soon for you to launch yourself into anything. Don't go getting into trouble."

"Don't worry your pretty head about me," Kiki told her.

Em let her gaze wander over the poorly hidden bald patches all over Kiki's scalp, her sallow skin and desperate attempt to cover it with too much blush.

"It's not my head I'm worried about," Em said.

As Kiki went off to give Kimo instructions, Em followed Delacruz out of the house. Pat had the bar all packed up and was carrying one last box to Kimo's pickup truck. Thanks to Sophie, the waiters were moving at warp speed as they cleared tables, pulled off tablecloths and napkins, and tossed the soiled linen into bins.

"I'm headed over to Delacruz's place," Em told her. "Did you hear what happened?"

"His art was stolen."

"One of the security guards is dead."

"Crapola."

"Worse than crapola. The police are on the way."

"Have you called Roland?" Sophie shifted an armload of cloth napkins.

"Yes. I'm waiting for him to call me back." Em looked around.

"Did Buzzy ever come back?"

"No. I hope nothing's happened to him, too."

Em chewed on her bottom lip. "That's all we need."

"Don't even think it," Sophie warned. "Don't even go there."

# 8

AS EM, DELACRUZ, and Jasmine passed the bar on the way back across the property, Pat winked at Jasmine and handed her a half-bottle of champagne.

"Compliments of the bartender," she said.

Jasmine thanked her, tipped up the bottle, and took a swig before she trailed after Delacruz. His short, marching steps made it appear as if he were about to take his compound by storm. They had just passed through the hedge when Delacruz took a dive and slid across the wet grass on his stomach.

"What the hell?" he hollered.

Em looked down and saw Buzzy sitting cross-legged in the damp grass.

"Where have you been?" Em asked him. "I've been looking for you all night."

He blinked and looked around. "I didn't want anyone slipping past. Something's happening here. What it is ain't exactly clear."

Delacruz rolled into a sitting position. Jasmine stood over him, swilling champagne from the bottle.

"Buffalo Springfield? Really? Who is this?" Delacruz shouted. "Who *are* you, and what are you doing squatting on my lawn?"

"He works for me," Em said. "I told him to watch for party crashers." She didn't add she'd been looking for him all night. "We just walked through here not twenty minutes ago, and you weren't here," she said to Buzzy.

He stared up at the stars. "That must have been when I was patrolling the beach."

"Did you see anyone skulking around?" Delacruz wanted to know.

"Like a person, you mean?" Buzzy asked.

"What else?"

"I thought I saw Desdemona."

"Who's Desdemona?" Delacruz got to his feet and stood over Buzzy, taking in his long gray hair and scruffy stubble. "What did you say your name was again?"

"Buzzy. Name's Buzzy."

"Do you have a last name?"

"No. Just Buzzy. Desdemona is my ex-fiancée."

"What was she doing on my property? How'd she get in?"

"She wasn't on your property. She's a dolphin. She was in the ocean out front. Just passing by on the way to Polihale."

Cameron clapped both hands against the sides of his head. "Did I hit my head on something? Is that hole in the hedge a portal into the Twilight Zone?"

"Buzzy and Desdemona had a psychic connection, not a physical one." The minute Em uttered the explanation she realized how insane she sounded.

"For the love of Cheetos!" Delacruz shouted.

Jasmine drained the champagne bottle, whipped back her arm, and slung the bottle over the top of the hedge into Wally's yard.

Em's relief knew no bounds when five KPD cruisers came screaming up the highway. She followed Cameron Delacruz as he ran past the house and down the driveway to meet them. Thankfully Leo had covered his Uncle Bass's body with a piece of plastic tarp. Mo was standing watch, or rather sitting beside it, talking on his cell phone.

When Roland stepped out of one of the unmarked sedans, Em hurried over.

"I got your message." He looked over her head at the scene in the driveway. "When I heard you whisper you needed me, I never guessed it was for this."

"Unfortunately, yes."

"Really, Em? Again?"

"Look, none of us was involved. In fact, all the Maidens were next door. Wally catered a big party to welcome Mr. Delacruz to the island and invited a lot of the people who live around here."

Roland looked at the house. "Neighbors in their tax bracket."

"You might say that. Lots of LA business connections. Delacruz was a friend of Fernando's."

Roland glanced at the body. Two uniformed officers had pulled back the tarp to give him a look. He stared at the victim and mumbled a curse. His jaw tightened.

He motioned for the officers to cover the body again.

"Until the medical examiner arrives," he told them.

"What?" Em had never seen him show any emotional reaction at a crime scene before. "What is it?"

"I know him. That's Sebastian Kekina. They call him Uncle Bass; some folks call him Uncle O'opu. He was an old friend of my pops."

"Oh, no."

"Did you see him earlier?"

"No, we were all next door."

"While you were all next door, someone was up to no good over here." He took a small black leather-bound notebook from his back pocket along with a small black pen. "So as far as you know, what happened?"

"Delacruz hired security guards from *Mahalo* Security to watch the place while he was gone. So many people partying right next door worried him. He owned two paintings worth multi-millions, and they were stolen. This Uncle Bass is related to the guy in charge. Leo."

"Leo Kekina. So somebody got past all of three of them."

"Someone overrode the smart house security system and broke in. Leo was at the party checking in with Delacruz. He was doing double duty as bodyguard and on house patrol while his men stayed over here. When they didn't answer their two-ways, Leo got worried and told Delacruz something was up. I walked over with them to see what was going on." Em looked over at the tarp-covered mound in the driveway.

Roland's words were clipped. "As usual, you thought nothing of rushing into what might have been a crime in progress?" Even though it was a moonless night, she knew Roland's expression had darkened.

"How were we to know what was going on?"

"The guards didn't answer, for one."

"I didn't expect this," she said.

"No one *expects* murder."

Delacruz came stalking over. He'd been haranguing the officers because he felt they were more concerned with the victims than with his stolen art.

"Are you the lead detective here?" He pinned Roland with a glare.

"Detective Sharpe."

"Let's hope so. I've lost a fortune in art. You need to put out a BOLO. Have everyone on the lookout for the thieves."

"A BOLO."

"That's right. Be on the lookout."

"You use that line in your mystery films?"

"Thrillers, actually. Not mysteries. Non-stop action thrillers."

"We don't work that way." Roland glanced down the driveway. Another unmarked car had just arrived. "Usually there's a lot more stop than non-stop action before a crime is solved."

Delacruz shot back. "I'm beginning to think nothing works on this island. You need to check out my living room, dust for prints, look for clues. My priceless Jackson Pollocks are gone."

"Right now the murder takes precedence over some stolen art."

"But I'm telling you this wasn't just a couple of giclees or tourist trinkets. I'm talking about a substantial amount of money. I'm talking about two of the larger privately owned Jackson Pollock paintings in the world."

"I'm telling you, we deal with the dead first. Show some respect."

"Respect? *Respect?*" Delacruz was bouncing from toe to toe, about to combust.

The producer was no threat to Roland, who was six-three and towered over him.

"Hey, Roland." One of the officers waved him over to the body.

"I'll wait here," Em said. She noticed Leo standing outside the knot of officers, staring forlornly down at his Uncle Bass.

While Delacruz fumed, Em watched Roland confer with the medical examiner for a few minutes before he returned.

"The body shows no sign of gunshot, knife wounds, or head trauma. No ligature marks or bruises on the throat. We'll have to wait for the autopsy to know more," he said.

"You think he might have had a heart attack?" Em wondered aloud.

"Or a stroke. He may have chased the thief or thieves down the driveway and keeled over." Roland watched the coroner's van back up the drive.

"Well?" Delacruz tapped his foot on the cement driveway. "What about my missing paintings?"

"Lead the way," Roland said. As they walked along side by side, he told Em, "You can go back to your crew."

She whispered, "I'm afraid to leave you alone with Mr. Delacruz. Hate for there to be a double homicide out here tonight."

"If I could, I'd walk away from this ass right now. Why don't you go on?"

"Wally is so overwrought, the least I can do is look after his friend for him," Em said.

"I hate to say it, but when isn't Mr. Williams overwrought?"

They reached the house, walked past Jasmine who was dozing on a wrought-iron chaise lounge on the front *lanai*. Roland didn't hide the slow once-over he gave the shapely model/actress. They stepped into the wide-open living area, and Roland immediately turned his attention to the scattered broken frames and empty walls.

"Do you have any photos of the paintings?" he asked Delacruz. "Anything descriptive you can give me?"

"There should be photos of them online. You'll find them if you google them. One is called *No. 17, 1946*, and one is called *Desperation*."

"How about you google the photos for me when you write that down?"

"I need to call my insurance agent first," Delacruz insisted.

"You should do that," Roland agreed. "*After* you give me the names of the paintings and some photos."

"Fine. I'll be in my office." Delacruz huffed down the hallway.

Roland took a few steps, lifted a frame with the end of his pen, and then lowered it to the ground. "Someone cut the canvases out of these frames. Roll them, pack them in a bag, and they'll x-ray like fabric."

"Have you ever worked an art theft case before?" She couldn't imagine any theft of this scale ever happening on Kauai before. "Do you think you'll find the stolen pieces before someone smuggles them off island?"

He shrugged. "I don't know. I *do* know that soon I'm going to know a whole lot more about art theft than I do now. Delacruz wasn't the only one whose paintings got lifted. I was on a call in Po'ipu earlier today. Last night someone hit a new gallery over there and stole a high-ticket piece. Nothing big as this, though. No one died."

"I'm really sorry about the old man," she said again.

"Whoever did this is the one who's gonna be sorry."

From the look in his eyes, Em didn't doubt it for a minute.

# 9

ONCE DELACRUZ disappeared into his office, there was nothing left for Em to do. Roland and the other officers started going over the crime scene, dusting for fingerprints and interviewing Mo and Leo in detail. Knowing he'd be busy for hours, Em told him goodbye and headed back to Wally's.

As she left she noticed Jasmine still asleep on the chaise. Further down the driveway, the police were setting up floodlights. A few yards away, between Em and the body that was still beneath the tarp, someone was pacing back and forth. Someone tall and lanky with a disjointed gait.

*Buzzy.*

Em sighed and walked down the driveway to see if he needed a ride home. No one knew where he lived, but rumor had it that he lived in a treehouse somewhere in the quickly disappearing acres of tangled jungle growth in the area. Many of the remaining undeveloped lots were being cleared, and despite disturbing ancient grave sites and sacred ground, the building continued.

As she walked closer, Buzzy heard her footsteps on the gravel drive and turned.

"Hi, Em." If he was surprised to see her, he didn't let on.

"What are you doing out here, Buzz?" He hadn't been around much all evening, and come to think of it, when she had seen him he'd been on the Delacruz property as much as at the party.

"Trying to commune with the poor dead guy."

"Ah." She should have expected as much.

"I thought maybe he'd tell me what happened. It's best to try and contact the dead while the spirit still hovers near the body. He's probably still wondering what happened, ya know?"

"Not really."

"It takes a while for the essence of spirit to move on. Best time to try and make contact is now."

"So are you getting anything?"

He shook his head. "He's a little confused. He's really sorry he couldn't stop the robbery."

"Did he get a look at the guy?" Em was only half joking and glad Roland wasn't close enough to overhear.

Buzzy shrugged. "If he did, he's not saying."

"We should get back to Wally's," she said.

"Yeah. One of the servers is gonna give me a ride up the road."

They left the artificially lit driveway and headed back across the lawn toward Wally's house. As they cleared the hedge, the garden still pulsed with the glow of tiki torches. Fernando's music flowed out of the place, and every light in the massive house appeared to be on, giving it the eerie appearance of a concrete pagan temple.

Em was relieved to see the tables and chairs had been folded and stacked and ready to be picked up with the tent in the morning. Suddenly without warning, shrieks and howls slashed through the music of the piano concerto. Em nearly jumped out of her skin until she realized it was only a cat fight. She'd recently read an article in the *Garden Island* about the North Shore being overrun by its feral cat population.

Buzzy stopped and slowly faced the direction of Delacruz's driveway.

"He hated cats," he announced.

"Who?" Em shivered.

"That Uncle Bass guy."

When they noticed Kimo across the driveway packing the last of his equipment into his pickup, Buzzy left Em to go help out.

Em found Pat was sitting on the back *lanai* having a beer and a cigarette.

"All packed up, boss." She saluted Em.

"Great. *Mahalo* for all the help and for keeping things running smoothly. You can pick up your check tomorrow."

After the night they'd all had, she planned to heavily tip all of her help. She'd gone all out on the food and liquor, and at this point she just hoped she could break even. When the smoke cleared, she'd have to think about whether or not she really wanted to expand to bigger catering gigs.

Inside, Sophie was checking to make sure all of their things had been packed up and carted away. Fernando's music still filled the house with not just sound but memories.

Em was almost afraid to ask, "How's it going?"

"Wally's in bed with an ice pack on his head. Lillian was hauled off to emergency even though the EMTs said there was nothing they could do for a broken coccyx. She insisted on an x-ray. Trish rode with her in the ambulance when Lillian said she'd pay her to film the whole disaster for her Facebook fan club in Iowa."

"Oh, great." Em rolled her eyes. "Now they'll all come flying to her aid."

"Some of them anyway."

Em looked across the expansive living area at the gigantic eighty-inch screen. Fernando was wearing a glittering crystal-encrusted suit in rainbow colors. He was still whaling away on the keyboard.

"No one can figure out how to turn that thing off," Sophie said.

"At least he made it to the party."

"Creeps me out," Sophie said. "So what's going on next door?"

"Roland is there. Odd thing is there was another art theft over on the Po'ipu side. It was last night, though."

"Way?"

"Yep. No one died over there though."

"Poor Leo. He's seems like a nice guy. He's really busted up about his Uncle Bass."

"So's Roland. Turns out Uncle Bass was a buddy of Roland's dad. When Roland went all quiet, I could tell he was seething."

"Uh, oh. I'd hate to be the guy responsible. You know how Roland never shows any emotion? Hard to even get him to smile? I have a feeling that's 'cause he keeps himself on a tight rein. If he ever lets go, look out."

"Maybe."

"I sure wish Uncle Bass could ID the killer," Em said.

Sophie stopped wiping down the island countertop. "Wait. He's dead, remember?"

"Right. Buzzy says his spirit is still hanging around, but the window is closing. Aside from Uncle Bass telling Buzzy he hated cats, the old guy hasn't been very helpful."

# 10

EARLY THE NEXT day, Kiki Godwin wrapped herself in a silk kimono, stretched out on an overstuffed chair on her *lanai*, and watched Kimo top off her morning coffee before he left for work. He'd been hovering over her every chance he got since she'd been released from Kukuoloko.

"How about a warm banana nut muffin?" he asked.

Kiki's hands started to shake so hard she was forced to set down her coffee mug.

"What's wrong? You need a pill or somet'ing?" Kimo's smile faded.

"Nuh . . . no . . . banana nut muff-fufin. Sorry."

He looked so stricken she couldn't bring herself to tell him that pairing the words *banana* and *nut* in the same sentence had set her off. *Bananas* reminded her of monkeys, and it was a monkey that sent her to the *nut* house.

*No banana nut muffin yet. Please.*

*Maybe never.*

She didn't remember much about the traumatic episode that had landed her at Kukuoloko. Kimo and her friends had been afraid to tell her more than bits and pieces. She did remember that the Maidens had just returned from a successful jaunt to Waikiki where they'd gone to support Uncle Louie when he participated in a big regional cocktail shake-off contest.

Upon their return, they'd landed safely on Kauai after the twenty-five-minute flight. Pat went to the parking lot to get her Jeep while Kiki had grabbed their bags and dragged the group's ice chest out to the passenger loading and unloading area at the curb. Pat arrived and was tossing bags in the Jeep when they heard loud thumping coming from the ice chest. There were cans of Spam inside, and Kiki thought they were settling. Pat opened the ice chest to take a look.

Just revisiting what she could remember had Kiki quivering under her kimono like a slick square of *haupia* pudding on a plastic *luau* tray. She took ten deep breaths and started frantically tap tap tapping on her forehead, then above her upper lip and then on her chin.

Tap, tap, tap. Breathe, breathe, breathe.

She closed her eyes and heard her therapist's voice in her head.

*Focus on something else. Visualize a radiant sunset. Visualize a silvery water-fall against the backdrop of a lush green mountain.*

*Horse-pucky.*

Instead, Kiki visualized Flora teetering on the brink last night before she rolled down the parquet dance floor like a giant runaway beer keg before she fell into Precious and Suzi, who took Lillian down with them like a pink-topped bowling pin.

Kiki pictured herself talking to Em. There was something she'd forgotten.

*Tap, tap, breathe.*

Someone had been murdered. A security guard.

Her breathing slowed. Her trembling lessened. It wasn't long before she reached for her coffee again.

Anyone else might think it odd that dwelling on a murder cheered her up almost instantly, but suddenly things were looking up. She was getting excited. Not at the idea that someone had been murdered—of course not—but because now at last she had something to keep her mind off her last few weeks in the hospital and the disjointed flashes of memory from that horrible night at the airport and the cursed capuchin monkey attack.

*There's been a break-in and a murder.*

Em's voice.

Kiki remembered what Em told her last night at Wally's house.

It was all coming back now. Not only had there been a murder, but a break-in. Kiki grabbed her phone off the coffee table and went online. There was nothing about the crimes on the *Garden Island* website; then again, they'd happen too late to make the local news. She tried the *LA Times* website and found a breaking story headline about a robbery and murder at producer Cameron Delacruz's Kauai compound. Over twenty million dollars in art was missing, and a security guard was dead.

Kiki set the phone down and finished off her coffee. The best, the very best way to rehabilitate herself would be to gather the Hula Maidens and solve these crimes. She wouldn't have time to think of anything else. By getting a dangerous thief and killer off the streets she'd not only be doing a service for the community, but she could keep her mind off the freaking monkey attack that almost ruined her life.

She dialed Trish first. The photographer lived the closest.

"I'm at home," Kiki said. "Can you come over?"

"You're home? That's fabulous! Lillian said she saw you at the party last night, but no one else did, so I thought she was delirious."

"How is she? I saw her go down."

"Oh, no! You saw us screw up last night?"

"Unfortunately, yes. So, how's Lillian?"

"She's okay. They didn't keep her in the hospital. MyBob picked her up. Her coccyx wasn't broken at all. She just hit the ground really hard and bruised herself."

"So can you come over?" Kiki asked again. "It's important. I'm calling a meeting."

"Sorry, but I've got appointments this morning. I'm taking photos for a feature story on the Kauai Writers Conference. I wish I could make it. I'm so glad you're back, Kiki! I'll see you soon."

Next she called Big Estelle, who lived with her ninety-three-year-old mother Little Estelle in Princeville.

"Big Estelle, hi! It's Kiki," she said.

"Kiki?"

There was a squawk on the line, and then it sounded like Big Estelle had muffled the phone. Within seconds, Big Estelle was back.

"Sorry about that," she said.

Kiki felt a sudden chill and drew the edges of her kimono together.

"What was that? Your mother?" Kiki wanted to know.

"Oh, you know her. She's watching *Family Feud* re-runs and whooping it up."

"Would you come over ASAP? I'm calling an emergency meeting. There's something important to discuss."

Big Estelle hesitated then said, "I really can't right now, but I'm so glad you're home. How wonderful, Kiki. Will you be at hula practice tomorrow at the Goddess?"

"Listen, if you have to bring Little Estelle, then bring her along. I don't mind. Just come soon."

"No, it's not that." A loud bang and then something shattering on Big Estelle's end of the line. She muffled the phone again.

"What in the heck is going on over there?" Kiki demanded.

"The window washers are here. You know how they are."

"Well, for heaven's sake, take it out of their fee if they break something."

"Will do. See you tomorrow." Big Estelle hung up.

Kiki stared at the phone. Since when did Big Estelle miss a meeting?

Or anything for that matter. She dialed Precious.

"Did your hair grow back?" Precious was a hairdresser, and hair was her first concern.

Kiki fingered a bald spot. "Not all of it. I'm going to need a creative style soon."

"You got it. I can't make it out there for an emergency meeting, though. I'm totally booked up today, but I can be at hula practice tomorrow."

It turned out Pat Boggs was working, too, painting an empty vacation rental, but she promised to be there as soon as she finished rolling a couple more walls.

Kiki was not about to call Lillian and listen to an hour of her whining about her bruised *okole*. She also decided not to call Flora, who was no doubt working at her gifts and sundry shop in Ching Young Village in Hanalei.

Like Trish, Suzi Matamoto was one of the most levelheaded of the group, and Kiki could always depend on her, but when she called the realtor, Suzi was just finishing up a breakfast meeting with a client.

"I can get there as soon as I wrap this up. Maybe thirty minutes tops," Suzi said.

"Perfect. See you then."

Kiki set the phone down, crossed her arms over her midriff, and closed her eyes. She drifted off to sleep dreaming of the mayor smiling his jovial smile as he handed her another framed, gilt-edged proclamation.

Holding the proclamation between them, they smiled for the cameras. The mayor said, "This small token of appreciation is from the County of Kauai and is bestowed upon Kiki Godwin and her Hula Maidens for their part in keeping our *aina* safe by flushing out yet another dangerous criminal and helping to put him behind bars."

Kiki nodded off for a cat nap with a smile on her face.

# 11

BY 9:00 A.M., EM had already spent three hours tucked in the sunlit office in the back room of the Tiki Goddess, savoring the quiet before the storm. The place officially opened at eleven every day, but posting the hours on the front door didn't necessarily keep the locals out if they wanted in. A gentle trade wind blew in through the old glass louvered windows. Her gaze drifted to the view outside: wide banana leaves backlit by sunlight, the empty parking lot, the row of palms that bordered it. The beginning of the small stone path that led between the trees to the beach house just beyond was visible.

Built in the old plantation style, the dark green wooden house with white trim was separated from the Pacific by a swath of dense green grass that ran down to meet the glistening white sand.

Her catering to-do list from the night before was nearly all crossed off. She'd called the tent rental company this morning and learned they'd arrived at Wally's by seven. The owner assured her they would load up the last of the rented chairs and tables, dismantle the dance floor, and take down the tent.

It was hard to concentrate. She kept thinking about Sebastian Kekina's tarp-shrouded body. He's been reduced to a small, lifeless lump beneath glaring klieg lights cutting through the dark of night as the generator that powered them growled incessantly.

She hadn't heard anything from Roland, though she hadn't really expected to yet. He worked every case diligently, and knowing the victim was a friend of his father's, Em was sure Roland would be more focused on finding the killer than ever.

Time ticked away as she checked her emails and then the new Tiki Goddess page on Facebook. Tourists posted photos, mostly of themselves hoisting one of her uncle's legendary tropical drinks decorated with festive umbrellas, fruit garnishes threaded on plastic swords, and translucent plastic mermaids or monkeys that hung over the lip of the glass by their curly tails.

There were photos of Uncle Louie sandwiched between couples

young and old alike. The consummate host, he'd hold babies aloft for kissable photo ops. One of his favorite lines was "Don't you just love to see babies in a bar?" He adored dancing with soon-to-be brides holding bachelorette parties at the Goddess. There were photos of Louie "lei-ing" guests on their birthdays and anniversaries, photos of the Hula Maidens dancing their hearts out on stage. They even squished between tables and danced on the floor. There were many nights when the stage was crowded with tourists overcome with enthusiasm and alcohol. An overdose of mai tais convinced them that they knew how to hula.

The quintessential tiki atmosphere was the backdrop in every photo. Woven mats covered the walls, colorful glass ball fishing floats and puffer fish lights dangled from the ceiling. Bamboo and tiki mask carvings, spears and swords and photos of the locals, not to mention the life-size portrait of Louie's wife Irene, made the Tiki Goddess the real star of every photo.

Em wrote out checks to her employees and the party supply rental company. After she checked her email again, she couldn't resist googling Cameron Delacruz to see if there was anything about the missing Pollocks on the news streams. She didn't expect the *Garden Island* to be on top of it yet. Besides, playing up murder in paradise wasn't all that popular with the Hawaii Tourism Authority folks.

All she found on Delacruz was what she'd heard at the party. He was a major force in the industry in Hollywood, a hard-to-deal with but successful producer until this past year when he'd had a couple of box-office bombs. Everyone seemed certain he'd bounce back. In every photo of him there was a leggy starlet on his arm. He didn't seem to care that they towered over him, because his eyes were level with their more-than-ample cleavages.

Em recognized the photos of his first wife Alanna Grant. Tall, bordering on skeletal thin but muscular, she had waist-length dark hair. She'd made a name for herself as a cover model before she turned to acting. Once Delacruz cast her as a female action-adventure lead, she catapulted to box-office heights. Not only was she a talented actress, but she insisted on doing most of her own stunts.

"Irreconcilable differences" was listed as the reason for their divorce three years ago. In Em's own experience that meant that Cameron Delacruz probably dropped his pants whenever and wherever he could, just like her own ex, the late Phillip Johnson.

Em skimmed the photos of Delacruz here and there around the world. She recognized his latest arm-piece, Jasmine Bishop, in a more recent shot. Apparently Jasmine was new on-the-Hollywood-scene, another model-wannabe-actress with no screen credits of note except for a few lipstick commercials.

Em decided that if she was an actress, and sleeping with a pompous ass like Cameron Delacruz was the only way to the top, she'd be looking for another career *wikiwiki*.

She'd told Sophie not to come in until ten thirty, so Em went into the Goddess to fill the ice bin and stash an extra ice bucket under the bar. She filled the white plastic bucket at the ice machine outside Louie's office door and hefted the twenty pounds of ice over to the bar. Heaving it up, she caught a glimpse of her bicep and chuckled as the ice cubes clattered into the stainless bin.

There was a knock at the front door as she was setting the empty bucket down.

"We're closed," she shouted. She hadn't even propped the wooden windows open yet.

"Em, it's me. Nat."

Nat Clark lived next door, among other places. He had a condo in a Waikiki high-rise and a home in Toluca Lake in the LA area. More than a part-time neighbor, he was a friend. More than a friend, actually. They'd dated a few times. He was intelligent and personable, a writer who was successful, handsome, in his late thirties, and a good kisser. Nat simply didn't set off sparks the way Roland Sharpe, her fire-dancing detective, did.

She walked over and unlocked the front door barely wide enough for him to scoot through and then locked it behind him.

"You look happy this morning," he said.

Her hand went to her hair which always seemed to be oozing out of an elastic hair band.

*Happy?* Hard to believe when they'd barely made any money on the party last night, and there had been a dead security guard in Cameron Delacruz's driveway.

"Why do you think I look happy?"

"You had a smile on your face when you opened the door."

"Actually, just before you knocked I'd lugged twenty pounds of ice from the back room to the ice bin." She made a muscle and showed off her toned upper arm. "I was laughing at myself because I used to pay a fortune for a physical trainer when I lived in Newport Beach and never got the same results. When did you get back?"

"Late flight from LA last night."

"Coffee?" She had a pot on behind the bar.

"Sure."

"Straight up? With cream?"

"How about a shot of Bailey's?"

"You got it."

He slid onto a carved tiki barstool while Em went behind the bar and poured two mugs of coffee. She laced his with a liberal shot of Bailey's Irish Cream.

"You don't usually imbibe this early. What's up?" she asked.

Nat blew gently over the rim of the coffee mug and then took a sip. Em walked around the bar and hiked herself up onto the barstool beside him.

"I'm waiting for the network to decide to renew *Death Do Us Part* for another season." He'd written for another long-running cop procedural series for years. When it ended he'd segued right into a new show.

"Are you worried the show will be cancelled? I thought it was doing great."

"It opened to big ratings, but now not so much. A show can be popular with a loyal fan base, but unless the numbers stay high, cancellation is always a possibility. Sometimes networks aren't willing to let the audience build." He took another sip of coffee and changed the subject. "So what's been happening around here?"

Em sighed. "I'm surprised you haven't heard yet."

"The usual drama? Maidens embroiled in some disaster or other?"

"We catered a big party last night at Wally Williams's place. A welcome-to-the-island bash for a producer. His name's Cameron Delacruz. Know him?"

"I haven't met him, but I know of him. He's produced a lot of hits. Mostly action-adventure."

"Starring his ex-wife. I read up on him a few minutes ago. A couple of his films recently bombed."

"Nuclear bombed."

"You wouldn't know it by his lifestyle. I heard he's in to his home here for six million."

"Bombing is all relative. He's made plenty over the years. Not to worry. He'll bounce back. So how was the party? Everyone happy with your catering?"

She shrugged. "Who knows? Everything was great until someone broke into Delacruz's home, stole his multi-million-dollar Jackson Pollock paintings, and left a dead security guard in the driveway."

Nat's blue eyes widened behind his tortoiseshell glasses. "Say it isn't so."

"Sorry. I can't help but think, here we go again."

# 12

KIKI WAS STILL on the sofa with her feet up, an empty martini glass beside her empty coffee mug. Suzi was curled up in a wicker chair nearby with a wine glass in her hand. Pat sat across from them on an ottoman nursing a beer. The trades luffed the curtains at the windows and carried in the never-ending sound of the surf from the ocean across the highway.

The Godwins' wood frame home sat perched on twenty-foot-high stilts, built to survive a tsunami. Though it was located in Haena, the same area where Delacruz and Wally Williams lived, it was a far more modest dwelling than the newer McMansions built on the beach.

Conscious of her bald spots, Kiki had developed a habit of smoothing her hand over them, parting her hair with her fingers and trying to arrange it to hide the exposed skin. When she realized Suzi and Pat were watching, she started to apologize but then noticed they were actually staring at her violently trembling hand.

"I'm still a wreck," she admitted. "So much for rehabilitation at Kukuoloko."

"Now that you're home, you'll snap out of it," Suzi said. "Wait and see."

"For sure." Pat nodded in agreement though she didn't look convinced.

Kiki shook her head. "I don't know. I'm still *so* jittery. I jump at every little sound. Last night the breeze slammed one of the doors shut, and Kimo had to grab me by the ankles and drag me out from under the bed. Nothing like that ever happens unless we're getting a little kinky."

"Want another drink? I'll get you one," Pat offered.

"No, thanks," Kiki sighed. "You could put some lemonade in the martini glass for me, though."

Pat got up and did Kiki's bidding while Suzi shifted around in her chair and tucked her feet beneath her.

"I'm going to bring you some of Tiko's newest smoothie mix," Suzi promised. Tiko Scott owned Tiko's Tastee Tropical, a line of natural fruit smoothie packets that were gaining popularity not only on Kauai but on the other islands and the mainland. "She's branching into herbal smoothies with restorative power. I'm sure she's got something to calm the nerves."

Kiki pretended to gag. "Herbal smoothies? Shoot me now."

"It certainly can't hurt," Suzi said.

"It will if I upchuck. I loathe all that healthy-green-sawdust-float-ing-in-a-blender crap."

Pat was back with the lemonade. Kiki motioned for her to set it on the table. She didn't trust herself not to slosh it all over yet.

"How about ack-you-punk-sure?" Pat plunked down on the otto-man again. "Get yourself poked all over with those itty bitty needles. It's supposed to work."

"You think I'm gonna let some pot-smoking moonbeam-dancing hippie quack stick pins in me like I'm some straw-stuffed voodoo doll?" Kiki fingered her head. "I don't *think* so."

Suzi sipped her wine. "So why are we here again? You know I can't sit through long meetings. Don't make me suffer."

"I wanted to know what happened at Wally's last night."

"I know. It was terrible," Suzi said. "It really wasn't our fault this time. That portable dance floor was sloped. Terribly tilted. It was an accident waiting to happen long before we started dancing on it."

"What are you talking about?" Kiki stared at Suzi.

"She's talking about the Hula Maiden pileup," Pat said.

"No. No. No. Not the pileup. I'm talking about the murder," Kiki said. "Kimo told me an elderly security guard died right there in the big shot's driveway."

"That was at the house next door," Pat said. "Before she went home, Em told me she heard there's a chance the security guard wasn't murdered. At least he wasn't shot or stabbed or garroted or hit with something, so they didn't know how he died."

"Well, whatever happened," Kiki said, "it's an open case that needs to be solved. I don't think there's anything that will help me snap out of this funk better than all of us working together again to solve a nice juicy murder."

Suzi frowned. Pat scooted to the edge of the ottoman.

"What do we do? Where do we start?" she said.

Kiki tapped her forehead and hoped they would think she was just drumming up an idea.

"I say we get as much information as we can right away. Maybe someone can hack into the police computer."

"Whoa!" Suzi held up her free hand like a traffic cop.

"We ain't a bunch of hackers," Pat reminded them.

Kiki shrugged. "Hula. Hacking. We're good at everything."

"You might be right. Solving this caper will help you recover, Kiki. You've already got some color back in your cheeks."

"That's my bronzer," Kiki said.

"Nope. There's some real color under the bronzer. If it will help you, I'm in," Suzi said.

"Me, too. I love this stuff. It don't pay the bills, but it sure beats painting houses," Pat said.

Kiki said to Pat, "Start the phone chain. Tell the girls we'll meet tomorrow at eleven. Tell them it's not hula practice, but something highly classified and important."

"Got it." Pat nodded. "Classified and important. VVP."

"What's VVP?" Kiki asked her.

"Very, very 'portant. At the Goddess, correct?" Pat said.

"No! Not there. We'll meet here. If Em gets wind of our plan she'll discourage us, especially after our last caper in Waikiki."

"But she has access to Roland. She can get us inside information," Suzi said.

"We can't sell ourselves short," Kiki said. "Besides, there are eight of us. Nine counting Little Estelle. If only one of us turns up a clue a day we can solve this in little over a week."

Pat and Suzi exchanged a quick look.

"I wouldn't count on Little Estelle." Suzi didn't make eye contact with Kiki.

"What's up with Little Estelle?" Kiki remembered the odd sounds she heard in the background when she spoke to Big Estelle earlier. "Is she ill? Is there something you're not telling me?"

It was no secret that Little Estelle was a nuisance. The ex-Rockette careened around on a motorized sit-down scooter, was a sex maniac who registered on iLoveCougars.com, drank too much, and snuck away from Big Estelle all too frequently. On their excursion to Waikiki she gave up her latest goal of becoming a rapper and decided to write her life story.

There was something else gnawing at the edge of Kiki's memory about Little Estelle, but whatever it was evaded her at the moment. No matter how difficult the little holy terror could be, she was one of the Hula Maidens, and Kiki didn't want to hear any bad news about her.

"Little Estelle's fine. In fact—" Pat started to say more but Suzi cut her off.

"She's busy working on her book." Suzi was digging in her bag for her keys.

Kiki noticed and was reminded of her own situation. "I'm not cleared to drive yet," she said.

Suddenly a rooster that had to be right under the house let out a long cock-a-doodle-doo that sounded like demented screaming. Kiki grabbed her head, rolled off the sofa, and ended up under the coffee table in a duck-and-cover position. Her vision blurred; her head began to pound.

She tried to tell the girls she was all right, but all that came out was an odd keening.

Pat dropped to her hands and knees and peered under the table.

"You're all right, Kiki. It's just a rooster. No need to moan like that. I'll help you out. Come on, give me your hand. That's it. Easy does it. Cut the catterwallin'."

Kiki opened and closed her mouth two or three times but still couldn't speak. Finally Pat coaxed her off the floor and helped her back onto the sofa.

"Are you gonna be all right by yourself?" Suzi hovered behind Pat. They were both staring down at her.

Kiki nodded, afraid to open her mouth and not be able to garble out a word.

"So we'll see you tomorrow. We'll call the others, don't you worry." Suzi patted her shoulder.

"I'll see if I can find out anything about the case from Em," Pat said. "I'll take notes if I do. Dwell on that, okay? Think about how much better you're gonna feel once we get going on this case."

As they let themselves out, Kiki wasn't thinking about the case. She was fuming, thinking about how much better she'd feel if she could only get her hands on the damn marauding monkey that did this to her. Thankfully, she'd never have to see it again. The wily stowaway was long gone and back on Oahu where it belonged.

# 13

IT WAS A SLOW night at the Goddess that evening; slow meaning there were only two Maidens dancing—Flora and Big Estelle. After the big party the night before, the others were home nursing sore knees, bruises, and resting up for Kiki's big emergency meeting. Every stool at the bar was taken, and all the tables were packed. There was a line of customers that trailed down the *lanai* steps and into the waiting area out front.

Em had given Sophie a well-deserved night off, which meant Uncle Louie was tending bar. Em helped him out when he was knee deep in drink orders. When she got a chance, which wasn't often, she helped Tiko Scott wait tables. Tiko worked the night shift part-time while growing her Tastee Tropical smoothie business.

Working the bar alone at the moment, Em felt a wave of relief when her Uncle Louie strolled back in. He'd asked her to take over, said he'd be right back, and then slipped out fifteen minutes ago. The tables closest to the stage were filled with a party of twelve women celebrating a twenty-second birthday, and they wanted a second round of drinks, and they wanted them now.

Her uncle finally returned, but with six plumeria *lei* around his neck and three hanging from each arm. The fragrance most synonymous with Hawaii immediately filled the air. He headed straight for the birthday party to *lei* the birthday girl, a blonde whose skin glowed so red she looked like she'd fallen asleep under a leaking nuclear plant silo.

Louie slipped the *lei* around her neck, kissed her on both cheeks, and then proceeded to *lei* each of the women in turn. They hooted, hollered, and thanked him by pressing their young sunburned selves against him and bestowing generous hugs and kisses.

Louie lingered by their table for a minute or two more, and then he took his time shaking hands, meeting and greeting old and new patrons as he made his way back behind the bar. Still fit in his early seventies, her uncle was Hawaiian-travel-poster perfect with his deep golden tan and head full of thick silver hair. He always wore a vintage Aloha shirt from his vast collection, baggy white linen pants, and when out and about he added a white Panama hat. Louie gave off a happy-go-lucky gentlemanly vibe that put people at ease the minute they saw him.

Tiko shouted orders to them over the noisy crowd, and together they lined up the various glasses needed to serve his most popular drinks: Great Balls of Fire, Horny Rum Rhinos, Mai Tais, and one of his latest, Sweet Coconut Balls.

"Sure wish we could serve some Flaming Manic Monkeys," he shouted to Em over the din. "They'll be great for special occasions."

"Not tonight, Uncle." It was all she could do to manage the many garnishes and paper umbrellas the specialty drinks required without having to light them on fire.

His Flaming Manic Monkey had taken top prize at the recent Western Regional Shake Off Competition in Waikiki, but the concoction called for igniting a float of 151-proof rum on top of the drink. Em put her foot down about serving them when the bar was overcrowded. They had already had a close call the night Lillian set her wig on fire. Em didn't want to go through anything like that again, let alone risk a lawsuit or burning the place to the ground.

At least time flew when the bar was jam-packed. Em hadn't realized the crowd had thinned out until she heard Danny Cook and the Tiki Tones calling her uncle up to the stage to lead the remaining guests in the closing song. It was an ode he wrote to his late wife, Irene Kau`alanikaulana Marshall, co-founder of the bar and his one true love. The lovely native woman he referred to as his tiki goddess had passed away over ten years ago. Every night at closing, the locals and *kama`aina* turned to face Irene's portrait and joined him in song.

All *pau* dancing for the night, Big Estelle and Flora bellied up to the bar.

"*Mahalo*, you two." Em lowered her voice while Louie was singing and slid complementary mai tais across the bar to the women. "Thanks for showing up tonight."

"I had to get out of the house." Big Estelle daubed sweat off her face and neck with a paper napkin.

Em completely understood. The woman's mother was a handful. "How is Little Estelle?"

"Obsessed with her new pet project twenty-four-seven."

"I'm sure writing ninety-plus years of memoires is all-consuming." Em waved to a couple of outrigger paddlers as they walked out.

"That too," Big Estelle mumbled.

"We're going to need another order of plastic stir sticks," Em told Flora. The shop owner ordered special stir sticks with the Tiki Goddess logo for Louie and also sold them by the dozens to tourists.

"Sure t'ing. I'll do it tomorrow." Flora had already polished off her mai tai. She went back to making sucking noises with her straw.

Louie finished his tribute to Irene and joined Em behind the bar.

"Congratulations on your big win in Waikiki, Uncle Louie." A couple from Anahola gave Louie the *"shaka"* thumb and pinkie hand wave. "You working on a new drink?" the man wanted to know.

"Always," Louie laughed. "Love doing the research." He hoisted a bottle of rum. Folks seated at the bar all nodded and laughed with him.

Not only were his original cocktails delicious, but he also wrote a legend to go with each and every one and had the stories printed up on the drink menus.

The couple wished him luck and left.

"What are you working on now?" Big Estelle wanted to know.

Uncle Louie's face brightened. "I've been thinking a lot about the time I went to New Guinea, back in the sixties. The nineteen sixties, not my sixties. Rumor had it there were still a lot of headhunters lurking in the jungle. You ever seen those tiki mugs that look like shrunken heads?" He frowned, thinking. "Used to have one somewhere. Maybe it's in the bar in the house. Anyway, I'm trying to think up a tall tale about that trip."

"Sounds like a wild trip all right," Big Estelle said.

"How about somethin' like a zombie?" Flora said. "I had a good one once."

Big Estelle choked on her last sip of mai tai. "You slept with a zombie?"

"Not. I had a *drink* called a zombie."

Em took an order from Tiko while listening to the exchange.

"Right," Louie said. "But there are already a lot of versions of cocktails named Zombie. I'm talking about headhunters."

"Probably already some of those too," Flora said.

"Speaking of hunting heads . . ." Big Estelle pushed her empty glass away. "Any news about the murder?"

"Murder?" Louie frowned. "What murder?"

"You didn't hear? You gotta be the only one."

He shook his head. "I was in Lihue all day. What happened? Nobody we know, I hope."

"Sorry, Uncle," Em said. "I haven't had a second to tell you about last night."

Flora and Big Estelle filled him in on the murder and robbery at the house next door to the party last night.

"You heard anything new, Em? Has Roland called?" Her uncle had reason to look concerned. Lately the Tiki Goddess staff seemed to be involved whenever anything newsworthy, good or bad, happened on the North Shore.

"Nothing at all. I haven't had time to talk to him."

"I hope none of us ends up in jail this time," Louie mumbled.

"We're all clear," Em said. At least she hoped so.

The band packed up their equipment, and Louie opened the cash drawer to pay them while Em signaled Tiko to make sure patrons knew they had time for one more drink. Big Estelle and Flora left when Em didn't offer to comp them another drink.

The crowd started to thin considerably once the music ended. There was no entertainment scheduled for the late-night crowd except on weekends. Within another forty-five minutes, the place had cleared out except for Buzzy. Now that the room was empty, Em saw him back in the corner of the banquette nursing a beer. Tiko looked worn to a frazzle. Em told her to take off.

Louie helped Em wipe down the bar and said, "If you've got this, I'm gonna head home and look for that shrunken head mug. Come to think of it, I think I brought home a genuine shrunken head souvenir from New Guinea."

Great, Em thought. *I've been living with a shrunken head somewhere in the house.*

"Go ahead. I'll be fine."

She was used to locking up alone and was hoping for an early night when Roland walked in. From the look on his face, he wasn't in any better mood than he'd been last night.

She wiped down the bar and tossed a rag into a bucket, poured herself a tall ice water, and asked if Roland wanted anything. He shook his head no.

When he sat down at the long banquette and stretched out his legs, Em walked around the bar to sit next to him.

"Any leads?"

"None. The ME said Uncle Bass wasn't murdered. He died of a massive heart attack. Probably chased the guys down the driveway, and his heart blew. Either way, whoever stole those paintings is responsible for his death."

"Can they be charged with murder?"

"Yes, under the state's felony murder rule. It allows someone to be charged with murder if he or she causes another person's death while committing or fleeing from a felony crime such as robbery—even if it's unintentional." He drummed his fingers on the table top for a minute, then turned his attention to Em again.

"What about the stolen art in Po'ipu? Any connection?" she asked.

"No idea yet. It seems like a huge coincidence, though. High-end art stolen two nights in a row. There have been a lot of vacation rental break-ins all over. Grab-and-run stuff when people aren't careful to lock their doors. The art heists took a lot more finesse. Breaking and entering, canvases cut off of their frames."

"The Po'ipu artist isn't anywhere near as famous as Pollock though."

"No, but according to the gallery owner, he's up and coming. His pieces command more money than an average buy, but definitely not even five figures. I haven't had time to research Delacruz's paintings, but I did find out that theft of works of cultural, historical, or artistic significance is a federal crime. Worst case scenario we'll have to call in the FBI Art Crime Team."

"Really? Would that be so bad if they came in and took this case off your hands?"

By now she knew Kauai Police dealt with the usual kinds of theft: small electronics like cameras, cell phones, iPads, wallets. Rental car break-ins. Home burglaries. Cars were rarely stolen because there was no way to drive them off the island. When a car was stolen, they were usually found abandoned in a cane field. Tracking down something as valuable as a Pollock was definitely not in Roland's wheelhouse. Then there was murder, which seemed to be happening a lot more and too close to home.

He stared across the room at nothing, his jaw set.

"I don't want the FBI collaring this guy. I want to hunt down whoever was responsible for Uncle Bass's death."

"I'll help in any way I can." She knew how he'd react to her offer. At least she thought she did.

He surprised her by saying, "I haven't had time to research the information on Delacruz's paintings or any of Pollock's work. I have no idea what we're dealing with here."

"I'd be happy to find out as much as I can."

"You're as busy as I am."

"I'll make time."

He reached into his shirt pocket and handed over a folded piece of paper.

"I'll get started tomorrow morning. Uncle Louie can set up the bar before Sophie opens."

Their fingers touched as he handed over the page.

"You sure you have time?" he asked.

"Of course."

His gaze drifted to the back of the room where Buzzy had rested his arms on the tabletop and had buried his head in them.

"Did you ever figure out where he was last night?"

Em shrugged. "Wandering around. Sometimes he's so stoned he doesn't know where he is, but he seemed lucid enough last night. I made the mistake of asking him to walk the grounds and watch for party crashers. He ended up on the beach trying to telepathically contact his ex-fiancée."

"Oh, yeah. The dolphin? You bought that?"

"Buzzy's nuts, but he's harmless."

Roland reached for her water glass. It was still half full.

"You mind?" he asked.

"Go ahead."

He drained it, set it down again. His hand slid across the table until it covered the back of hers. "Too bad you never get a night off."

"Look who's talking. When you're not busy detecting you're dousing knives with gas, lighting them on fire, and dancing around half naked."

"Not really."

"More than half naked?"

"I prefer half dressed," he said.

Em laughed.

"Your uncle home tonight?" His thumb was slowly cruising back and forth over her hand.

"You bet."

"When are you going to get your own place?"

"When are you going to invite me over to yours?"

# 14

"THIS IS A great shrimp salad, Suzi. Will you email me the recipe?" Precious was seated on the floor in Kiki's large comfortable living room with a plate of food balanced on her thighs.

Suzi Matamoto's mouth was full, so she nodded and kept chewing.

Kiki looked around the room at the gathering of Hula Maidens and worked hard to keep from bursting into tears. Three weeks ago she was too messed up to dream she'd ever be released from the hospital, and now here she was back in her own home hosting a luncheon, surrounded by her hula sisters.

She loved nothing more than filling the house with friends for dinners and special occasion parties, but she was still fragile. This morning's gathering was only supposed to be a meeting until Suzi volunteered to bring a salad. Pat signed up for three bottles of champagne, Precious lugged in a box of cinnamon rolls as big as her head, and Trish came over early to make coffee and set the table for buffet.

When Flora arrived she added a tall tropical bouquet of flowers and lined fragrant green *laua`e* leaves down the middle of the tropical print tablecloth. Big Estelle came in huffing and puffing from the long flight up the stairs carrying a plate of fried Spam slices garnished with grilled pineapple rings. She said Little Estelle sent her regrets, but she was busy with her project.

Kiki was just thinking of the old saying, *lucky I live Kaua'i*, when Trish lifted her champagne flute for a toast.

"Here's to Kiki," she said. "We're so glad you're home!"

The women raised their glasses in Kiki's direction then sipped champagne drizzled with *likiko'i* syrup. Once the toast was over, Suzi said, "Okay, Kiki. Tell everyone what's up."

"Do we have a show or a competition coming up?" Trish popped a piece of cinnamon roll into her mouth.

"Not actually a show, but we will be dancing this weekend. You all know about the robbery and the murder at the house next to Wally's party. Uncle Sebastian Kekina's funeral is Sunday, and we're going to dance."

"What'll we wear?" Flora wanted to know.

"What dances are we gonna do?" As the newest member, Precious's biggest concern was what songs to practice before gigs.

"Do we smile or not? I never know what to do when we dance at funerals," Trish said. "It doesn't seem *pono* to smile."

Kiki rubbed a bald spot. "I don't know yet. Don't ask me hula questions right now."

From her chair near the window Pat barked, "Yeah, shut up, y'all. She don't need badgerin'."

"Right. *Mahalo*, Pat," Kiki said. "Anyway, I'll let you know more about Uncle Bass's celebration later. Right now, we have to put our heads together. There's a murderer, or murderers, out there somewhere, and we have to track them down."

"Wait a minute." Trish shook her head. "We've been warned not to butt into police business, Kiki."

"We have a successful track record of solving crime on this island *and* a proclamation from the mayor to prove it," Kiki shot back. "I'm not in favor of backing down, and neither are the others." She slowly eyed the rest of the group. "*Are* you, ladies?"

No one dared contradict her.

Pat raised her hand.

"What?" Kiki said.

"I got something to say about why we gotta do this."

Kiki was hesitant but said, "Okay."

Pat looked at all the others. "We ain't doin' this just for the fun of it or because we wanna be famous detectives or nothin'. We gotta do this 'cause it'll be good therapy for Kiki. She needs to get her mojo back, and working on the robbery case will keep her from thinkin' about what happened after Waikiki."

Afraid Pat was actually going to *say* what had happened, Kiki slapped her hands over her ears and closed her eyes so she couldn't hear or lip-read.

"It's okay, Kiki," Precious yelled. "All clear."

Kiki lowered her hands, tried to smile. "*Mahalo*, Pat, for that. It's true. I think focusing on the robbery will help me out of the crazies."

"Then of course we'll do it," Flora said. "We'll find the murderers."

"I heard Uncle Bass wasn't murdered. He died of a heart attack," Trish said.

Kiki nodded. "That might be, but I read on Facebook his family thinks it was the robbers' fault that the poor old guy is dead. If there hadn't been a robbery, he wouldn't have been running down the driveway. Besides, the bums stole a couple of famous paintings. Who does that? Nobody with any soul, I say."

"I read in the paper there is a reward for the return of the stolen art. No questions asked. I'll bet it's a big reward." Big Estelle was sitting beside the buffet table. She reached over and forked up a couple slices of Spam. "If we find 'em we can split the money."

"Or put it in the hula kitty," Pat said. "Maybe go on another road trip."

"All right then, that's settled." Kiki was all smiles. "We go for it."

"So what do we know? Where do we start?" Suzi set her plate aside and took out her notepad.

The women exchanged looks and shrugged.

"All we know is what's been in the paper," Big Estelle said.

Kiki set her half-finished plate aside. "I must report, Kimo called this morning. When he got to work, Em was on the phone with a California art dealer she knows on the mainland. She was asking him to look into the history of the missing pieces. But you didn't hear that from me."

"You think Roland asked for her help?"

"I'm thinking she's got more to do than research the stolen paintings for her own curiosity. If Roland asked her to help, then that's kind of like asking all of us, right? But we'll need to track down some viable clues on our own," Kiki said.

"We should go over to the scene of the crime and look around," Suzi suggested.

"I've gotta run the shop today." Flora didn't sound all that sorry to miss the excursion.

"I've got clients booked starting at one thirty, so I'd better hit the road." Precious's salon was forty minutes away in Kapa'a.

"Whoever goes to Delacruz's, we can't just waltz right in," Pat reminded them. "There's a security gate."

"A lot of good that did them the other night," Big Estelle chuckled. She wet her napkin in a glass and tried to wipe a spot off her dress, but it wasn't budging.

"Is that paint or food?" Precious wanted to know.

Big Estelle stopped wiping.

"I could tell them I'd like to take photos for a feature article," Trish suggested.

Kiki was silent, thinking. Finally she drained her champagne flute and yelled, "Fruit basket!"

"Uh, oh." Pat jumped up, ready to assist. "She's losing it again."

"Sit. I'm perfectly sane," Kiki shot back. "We'll take over a fruit basket. Pay a friendly welcome-to-the-neighborhood call."

"Mr. Delacruz is a bazillionaire. No need fruit." Flora rolled her eyes.

"What then?" Kiki said.

"*Poi*," Precious suggested. "Bet they don't have any *poi*."

"*Haoles* don't eat *poi*," Flora sniffed.

"*Haoles* do eat *poi*. I eat *poi*," Trish reminded her.

Everyone else said, "Me, too."

"Okay, then." Flora was adamant. "*Malihini* don't eat *poi*."

Kiki nodded. "You're right. Newcomers don't usually like *poi*. A fruit basket will do. Hopefully it will get us through the front door."

"Maybe throw in some nuts from Kauai Nut Roasters."

"Sounds good," Pat agreed. "Along with a bottle of Koloa rum."

"It'll be a welcome and a condolence call," Kiki said. "Sorry about your loss. We can ask about his paintings, find out if they saw anyone suspicious snooping around when he moved them in or the day of the party."

"So exactly what will we do when we get there?" Suzi had been typing notes into her notebook. "Assignments?"

Kiki tapped her fingers against her chin and stared at the ceiling a minute.

"When we finish here those who can will go over with a basket of goodies. Big Estelle can drive her van. If we get through the gate I'll make nice and chitchat while the rest of you snoop around. Walk around and pretend to be looking at stuff. Check out the garden and the possible break-in points. Maybe we can find out where the guards were stationed. Trish, take photos of anything out of the ordinary, anything at all."

"The police were all over the place for hours," Pat said. "You think they missed something?"

Kiki said, "All we need to find is one itty bitty little clue."

# 15

EM WALKED OUT of ocean water as clear blue as the sky. Trade showers were supposed to blow through later in the day, but for now the sky was clear except for an occasional passing cloud. She pulled off her snorkel and tossed it on the towel she'd spread on the strip of sand between the edge of Louie's yard and the slabs of coral barely submerged in the water along the shoreline.

She swam using a snorkel so she wouldn't miss the show put on by the tropical fish, loving the world that existed below the surface of the water. She'd memorized a few of their Hawaiian names: the long silver needle cornet fish were *nunu peke*, Moorish idols were *kihiki*, eels were *puhi*, and the Hawaiian state fish, the *humuhumunukunukuapua'a*, was an artfully striped triggerfish.

There was a host of wonders everywhere she chose to look. One of her favorite thrills was spotting a green sea turtle and swimming along beside it for a while. One of her least favorite was seeing the outline of a small white tip reef shark far below her in deeper water. The first time it happened to her, she'd mastered swimming backward in seconds.

There were days she wished she were a mermaid so she could stay underwater as long as she wanted.

Em sat on her towel and shook water out of her shoulder-length blond hair by running her fingers through it. She was just about to stretch out when she heard footsteps crunch in the coarse sand behind her. She shaded her eyes, looked up, and found herself staring at Nat Clark in silhouette against the sky.

"You planning to take a snooze? If so, I'll keep walking," he said.

Em sat up again. "No, what's up? Did you hear anything about your show yet?"

"Nothing about the show. How about you? How did you manage to get away from the bar?" He sat down on the sand beside her towel.

"It's really slow right now. Sophie can handle it for a while. On sunny days people stay out on the beach longer. Late afternoon when the tourists are all sunburned, tired, and hungry, then we'll be slammed.

The kids will be sandy and cranky and the parents frazzled."

"You'd think they'd be relaxed after chillin' at the beach," he laughed.

"You'd think."

"Heard anything new about the robbery?" he asked.

"The security guard died of a heart attack."

"I saw that on the *Garden Island* website."

"Roland asked me to research the stolen Pollock pieces. They were worth over twenty-two million."

Nat whistled in appreciation and nodded. "Last night I remembered reading something about Delacruz collecting Jackson Pollock pieces. He and his ex Alanna went toe to toe over them when they divorced. He ended up keeping them, and rumor has it that was in exchange for Alanna Grant being cast as the lead in three more of his films."

"Is that why the films tanked?"

Nat shook his head no. "Not at all. Over the last couple of years, Delacruz stepped out of the box. He produced a period piece set in Burma and a spy film starring a whole raft of aging action heroes."

Em watched Norwegian Cruise Line's *Pride of America* slide slowly along the horizon, making its way toward the Na Pali Coast, an area inaccessible except on foot or by boat. Em personally considered the Na Pali the number one Wonder of the World.

"You think his ex would steal the paintings from him?" she said, thinking aloud.

Nat laughed again. "Not for money. She's got more than she can count. The woman commands eighteen million or more per film. I can't see her slinking around Kauai putting her career, not to mention her freedom, on the line just to get back at Delacruz."

"You're probably right." Em brushed sand off her knee. "Roland has his mind set on solving this before the FBI has to be called in. Sebastian Kekina was a friend of his dad's."

"I'd hate to be on that guy's seek-and-destroy list."

"Roland's?"

"Right."

They sat side by side in silence with only the sound of the waves lapping over the slabs of coral. Em sifted the coarse golden sand through her fingers.

"Is there any chance of me taking you out for dinner soon, or are you two getting really serious?"

Em felt his gaze riveted on her and kept her eyes on the cruise ship. A few weeks ago Roland had flown to her aid on Oahu when she ended up a suspect in her ex's murder. Nat was the one who called Roland in the first place and asked if he'd help Em.

She and Roland ended up spending the night together in Waikiki after the case was solved. She was supposed to meet him tonight at Hukilau *Lanai* for dinner and share the info she learned about the paintings over a leisurely meal.

So was their relationship *serious?*

It was hard to say. Roland was a man of few words and fewer outward expressions of emotion. She was recovering from her messy divorce when her ex Phillip Johnson was killed. The last thing she wanted at this point was *serious.*

Still, she was positive she'd never be able to successfully handle being semi-serious with two men at once.

"Serious might be a bit too strong a word to describe what Roland and I have going, but we've moved a few steps past casual." When she turned his way, she saw Nat smiling at her and almost regretted turning him down.

"Say no more," he said. "It serves me right for living and working on the mainland and another island. You know my cell number in case you ever change your mind and want to take a few steps past casual with me, too."

# 16

WHEN THE MAIDENS' brunch meeting finally broke up, Pat, Flora, and Precious headed back to work. Kiki and a skeleton crew—Suzi, Trish, and Big Estelle—climbed into Big Estelle's van and headed for the Delacruz compound. As they pulled up to the security gate flanked by tall lava-rock columns, Big Estelle stared at all the buttons on the intercom.

Trish hung out of one of the back windows, snapping photos of the statues Delacruz had commissioned for the tops of the columns. One was an overtly muscular Poseidon wielding his trident.

"I know who the guy is, but who's the woman with the dolphin beside her?" Kiki stared up at the other statue.

"Amphitrite," Suzi piped up. She had her cell in her hand and read, "She was the wife of Poseidon, Queen of the Sea in Greek mythology. Also known as the loud moaning mother of dolphin, seals, and fish."

"I have a loud moaning mother," Big Estelle mumbled.

Trish adjusted her shoulder to get a better shot. "Has Buzzy seen that dolphin statue? The thing is half the size of Amphrawhatzit, the queen of the seas."

"What should I do?" Big Estelle gripped the wheel and stared straight ahead as if she planned to gun the engine and bust through the security gate.

"Try pressing that red button," Kiki said.

Big Estelle pressed. Then pressed again.

Finally a woman answered. "Yes?"

Kiki leaned across Big Estelle and shouted toward the intercom.

"Aloha! I'm your neighbor Kiki Godwin. I'm with a couple of the Hula Maidens who entertained at the party at Wally Williams's. We're just stopping by to welcome Mr. Delacruz to the neighborhood, and we have a gift to drop off."

There was a moment of silence and then, "Oh, hi. This is Jasmine. I was with Cameron at the party the other night. Come on up to the house."

There was a click and then a loud buzz, and the gate slowly swung open.

"Wow," Trish said. "I never thought we'd get in."

Kiki snorted. "Are you kidding? I have a knack for getting into places where I don't belong."

Big Estelle headed up the drive.

"I wonder where they found Uncle Bass?" Suzi stared out the window. Trish snapped photos.

"Gotta be around here somewhere. They said he was in the drive-way, probably chasing down the perps." Kiki felt renewed with every passing second.

"Remind me not to chase anybody," Big Estelle told them.

Kiki leaned forward and studied the huge house up ahead.

"I haven't been here since Fernando was killed and Em was kid-napped and held in the safe room in this place."

"Don't remind me." Suzi shivered. "That was some bad monkey business."

"Wh . . . what did you . . . just stay? Say?" Kiki's head started throb-bing. She drank in some quick, deep breaths.

"I'm sorry. I'm so sorry. That was some nasty *business*," Suzi cor-rected.

Kiki ignored her, tapped her forehead, and focused on the house as they pulled into the circular drive. The lovely Jasmine was standing on the *lanai* waiting to greet them.

"Aloha," Kiki said, stepping out of the van.

She reached back for the gift basket, one she'd thrown together before they left the house. She'd filled it with huge papayas, bananas, and limes from Kimo's garden, a bottle of Made on Kauai Koloa rum she'd stashed away for emergencies in her hurricane closet, and a can of fla-vored macadamia nuts. She'd quickly woven some *ti* leaves into what looked like a natural decorative bow and had tucked in a couple sprays of white orchids.

Jasmine greeted them all warmly and *oohed* and *aahed* over the basket after Kiki handed it to her.

"I hope we aren't interrupting anything." Kiki tried to peer around Jasmine and look inside. "I'm sure Mr. Delacruz is busy."

"You aren't interrupting anything. In fact, you ladies have saved me from complete boredom. Cameron flew over to Honolulu to appear on a segment of *Extra Hot Style*, you know, that gossip magazine show? They're going to film him at the affiliate station on Oahu since he couldn't really set up much of a press conference over here. Anyway, he left me home alone, and all I've done so far is lie around by the pool and read magazines."

"So lucky we came over then," Kiki said. She introduced the others.

"Come on in," Jasmine invited. "In fact, I was just about ready to sit down and watch the show. Cameron should be on in a couple of minutes. I almost forgot what time it is on the mainland. I would have missed it."

They kicked off their sandals and rubber slippers and followed Jasmine through a sliding door off to the side of the *lanai* into a screening room complete with a huge flat screen on the wall and an acre of cushy sofas and pillows scattered around.

Kiki studied the room but saw nothing unusual as she climbed into the deep sofa. Suzi's feet barely made it to the edge. Jasmine flicked on the remote, and the television filled with the logo of the *Extra Hot Style* celebrity magazine show. The smarmy host gave a rundown of the night's feature stories.

"Tonight we'll hear from one of Hollywood's most well-known producers, Cameron Delacruz, whose multi-million-dollar beach home on a remote outer Hawaiian island was broken into earlier this week." Thankfully Cameron's account of the robbery was going to air first.

"Remote outer island? He makes it sound like we live on a deserted atoll," Trish said.

A second later the screen filled with Delacruz wearing an Aloha shirt and an orchid *lei*. He was seated in front of a backdrop of Waikiki. On camera, his bottled tan took on an orange glow. Teetering on the edge of a wrought-iron stool, he looked like a spray-tanned elf.

From somewhere off camera the host asked, "Tell us how the robbery went down, Cameron. I'm sure you were horrified. Did you fear for your life?"

Kiki snorted. "He wasn't even there."

Someone shushed her.

"I can't go into all the details since the authorities are in the process of hunting down the criminals as we speak," he said. "I will say that they got away with my Jackson Pollocks, two huge works worth over thirty-five million."

The host feigned shock. "What a tragedy. I understand a security guard was killed in the line of duty."

"That's true, but let me just add that I . . ." Delacruz leaned toward the camera. "I just want my paintings back. Please. We're offering a *huge* reward for their return. *Huge*. No questions asked."

"He didn't even mention poor Uncle Bass," Suzi said. "What a putz."

"He's always very focused," Jasmine said.

"If you ask me, he's way out of focus," Kiki mumbled, thankful when the show moved on to another clip of a movie premiere on Hollywood Boulevard. Jasmine clicked off the television.

"What can I get you ladies?" she asked. "I have ice tea and fruit juices. Do you drink wine? Or I can make you a great coconut nutmeg rum shake."

"Now you're talking," Big Estelle said. "I'll try one of your rum shakes."

After two drinks each, all but Kiki had forgotten the true reason for their visit.

She set down her glass. "I'm really sorry about the robbery. That sort of big-time crime doesn't happen out here much. Small stuff like phones and tablets and cameras get stolen, mostly from vacation rentals, but art? Who woulda thunk it?"

Jasmine said, "I'm just glad we were at the party and not here alone. What if it had turned into a home invasion? It's bad enough the older security guard had a heart attack chasing the guy down."

"Is this where it happened?" Kiki looked around the screening area.

Jasmine stretched. "No. The paintings were all on display in the main room at the front of the house. Would you like to see?"

"Love to." Kiki scooched over to the edge of the sofa and stood up. Big Estelle was nodding off. Trish shook her awake. She sputtered and sat up.

They all followed Jasmine into the wide open living area. Even though she pointed out the bare nails on the bare walls, it was easy to see where the paintings had been. Broken frames and stretcher bars were still leaning up against the sofa.

"So, these were huge pieces?" Kiki stared at the frames.

"Very huge. Cameron had the furniture and lighting placed so the Pollocks would be the focal point of the room." She pointed to an expansive area above the sofa that was completely bare. "These were oil on canvas. Cameron paid over twenty million for them."

"Twenty million. As in dollars?" Big Estelle stared up at the empty wall.

"This is a beautiful place." Kiki looked around the room.

"Would you like a tour?" Jasmine asked.

"I thought you'd never ask." Kiki smiled, and as she began to follow

Jasmine toward the dining room, she wiggled her brows at Trish, the high sign for the photographer to mosey around on her own with Suzi.

"I thought this was a smart house." Kiki ran her fingertips along the polished surface of the solid *koa* wood dining table with twelve matching chairs. "How did the thieves get in?"

Jasmine shrugged and twirled a lock of her long dark hair around her index finger.

"Cameron has no idea. He is the only one with the code. Well, he and his lawyer on the mainland in case of an emergency. He hasn't even given it to me."

"Better hope you don't get locked out."

"Right, huh? I'd have to spend the whole day by the pool until he got back." They headed for the kitchen. "It's amazing, really. From anywhere in the world Cameron can lock up the house, turn the AC up and down, view each room from his cell phone camera, and I don't know what all else."

"But all that doesn't matter if someone can just walk in," Kiki pointed out. She saw Big Estelle and Trish standing by the water fountain in a small garden off to the side of the pool.

"What about cameras? A place like this must have cameras."

"It does. They're hidden all over, but they were turned off by whoever used the code to walk in."

She wandered over to a carved sideboard that matched the *koa* wood table and chairs and almost moaned; it was so very lovely and so very far out of her price range.

"There's a safe room, too," Jasmine volunteered. "It's in the middle of the house."

"I know. The gal who catered the party over at Wally's was kidnapped and locked up inside it a couple years back."

"No kidding? I never heard that."

"It's a long story." Kiki noticed Big Estelle and Trish already back inside and headed their way. She turned to Jasmine again. "Thanks for the tour. We'd better get going."

"I need to get to work," Trish said, which was code for *I may have found something.*

Kiki thanked Jasmine for the tour and the drinks.

Once they were all in the car again, Kiki turned to Trish. "Well?"

"I think we found something," Trish said.

"I found them," Suzi announced.

"What? What did you find?" Kiki was bouncing up and down on the seat.

"Footprints in the flower bed," Big Estelle said.

"Surely the police saw them," Kiki said.

Big Estelle carefully negotiated the road as it curved around a red dirt cliff side.

"It doesn't matter if they saw them or not," Big Estelle said. "Now we know something that wasn't in the paper. The footprint was smallish. It was an athletic shoe of some kind, no heel."

"I'm a size seven," Trish jumped into the conversation. "I put my own foot alongside the print, and it was almost exactly the same size."

"Isn't that evidence tampering?" Suzi said.

"The police are done here," Kiki reminded them. "The size narrows the burglar down to a small man or a woman with around a size-seven shoe."

# 17

EM LEFT THE Goddess parking lot around four fifteen to give herself enough time to meet Roland by five thirty. Kapa'a was only forty minutes away without traffic, but this time of day the highway was usually choked with cars. Throw in a fender bender, and she'd be sitting for hours, not that that would be so terrible with the Pacific on her right and the lush green Kauai mountains on her left, except that Roland's schedule was erratic. She looked forward to spending some quality time with him, something they hadn't had time for in weeks.

But traffic was light, and she breezed through to the Hukilau Restaurant in the Beachboy Resort behind the Coconut Marketplace, so she headed out to the poolside bar for happy hour and decided to try a Loco Lemonade with tequila, ginger liqueur, lemonade, and honey. It was great, but Roland was late. She nursed the drink for forty-five minutes and alternated with ice water. When her cell rang at six o'clock she knew it was him even before checking caller ID.

"I'm sorry," he said. "I got hung up. No time for a nice leisurely dinner tonight."

Her mouth had been watering while thinking about digging into the Hukilau Mixed Grill. She could almost taste the island grilled seafood and sugar cane skewered shrimp, so she decided she'd stay and have dinner alone.

"It's all right," she said. "Can't be helped."

"We can't *dine*, but I've got a few minutes to spare. I'm just pulling into Paco's Tacos in Kapa'a."

"The restaurant, not the food truck?"

"Right. Want to meet me?"

"I'll leave right now."

"What would you like?"

"The fish taco plate. Please."

"You got it."

She paid for her drink, happy she'd just had one.

Roland was waiting for her at an inside table in the back corner. Em hung her purse on the back of her chair and sat down with a smile.

"Hey, I'm really sorry about dinner at Hukilau."

"I'll force you to make it up to me, don't worry."

Their orders came right out—one of the perks of eating with a police officer. As soon as Em took a bite of one of her three delicious tacos heaped with fish and coleslaw, Roland dug into his huge enchilada-style burrito slathered in sauce and draped with avocado slices.

"Have you got any leads?" She took a sip of her Jarritos mango drink.

He shook his head no.

"I spoke to a contact in Honolulu about stolen art. It's pretty hard to recover right after a heist. The thieves usually hide it until the dust settles, especially if it's high-end. That kind of stuff is hard to get rid of."

"Which means Delacruz's Pollocks won't be easy to sell off."

"Unfortunately, stolen art can disappear for decades. We may never find it."

"But you're not going to give up that easy because of Uncle Bass," she said.

He swallowed another bite of burrito. "You can bet on that."

"I heard from Kiki that Delacruz avoided any mention of his death on television today."

"All he cares about is his stolen art. He's been calling every two hours to see if we've found anything and keeps threatening to bring in his own detectives from the mainland. I told him to go right ahead."

"Uncle Bass's memorial is this weekend," Em said. "Kiki said the Maidens are going to be dancing."

Roland looked less than pleased.

"You don't want them there?" Em picked up her taco again.

"I don't mind them dancing. It's the trouble that comes with them that I care about. It's apparently some kind of package deal."

"The memorial is scheduled for the middle of the day. What could go wrong?"

"I don't even want to imagine. Let's just eat."

They focused on their meals for a couple of minutes before Roland said, "Delacruz isn't doing us any favors going on television and blabbing about how much his collection is worth. I saw him on KITV late news last night saying it was valued at over thirty million dollars."

"He was on *Extra Hot Style*, too," she said and pushed her plate toward him. "I saw a clip on the Internet. I can't eat that last taco. You want it? Two is plenty."

"Have them box it up for you. I'm *pau*," he said.

She expected him to signal the waiter for the bill, but instead, he glanced at the time on his cell phone and then leaned back in his chair.

"My friend said museums usually don't say what stolen paintings are worth because the media hype will make them all the more valuable and less likely to be recovered," he said. "I doubt Delacruz's insurance company will take his word for it that he's out over thirty million."

"He recently had a couple of films go belly up," she said.

"Convenient timing."

"I talked to Nat Clark this morning. He said Delacruz and his ex-wife got into it big time over the paintings in the divorce settlement. She let them go for three guaranteed movie roles. I immediately thought of her, but Nat said no way would she risk everything just to get her hands on the Pollocks."

"You think Delacruz would try to pull a scam?"

She shrugged. "Who knows how desperate he is? He seems genuinely upset over the loss of the paintings. Nat thinks his reputation as a box-office giant could take a hit, in which case he'll need the insurance money."

Roland crossed his arms. "So you saw Nat Clark? How's he doing?"

"Fine. I was out on the beach, and he was just walking by." She felt her cheeks bloom with heat and wondered why he made her feel guilty for talking to Nat. They were still only slightly serious.

"If Delacruz keeps running up the price, we may never find any of it. If the paintings get smuggled out of Hawaii they could end up anywhere: Asia, Europe, some Middle Eastern sheik's collection. I found out hard-core international criminals use art to secure loans. Paintings become bartering chips and change hands over and over."

"Not very hopeful news," Em said. She reached into her purse and dug out the pages of information an art dealer from Newport Beach had emailed her that morning. "Have you found anything out about the collection?"

"No time to look. Besides, I knew you were working on it."

"An old friend from college married a high-end art dealer in Newport Beach. I immediately thought of him and got in touch. He was able to get on auction and dealer sites online and found out what Delacruz paid for the Pollocks."

She didn't add that when the old friend called to tell her the email was on the way, he asked if she was still single. When she said yes, he told her if she ever got back to the mainland that they should meet for drinks.

"Great," she had said. "I'd love to see you both again."

There was a pause, and then he said, "I was hoping we could meet alone, Em."

"Oh, no. Have you and Marsha split up?" She was definitely out of the loop, so she wouldn't be surprised to hear it was so.

Again, there was a pause. "No, we're fine."

"But you want to have a drink with me alone?"

"Can't blame a guy for trying."

"Trying to console the lonely divorcee, is that it?"

"Just trying to be friendly, Em. That's all."

Too friendly as far as she was concerned. She'd given him a curt goodbye and left off the thanks she owed him for the information. He wasn't the first of her friends' husbands to hit on her. It had happened a couple of times right after she and Phillip split up.

As far as she was concerned, until proven innocent, all men were hound dogs sniffing on the trail of any willing woman, single or married.

She must have been studying Roland for a second too long.

"What's wrong?" he asked.

Em shook her head, trying to shake off the humbug feeling. Maybe it wasn't fair throwing all guys in the same basket. Maybe there were one or two good guys left out there. Hopefully Roland was one of them.

"Where was I?" She frowned.

"You were about to tell me what you found."

She looked down at the pages again. "The oil paintings are on canvas, which we know. One sold for twenty million, and the other was three and a quarter."

Roland let out a sigh. "I'm in the wrong business."

"Aren't we all?"

He looked thoughtful for a moment. "So they cut the two canvases out of the frames and probably rolled them up. So that would be easy enough to walk out with and easy enough to pack."

Em handed him the information. Roland stared down at the photos of the paintings.

"These look like something a kindergartner could do. Who can't spatter paint all over a canvas? I don't get it."

"I asked the same question. Anyone can do it, but when Pollock started working in abstracts he was a pioneer. An artist is deemed a true genius not because what he's doing is difficult, but because he or she changes the way things were done previously."

"Like inventing a new technique."

"I guess so."

"I've got an idea," he said. "Why don't we melt crayons with my fire knives and dribble the wax on canvas? Then we could buy an island somewhere and retire."

She was thrilled he could picture them alone together on an island somewhere.

"Dribbles and spatters are overdone," she said. "Think of something new."

"Get naked, paint each other, and roll around on canvas?"

"Done *and* over-done. I kind of like the way your mind is working though."

He paid for their meals, and they headed outside. "Where did you park?" he asked.

A steady stream of cars was still going through Kapa'a though it was dark. Some of the shops along the highway were still open, hoping to attract one more tourist, one more sale.

"I'm around back in the parking lot."

"Good. I've got a new technique I'd like to try. It doesn't have much to do with art."

"Detective Sharpe, you're on duty."

"I won't tell if you don't tell."

His technique turned out to be a steamy good night kiss that he planted on her as they lingered behind a van in the parking lot on the back road.

"I hate to think of you driving home in the dark. Watch the road, Em. You know how many head-ons we have a year?"

"No, and don't tell me. I'll be careful. It's supposed to be a clear night."

"Call me when you get home, okay? Leave a message if I don't answer."

"I will." She hit the unlock button on her key and paused. "Roland, is what we have serious?"

"You think I kiss everybody like that?"

"I don't know. Do you?"

Once she was in the car and headed back to the North Shore, Em realized he'd smiled but never really answered.

# 18

THE MEMORIAL celebration for Sebastian Kekina a.k.a. Uncle Bass or Uncle O'opu was held at Anahola Beach Park. Kiki and Em rode to the event with Suzi in her Prius. They pulled into the huge grass lot across from the bay and were directed by volunteer parking attendants.

A gigantic tent filled the south end of the park area where a good two hundred or more local people had already gathered. There weren't many *haoles* in the crowd.

"Are you sure we're supposed to be dancing today, Kiki?" Suzi looked around.

"Trust me. We were invited." Kiki adjusted a variegated green and white stem of Song of India leaves to hide one of her bald patches.

"That's exactly what you said right before we were all hauled off to jail in Waikiki for performing at the Hau Tree Bar without permission."

"But this time it's true. I swear. A friend of Flora's invited us."

"You sure she didn't just invite Flora?"

"Nope." Kiki got out of the car and noticed eighty-five percent of the crowd was Hawaiian. "Flora said the invite was for all of us. We're supposed to go on at two. Hawaiian time."

"Oh, no," Suzi said.

"What now?" Em looked worried. Then again, Kiki thought Em always looked worried.

Suzi said, "By two o'clock Flora might be in the bag." Flora was known for sipping more than just Gatorade out of the plastic bottles she carried in her oversized bag.

"She promised not to drink until after we perform," Kiki said.

"Let's hope she keeps her promise. Looks like that's the line to get into the tent where the tables are set up." Em started across the grassy field.

There was another tent where buffet tables were lined up for miles. A row of men and women waiting for the buffet to begin were armed with tongs, ready to serve from steamer trays heaped with mountains of food. Others were assigned to wave *ti* leaves over the food to keep flies away.

Hawaiian music was playing, filling the air with traditional *mele* or song. As a former police officer and well-known figure on the island, Uncle Bass was getting the send-off he deserved. When they reached the edge of the tent, Kiki let Suzi and Em get in front of her in the line at the reception table.

They each signed the guest book and then pulled white envelopes with cards and cash donations out of their purses and dropped them into a wooden calabash already overflowing with cards. Kiki changed her estimate. There had to be close to three hundred people milling around and lots of uniformed officers in the crowd.

Once they left the guest book table, the line snaked past a long plywood photo wall filled with photos of Uncle Bass from present day back through to his childhood. Kiki paused to study the photos and found it hard to imagine the seventy-five-year-old with white hair as the smiling brown boy on the beach holding an old *koa* plank surfboard. Walking past the photographs was like witnessing history unfolding. There were his years at Kamehamea School on Oahu, his freshman year at the University of Washington, and then photos of Bass back on Kauai. Like so many of the Hawaiian kids, he'd missed home too much to stick it out for four years away from the islands.

"Look, Em," Kiki said, spotting a photo of Uncle Bass with another man on the beach at Waikiki. "That has to be Roland's dad. He's the spitting image of him."

Em leaned closer to get a better look at the small black-and-white image.

"It sure is. That looks just like Roland."

"Did I just hear my name?"

Kiki turned around, and Roland was right behind them, watching Em. There was no hiding the fact the two had a thing for each other, even though they thought they were playing it coy.

"I'll go get us some seats," Suzi told Kiki before she headed off through the sea of wooden picnic tables covered with white butcher paper.

"So . . ." Kiki looked up at Roland. "Are you getting close to an arrest?"

"I can't comment on a case in progress," he told her.

"Some of the Maidens and I went over to the Delacruz house this week to look for clues. We found a good footprint in the flower bed. It was narrow, the length of a woman's size-seven shoe." She nodded with a *so there* look.

"Jasmine Bishop, Delacruz's girlfriend, is a size seven," Roland said.

"Oh." Kiki deflated like an old party balloon. "So is she a suspect?"

"She was almost always with someone at the party that night," he said. Then to Em, "What's going on?"

"Nothing, I swear," Em said. "At least nothing I know of. Kiki, what have you been up to?"

"A few of us went to see Mr. Delacruz, ostensibly to welcome him to the neighborhood. Of course, we were really there to see if we could find anything that would lead to the arrest of the perps. We found the footprint in the planter, deduced it was from a size-seven shoe, and photographed it."

"I'm sure you used a state-of-the-art measuring technique?" Roland wasn't smiling.

"Of course. Trish put her own foot right next to it. She's a size seven, and they matched. So, are you looking for a small man or a woman with a size-seven shoe? And why *not* Jasmine? Are you sure she was at the party all night?"

"I can't give you any information on this, Kiki," he said. "I won't jeopardize the case. I'd really appreciate it if you and the Maidens would step down and stay out of it."

"How about we get some food?" Em suggested to Roland.

It irked Kiki that Em was always playing peacemaker. "I'll see you later. We dance at two," she reminded Em.

Kiki walked over to where Suzi was sitting at the end of a table saving two seats.

"What's wrong? You look pissed," Suzi said as Kiki slid onto the picnic bench beside her.

"Roland told us to stand down and not snoop around." Kiki tried to ignore the little *keiki* running around the tables, chasing each other in an impromptu game of tag.

"So, are we going to back down?"

"What do you think?" Kiki snorted.

"Hey, look," Suzi said. "There's Sophie on the other side of the tent. Everybody's here."

"I don't see Louie." Kiki squinted but didn't see him anywhere. "Someone has to tend bar, I guess."

Suddenly one of the *keiki* let out a loud whoop and then a sharp, high-pitched wail. Kiki levitated off the bench, covered her head with her arms, and ran. Suzi followed her out of the tent and found her cowering behind a long row of blue porta-potties.

"Maybe it's too soon for you to be out in public." Suzi took hold of Kiki's elbow and tried to help her to stand.

"No . . . no." Kiki shook her head. Out of the corner of her eye she watched one of the orchids from her hair adornment fly off and hit the ground.

"Maybe it's too soon to dance. You can direct. How would that be? Sit in the front row and give us encouragement."

Embarrassed when her eyes stung and flooded with tears, Kiki hid her face in the crook of her arm and tried to collect herself. She hardly ever cried and certainly not in front of anyone.

"I have to dance. Hula is life. You know that. Hula heals. We've been invited to dance for a predominately Hawaiian crowd. I *have* to dance. I'm so honored."

"But what if someone hoots or cheers or whistles too loudly? What if a truck backfires? What if another kid screams?"

"I'll be all right," Kiki promised. If she could only stand up.

Someone slammed the porta-potty in front of them. Kiki jumped up, but she didn't bolt. She was shaking, but she was on her feet again.

"I may have been broken. I may never have hair in some spots on my head again, but I refuse to give up or give in to that . . . that . . ."

"That freaking monkey!" Suzi finished for her.

Kiki felt the blood rush from her head. While she was in the hospital her visitors and the staff had been instructed not to use the *M* word. Kimo had sworn he'd never ask her for details about the attack. Now, the minute Suzi had said the word *monkey*, Kiki had a flashback. Those long hairy arms and legs. That tail, that horrible skinny tail. That mouth full of sharp teeth and the insane screeching and chatter coming out of it. The horrific shock and fear that overwhelmed her when the capuchin leapt out of the ice chest and latched onto her hair all came rushing back.

She'd blocked that night for so long that the vision sent her reeling back against the plastic porta-potty. She slid down the side of it and was sprawled on the ground, staring up at a clear blue sky that faded to black.

# 19

*"KIKI? KIKI!"*

The voices drifted to her from somewhere far away. Kiki slowly opened her eyes and saw the circle of Hula Maidens crowded around her. She tried to sit up.

"Where yam?" she mumbled.

The ring of heads looking down at her didn't budge. Kiki recognized Lillian as one of them, probably because of the pink hair. Lil started to cry and shouted, "She has brain damage!"

"She don't have brain damage, but so help me Pete, you will if you keep up that catterwallin'." Pat was there. Her voice was easily recognizable. Kiki relaxed a bit. At least someone was in charge.

Kiki looked up at the sky behind their flower-studded heads and tried again.

"Where. I. Am?" she muttered.

"Anahola Beach Park. Uncle Bass's funeral," Pat said.

"Smell. What? Smell. Some. Thing."

"You took a dive behind a porta-potty, which is good because nobody saw that but me," Suzi said.

Lillian sniffed. "We saw a flash of purple when you ran out of the tent earlier. Pat led us over here thinking you might be practicing, and we found you passed out cold."

"They aren't serving martinis, so we figured something bad happened," Precious deduced.

Pat reached for Kiki's arm. "I'm gonna pull you up now. You ready?"

Kiki nodded slowly. Once she was on her feet, Pat looked her in the eye.

"We talked it over while you was out," she said. "You're gonna sit this one out. You can introduce the girls, but you ain't dancing. Get it?"

"Buh." It was all she could manage.

"No buhs about it." Pat stared around the circle of women. "If any of you ever says the *M* word again, you'll be suspended from hula for six months. Got it?"

Kiki recovered her composure and was soon standing off to the side of the stage set up in the center of the tent, watching the Maidens line up just outside. The picnic tables in the tent were jammed with people. No one paid much attention to the entertainers. They were content to enjoy the *luau* food, music, and conversation. She was about to step to the center of the stage to introduce them when Cameron Delacruz walked up on stage and took the microphone from one of Uncle Bass's family members acting as the master of ceremonies.

"Aloha, everyone. My name is Cameron Delacruz," he began.

Immediately the lighthearted chatter died down to dead silence. It was so quiet even the *keiki* sensed something was up and stopped running around. There wasn't a soul in the crowd who wasn't aware of how Uncle Bass met his fate or that he'd died at Delacruz's home.

Kiki wondered who, if anyone, invited Delacruz to speak, let alone attend the memorial. Leo Kekina had nothing good to say about Cameron Delacruz or the way he'd behaved the night Uncle Bass died. If anything, the story had grown with each telling. Kiki found Em and Roland seated at a nearby table. They both looked as stunned to see Delacruz as everyone else.

Delacruz tapped the microphone and smiled. "I just wanted to convey my condolences to the family for your loss and to let you know I intend to see the criminals brought to justice, even if I have to bring in detectives from the mainland. I'd also like to reiterate that I am offering a sizable reward." He paused and slowly looked around at the crowd, staring at each table, letting his gaze wander from one side of the tent to the other.

"We're talking a *lot* of money. A *size-a-ble* amount for the return of my paintings. No questions asked. So if you know of anyone or you hear of anyone who might have them stashed in a closet somewhere, please call me or the KPD. The reward is enough money to change your life. You could buy a fancy new home or send your kids to the mainland." He must have seen the shock and anger written on the faces in the crowd and suddenly stopped.

Silence echoed louder than sound in the tent.

Kiki couldn't believe the man's audacity. He knew nothing about the close-knit local community or how things worked on Kauai. He might or might not get his paintings back, but if he did, it certainly wouldn't be by insulting the locals.

"We don't need your money," someone shouted from the back.

As Kiki stared at Delacruz, all she could think was *run, sucker, run*.

Suddenly Roland was there, standing beside Delacruz, who looked like he was foolish enough to say more until he caught sight of the detective and closed his mouth.

Kiki hurried up to take the microphone.

Delacruz added insult to injury when he said, "My halo," instead of *mahalo*.

There was a chorus of boos as he left the stage. Roland smoothly escorted him out of the tent and across the lot to his car.

Kiki was hesitant to follow the producer to announce the Hula Maidens. At a loss, she looked around for help, and it came in the form of Sophie, who emerged from the middle of the sea of picnic tables. Kiki gladly surrendered the mic.

"Aloha. My name is Sophie Chin, and I work at the Tiki Goddess. I'm sure most of you know the next *halau* by reputation even if you haven't seen them dance. They've performed all over the island, they dance almost nightly at the Goddess, they've danced in the competition at the Kukui Nut Festival, and they recently performed on Oahu. They may not be Hawaiian, but I know these ladies, and they are Hawaiian at heart. So how about joining me in giving them a warm Anahola welcome?"

She stepped back and waited beside Kiki as the Maidens took the stage to scattered applause.

"You okay, Kiki?" Sophie whispered.

"I'm good. *Mahalo*," Kiki whispered to the young bartender.

Sophie winked, "No worries, auntie. Happy to help my bleached-out Hawaiian sisters."

# 20

MONDAY EVENINGS were traditionally mellow at the Goddess until the airing of *Trouble in Paradise*, the reality show based on the bar. Because one of the cameramen on the crew had ended up dead, the show was short-lived, but reruns and YouTube clips added to the already popular bar's appeal to tourists and locals alike. The only time the place was semi-deserted was when the Hanalei River flooded, and the only road into the North Shore was closed until the rain let up or the tide went down.

Most of the Maidens decided not to show up the night after Uncle Bass's celebration, so when Pat called to say she'd rounded up Suzi, Flora, and Lillian to dance, Kiki told Sarge that she had to make a comeback sometime, so Pat gave her the okay.

Adult audiences could be as rowdy as kids, but Kiki figured they were less likely to sneak up on her and scare her sideways into stuttering muteness.

She and the others had a last-minute meeting in the ladies' restroom. They used their hair pieces from the day before.

"Congratulations, ladeez!" Pat boomed. "Nobody fell over yesterday. Let's see if we can keep the streak going."

Suzi applied another coat of lipstick. Lillian fanned herself with a menu. Flora made sucking sounds on her Gatorade bottle.

Pat didn't like to be ignored. "So, Lillian, howz your coccyx?"

Lillian's eyes sparkled, and her cheeks pinked up. "It'll never be the same, of course, but I've rallied for my fans. You should see all the baskets of Iowa goodies my hometown fans sent. I got corn-shaped cheese, a corn sucker, popcorn on the cob, corn salsa, bacon-flavored jelly beans, and my favorite, chocolate cow chips. They came in a box printed in black and white like cowhide."

"Be still my heart." Kiki tried to picture a chocolate-covered cow chip. Was it like a potato chip covered in chocolate? Or was it something that looked like a cow patty from the pasture?

"Thanks for not sharing," Flora said.

"Oh, but I did bring some bacon-flavored jelly beans for later." Lillian smiled.

"Okay, ladeez, line up, you're goin' on." Pat ducked out the door to alert Danny and the Tiki Tones.

"What are we dancing again?" Suzi wanted to know.

Kiki said, "Old *hapa haole* tourist favorites. Waikiki, Blue Hawaii, Tiny Bubbles. Oh, and Kaimana Hila. The Japanese love that one, and there's a table of ten of them in back."

"Wait!" Lillian stopped in her tracks. "Kaimana Hila? We haven't practiced that one. I don't think I know it."

"So step off the stage when they play it, and let the rest of us dance."

"Step off the stage? Step *off* the *stage?*"

"You act like I told you to set yourself on fire again." Kiki stepped around her to lead them out.

"But . . ."

"Step down or dance behind someone else, but you better be able to follow and not crash into us. No matter what, *do not fall down.*"

"Got it."

When Kiki turned her back to them, she smiled. She was back. She was focused. She was ready to dance.


BY THE THIRD number, she was out of breath and happy the performance was relatively short. The audience was still yelling *hana ho*, demanding an encore. She ignored them and headed off the stage and went straight to the bar where she hopped onto an empty stool.

Sophie was tending bar. She hurried over and set a cardboard Goddess coaster in front of Kiki.

"Good job dancing, Kiki. What'll it be?"

"Something double-fisted."

Not far from Sophie, Louie overheard. He stepped closer, and Kiki noticed Sophie whispering something in his ear. Louie nodded and said, "Thanks for the reminder. I won't say it."

Then he turned to Kiki. "I've been working on something new for the heavyweights. Nothing fruity about it. Not like a traditional Zombie. Naturally, I'm putting my own spin on it. Thinking of calling it Night of the Living Dead."

"That's a lot of words. How about Meet the Mummy?" Kiki suggested.

"Also too long."

"How about Thriller?"

He smiled. "Closer. I'll think about it."

"What's in it?"

"Mostly tequila and Hawaiian chili pepper water. I'll serve it to you in my special shrunken head tiki mug."

"Okay, I'm game. Where's Em?" Kiki was used to seeing her in the bar every evening. "Out with Roland?"

"Not tonight," he said. "She'll be over soon. She's taking a break. Nice dancing tonight, Kiki. Good to have you back."

"*Mahalo.*"

He dumped a jigger of tequila into a shaker. "The Japanese sure loved it when you did Kaimana Hila. Some of them were back there dancing along. Lillian looked a little out of it, though."

"She always looks a little bit out of it. I felt pretty out of it myself tonight, but I'm doing better every day." She noticed her hands were still shaking.

"If you were off, it wasn't noticeable. You kept right on smiling."

"It's slow going. I want to get better faster but, you know." She shrugged.

"Sophie just reminded me not to say the *M* word. Is it really that bad?"

She watched him fill a jigger with chili pepper water, and then he tossed a whole red chili pepper in the shaker. Kiki winced. "That's gonna be hot. Back to how bad is what I've got? It's bad if I have a flashback. I'm losing sleep. I need a cause, something to keep my mind from replaying the incident at the airport. I thought if I could just get the Maidens involved in solving the Delacruz case, I'd bounce back faster."

Louie poured the Thriller over rocks in his collector's edition shrunken head mug, slid a straw in the drink, and set it in front of her.

"That mug is part of my private collection." He beamed.

The mug looked like a cross between a shrunken head with its lips stitched shut and a skull. Her hands were shaking, and the mug was oversized and heavy. She couldn't trust herself to lift it, so she slid it closer and took a sip out of the straw.

"Whoa." The liquor and pepper hit the back of her throat, and she started coughing.

"Like it?" Louie looked hopeful.

"Have you tried this on David Letterman yet?" Letterman was Uncle Louie's cocktail-taste-testing parrot. Usually Louie didn't ever serve a drink without Dave's approval first.

"Nope, just you."

"It's pretty spicy. Maybe Dave should have a go at it before it hits the menu."

"Okay. Listen, if you'd like a job, Kiki, I can put you on as a hostess. You could work the front door, chat up folks waiting in line for a table, greet them with aloha the way my Irene used to." There was a wistful look in his eyes as he spoke of his late tiki goddess. "That'll give you something to do."

"A greeter? That's a sweet idea, Louie, but I need to be busy with something grittier than that. I share aloha through my dancing."

As soon as Em walked in through her uncle's office and joined him behind the bar, Sophie announced she was going on a break.

"How's the new cocktail?" Em pointed at the mug sitting in front of Kiki.

"Fire hot. That's the good news, I guess."

"Uh oh." Em was looking at the front door.

Kiki turned around in time to see Roland Sharpe walk in leading two uniformed officers. He stood inside the doorway for a minute and scanned the room before he looked toward the bar. Roland ignored them all and headed toward the back corner where Buzzy sat with some braided Rasta guys in knit caps.

"What's going on?" Louie wondered.

"They're talking to Buzzy," Kiki said.

"Buzzy just stood up," Em said.

"They're putting cuffs on him!" Louie started around the bar.

Em caught his arm. "Wait a minute, Uncle Louie. People are always watching you to make sure they don't miss anything. I'll go see what's up."

Kiki drank half the Thriller and thought better of finishing it since she had already lost all feeling in her lips. She followed Em around the corner of the bar. As they neared the back table, she heard Buzzy's languid voice.

"Whazzup, man? I'm not driving or nothing. I don't even have a car."

"You have the right to remain silent," the young officer began.

Em had reached Roland's side. Kiki was on her heels.

"Roland, what's going on?" Em asked.

"This is official business. We're arresting Buford Burney the Third in connection with art theft, assault, and felony murder."

"Who's Buford Burney?" Uncle Louie looked around.

"That must be Buzzy's real name," Kiki guessed. Right now by any name, Buzzy looked more confused than ever.

Kiki tugged on Roland's arm. "You have to be kidding. Buzzy wouldn't hurt a fly. He's probably never even swatted a mosquito."

The officers were guiding Buzzy out the front door.

"I've got to go, Kiki. Sorry." Roland shook her off and followed them out. She and Em stayed close on his heels.

Cell phone cameras were going off all over the bar. The Japanese tourists were the first out the door behind Buzzy's entourage. They posed next to the police car, making *shaka* and peace hand signs and snapped photos.

More tourists came pouring out of the bar along with Pat and the three other Hula Maidens.

Em stepped up to Roland. Kiki heard her say, "Do you really think Buzzy could get it together enough to disable the security system, sneak past the security guards, get inside and take the paintings off the wall, and carry them out of the house without anyone seeing him?"

"Exactly. In what universe, Roland?" Kiki added.

The youngest officer was assisting Buzzy into the back of the patrol car. Buzzy wasn't protesting. Instead, he stared toward the roof of the car, disoriented. One of the Rasta boys started to boo. The patrol car began to inch forward. A Japanese girl who'd been posing on the hood jumped off. The crowd finally parted enough to let the car through. Once it was out of the parking lot and turning onto the highway, Roland turned his full attention to Em and Kiki.

"You've got the wrong man, Roland." Kiki felt herself getting riled up.

Em gently laid her hand on Kiki's arm to calm her.

"What makes you think he's responsible?" Em asked her detective.

Kiki was impressed but not happy. Roland was all business tonight. He never cracked a smile, not even for Em.

"Here's what we know. Buzzy was MIA for most of the Delacruz party. You said so yourself, Em. The other night when I was here I picked up his empty beer bottle and ran his prints."

"I didn't see you lift any bottle."

"I'm a pro, remember? Turns out his real name is Buford Archer Burney the Third, a.k.a. Buzzy, and he's been on an FBI watch list since 1973."

# 21

KIKI STOPPED BY the Goddess on her way to Princeville early the next morning. Em and her uncle were still at the beach house.

Em greeted Kiki and opened the door to the screened *lanai*. "Are you driving yourself?"

"I am. I have to get some of my getup-and-go back." That morning Kiki decided it was do or die. If she was going to get anything accomplished, she needed to get behind the wheel again, clearance or no clearance.

She followed Em across the *lanai* and into the large main room of the old wooden beach house. Uncle Louie was behind the kitchen counter, pouring himself a mug of coffee.

"Hey, Kiki," he called out when he saw her. "Wanna cup?"

"Sure," she said, nodding.

The image of a 1940s film star, with his perpetual golden tan and slicked-back shock of white hair, he carried off the look in a long silk kimono-style robe tied over his bare chest and white Bermuda shorts. He set a platter of fresh island fruit on the counter that separated the kitchen from the living area and then three mugs of steaming Kona coffee. He joined Kiki and Em on barstools pulled up to the counter.

Kiki loved Louie's house for its perfect location right on the beach. Her own place was close to the water, but it was across the highway. An affordable beachfront home passed her and Kimo by years ago. No way could she afford a waterfront view since Kauai had become the Aspen of the Pacific.

"So, what are we going to do about Buzzy?" She picked up her coffee, blew over the rim, and looked at Louie and Em in turn.

"We?" Em poured non-dairy creamer into her coffee, ruining it as far as Kiki was concerned.

"Yes, all of us. The Goddess staff and the Maidens. Buzzy is one of us." Kiki set her coffee down. "We can't let him sit in the pokey."

"You aren't cooking up a jailbreak, are you?" Em was not joking.

"I know a guy in explosives," Louie volunteered. "He lives in Lawai."

"Uncle!" Em set her mug down so hard coffee sloshed over the rim.

Kiki laughed. "Actually, I was thinking about a fundraiser for his legal fees."

Em picked up a slice of pineapple, took a bite, and then said, "I couldn't sleep last night so I googled Buford Archer Burney the Third." She polished off the slice.

"And?" Kiki leaned forward.

"I couldn't find any information on Buford the Third, but Buford A. Burney the Second, Buzzy's father, is a very, very wealthy man."

"How wealthy?" Louie asked.

Em said, "You know the Fortune 500?"

Kiki and Louie nodded.

"He's personally worth a billion dollars. The family owns more companies than they can count. I doubt Buzzy really has to worry about legal fees," Em said.

Kiki mulled over the information for a moment.

"If his family was footing the bill, he'd wouldn't be living in a tree, doing odd jobs, and bussing tables at the Goddess, would he?" she said.

"I did wonder," Em said. "I sent emails to the corporations listed under Buford the Second's holdings, explaining that I'd like him to email me regarding his son. So far I've gotten no response."

"Let's hope he gets in touch soon," Louie said.

"Or at least let's hope someone does from the family does. Buzzy's father is in his nineties," Em said.

Kiki frowned. "Does The Second have any other children?"

"If so, I couldn't find anything on them, but I'm not an expert at this. I can only find what's available to everyone."

"We sure need a techie," Kiki said. "With a techie around we could go legit and do some big-time detecting as a group. Maybe we can convince one to join the Maidens."

When Louie stood up to get a refill for his coffee, his parrot Letterman started dancing around on his perch looking hopeful.

"He hated the new cocktail, by the way," Louie admitted.

"Good, then it wasn't just me," Kiki said.

The parrot started squawking.

Kiki ducked then took a deep breath to calm herself. "Give that poor bird a drink."

"I want his palate clear when I start working on another version of

Thriller later." Louie raised the coffee pot. "More, anyone?"

"No, thanks," Em said.

"Not me, either," Kiki added. "I'd better get going. I'm meeting Big Estelle at the Princeville Center in the food *lanai* for more coffee. We're going to put our heads together and come up with a fabulous fundraising idea. She can reserve the Princeville Community Center for the event."

"You're welcome to have it at the Goddess." Louie looked hurt that she hadn't already planned on it.

"Oh, don't worry," she assured him. "We'll have a second fundraiser in the bar. I'm thinking we'll kick off the drive at Princeville with something elegant. All the folks Buzzy works odd jobs for up there can contribute. Then we'll have something at the Goddess. Maybe something a little more casual for the Hanalei and Haena crowd."

"How about a *lau lau* sale?" Louie suggested. "I love *lau lau*."

"That's a possibility," Kiki said. "Lotta work though."

"You can make them in the *luau* shack by the *imu*," he said. "Steam 'em in the *imu*?"

"*Mahalo* for the offer. I'll ask Kimo if that would work. I'll discuss the idea with Big Estelle." Invigorated, Kiki looked at her watch. She was feeling better than she had in months. Once more she had a goal, a purpose.

"Well, I'm going to take off," she announced.

Em stood up and gave her a hug. So did Louie.

It was still a little too early to meet Big Estelle, but Kiki was too excited to wait any longer.

"Thanks for the coffee," she called out as she headed for the door.

Em followed her. "Don't overdo, Kiki."

Kiki had her hand on the screen door. "I feel like a new woman. I feel like a million bucks. I'd kick my heels together if I didn't think I'd end up on the ground."

Letterman squawked, "Yo, ho, ho and a bottle o' rum!"

# 22

IT WAS A STUNNING morning. Kiki left the Goddess and headed for Princeville. No matter how many times she saw the various views of the ocean and Hanalei Valley from the winding highway that passed over quaint one-lane bridges and around sharp curves, she never took the scenic grandeur for granted.

The lookout above the one-lane bridge over the Hanalei River was already backed up with tourists taking photos. A man holding a selfie stick had lined up his family, and all five of them posed against the breathtaking backdrop of Hanalei Bay.

Around the corner, past the fire and police substations, there was another crowd of tourists at the Hanalei Valley Lookout, one of the premiere photo ops on the planet.

Kiki turned in at the Princeville Center where the parking lot was already choked with cars and pickup trucks jockeying for spaces so small compact rental cars barely fit in them. She started hyperventilating and decided she simply wasn't ready to face fighting for a parking space. Glancing at the clock on the dashboard, she figured Big Estelle hadn't even left home yet, so she decided to head over to the house.

Big Estelle lived on one of the Princeville loops. Kiki hated the loops. The semi-circular streets provided the perfect way to get lost in the bowels of the planned resort community laid out around three nine-hole golf courses. The only things she really liked about Princeville were its spectacular views of the ocean and the mountain, Makana, in the distance. The tourists and tour guides referred to Makana as Bali Hai because it was featured as the dreamy, mist-shrouded island in the 1950s film *South Pacific*.

She drove up to the Estelles' two-story house with a wide front *lanai* and parked in the driveway. The house was a derivative of beige, one of the few approved colors of the complex. She set the parking brake, got out of her car, and started up the walk. She heard a baby squeal, looked around, and spotted a minivan with kiddie car seats parked in the driveway next door. She crossed the *lanai* and knocked on the front door. It took a minute or two for Big Estelle to answer. As soon as she saw Kiki, she stepped outside and shut the door behind her with a loud snap.

Kiki blinked.

"What are you doing here?" Big Estelle didn't even try to hide her irritation.

"I was early, so I decided to stop by instead of meeting you at the coffee shop. Is that paint on your skirt?" Kiki pointed to a purple blotch on Big Estelle's *muumuu*. Then she noticed another one in yellow.

"Home improvement. Okay, so let's go, I'm ready." Big Estelle headed for the steps.

"But you don't even have your purse." Not that she minded paying for Big Estelle's coffee, but she found it odd the woman was ready to walk away without her purse.

"Oh. I'm out of cash. We're only having coffee. You can surely shout me one."

"What about your mother? Don't you need to tell her you're leaving?"

Big Estelle usually hesitated to leave her mother at home alone, seeing as how Little Estelle was a well-known mischief-maker. Come to think of it, Kiki realized Big Estelle had been leaving her mother home alone quite a bit lately.

"You know, I haven't seen your mom since I left the hospital. I should really tell her hello," Kiki said.

Big Estelle blocked the way to the door.

"Not now. Maybe when we come back. She's not that great in the morning."

Suddenly suspicious, Kiki wondered why Big Estelle was keeping her away from her mother. Elder abuse, maybe? Or worse? There could be a Bates Motel situation going on right under her nose.

Kiki slapped her hand to her forehead and closed her eyes. If there was one thing she couldn't stand, it was someone telling her no. She was more determined than ever to get into the house.

"What is it? What's happening?" Big Estelle gently took her by the arm.

"I'm feeling a bit dizzy, is all." Kiki opened one eye and peered around her hand. "Maybe a glass of water will help. Maybe I'm dehydrated."

Big Estelle hesitated long enough for Kiki to surmise there was definitely something up. Instead of taking her inside, Big Estelle tried to lead Kiki to a wicker chair on the *lanai*. Kiki balked and sagged against her.

Just then the door opened, and there was Little Estelle, leaning on her aluminum walker.

"Kiki!" She actually cackled. "I heard they let you out of the booby hatch. Congratulations!"

"They did." Kiki nodded. "How are you? I haven't seen you since I got home. Is that paint on your face?" Kiki blinked. Sure enough, it looked like there was a green streak of paint down Little Estelle's left cheek.

"I thought you were dehydrated." Big Estelle stared at Kiki.

Kiki pretended to have trouble swallowing. "I am."

Big Estelle said, "Get her some water, Mother. We'll wait out here."

"You don't have to do that, Little Estelle." Kiki glared at Big Estelle. "How's she supposed to carry water and use a walker?"

Just then, a low chattering started somewhere inside the house followed by a loud bang. Then came the howl of a banshee. But it wasn't a banshee. It was a sound embedded in Kiki's brain. A sound she'd never, ever forget.

Kiki's hair stood on end. The bald spots on her head started to throb. Her heart nearly stopped beating. She grabbed hold of Big Estelle.

"What? Wh-wha-t . . . was that?"

"Close the door, Mother! Close the door!" Big Estelle screamed as she dragged Kiki down the steps and off the *lanai*.

The door slammed shut but not before Kiki heard another earsplitting howl and frantic pounding on the other side of the door.

# 23

"I'LL BE RIGHT there." Em shoved her cell phone into the pocket of her shorts and headed toward Louie's office.

"I've got to run." She called out to Sophie, who was behind the bar. "Something's wrong with Kiki. An emergency."

"When isn't it an emergency?" Sophie shook her head. "Where is she?"

"She's at the Estelles'." Em was in the office now. Sophie had followed close on her heels. Em opened the file drawer where she kept her purse and hooked the strap over her shoulder.

"Big Estelle called, and she was crying. She said something about Kiki collapsing. She wanted to know where Kimo was, and I told her the farmer's market in Kilauea."

"Did you tell them to call 911?" Sophie planted her hands on her hips.

"They did, but they want me there anyway." Em ran out the back door yelling, "Tell Kimo what's up when he comes back."

"Call me later, and let us know what happened."

Em climbed into Louie's Honda pickup and flew up the road. Thankfully, it was still early, and most of the tourists were headed in the opposite direction toward the dry cave at Haena Beach Park and Ke'e Beach at the end of the road.

By the time she reached the Estelles' place there was a KFD hook-and-ladder truck, their EMTs, and the American Medical Response ambulance parked out front. Big and Little Estelle were off to one side of the *lanai* huddled together.

Em jumped out of her uncle's truck and sighed with relief when she saw Kiki lying in the center of a circle of emergency responders. At least help had arrived, and none of the men looked overly concerned. Em cleared the steps and walked around the knot of men in uniform.

"Oh, Em, thanks for coming." Big Estelle rushed over to her.

"What happened?"

Little Estelle was seated on a wicker chair, her walker parked beside her.

"She freaked out. Her eyes rolled up into her head, and she passed out cold as shrimp cocktail on a bed of ice," she said.

"I thought you were meeting at the coffee shop," Em said.

"I thought so too." Big Estelle shook her head. "She was early, so she decided to come over here and meet me here instead. We weren't expecting her, poor thing. We didn't have time to prepare."

Em couldn't imagine what they had to prepare to welcome Kiki, who totally embraced the casual Kauai lifestyle. She did notice they both had small spots of paint on their clothes, and Little Estelle had tried to wipe a blue streak off her face but only succeeded in smearing it.

Little Estelle turned on her daughter. "I told you she was bound to find out sooner or later. Better sooner. Now she'll just have to get over it."

"Get over what?" Em looked back and forth between them.

"Don't blame me." Big Estelle's face glowed with perspiration. "I said this was a bad idea, but mother refused to listen. I didn't want that thing here."

"He's not a thing. He's as smart as you are. Besides, this is still *my* house." Little Estelle shook her finger at her daughter.

"It's my house, too."

"Only thirty percent."

"Stop!" Em glanced over and noticed Kiki now still sitting up, but her eyes were closed. "Who is *he*, and what's going on?"

"*He* is Alphonse," Big Estelle whispered.

Em's stomach dropped to her toes. She stared at Kiki. The woman was as white as bleached coral.

"Alphonse the monkey?" Em whispered back.

"Is there another Alphonse?" Little Estelle obviously didn't care if Kiki heard.

Em thought back to two months ago when the capuchin monkey had escaped his owner, stowed away in the Hula Maidens' ice chest, flew from Honolulu to Lihue, then leapt out and attacked Kiki when Pat opened the ice chest at the airport. He clamped onto Kiki's head as she ran screaming through the ticketing and baggage claim areas until she passed out. TSA agents had to tranquilize Alphonse before they could remove him.

"You've had him here all this time?" Em was aghast.

"He's a treasure. He's my little precious," Little Estelle said.

"He's obnoxious vermin," Big Estelle countered. "He's shredded our drapes, ruined most everything in the house, and he refuses to wear a diaper."

"We wanted to get shutters anyway. It was either adopt him, or the Kauai Humane Society was going to put him down." Little Estelle glared at her daughter. "He only poos a couple of times a day."

"What about the Shriner on Oahu who owned him? Doesn't he want him back?" Em asked.

"Would you?" Big Estelle leaned over and wiped her upper lip with the hem of her skirt. "Believe me, that man was happy to see the little bastard go."

"He's not a little bastard," her mother shouted.

Her shout was punctuated by the sound of breaking glass inside the house. Little Estelle grabbed her walker.

"Better go see what's up," she said.

"See what it's broken now, you mean," Big Estelle grumbled.

"He's not an *it*, either." Little Estelle thumped her way over to the door, opened it as wide as she dared, and after a bit of banging, managed to get herself and the walker inside without letting Alphonse escape.

"What about Kiki? Please don't tell me she was attacked again." Em doubted the woman could take another monkey ravaging.

"He didn't get to her. I kept her out on the *lanai*, but I think Alphonse must have seen her or recognized her voice because he went crazy. Kiki heard him and passed out cold. Do you think she'll throw me out of the Hula Maidens?"

The EMTs were moving away from Kiki. One of the firemen patted her on the back. Another waved Em and Big Estelle over to join them.

"She's feeling better," he told them as the other responders started packing up. "She doesn't want to stand up yet. Oh, and this is hers." He held out his closed hand.

Em extended her hand. He dropped a thick, fuzzy eyelash strip on her palm.

"Thanks, I think," Em said.

"How are you, Kiki? I'm so sorry," Big Estelle apologized.

Kiki tried to wave Big Estelle away. She pointed at Em and tried to speak.

"Her. I waa. I waaan tttt her. Nnnn. Not. You."

Crushed, Big Estelle backed away. Kiki focused on Em, took a deep breath, and spoke very, very slowly.

"I heard it. I caught a glimpse. They. They have that. Monster. In house."

"He's not a monster!" Little Estelle yelled from inside. "He has as much right to be here as you do."

Kiki's tears had softened her false eyelash adhesive. Sure enough, the right one was missing. Her left lash strip drooped. Em resisted the urge to reach out and poke it back into place. She looked around and noticed the firemen had all left the *lanai*. Em waved Big Estelle over. Kiki shivered and started thumping her forehead. Big Estelle waited in silence.

"Listen." Em took Kiki's hand and also Big Estelle's. "You are hula sisters. There's always a way to work this out. Now, who has an idea?"

Finally, Kiki took a deep breath and stopped knocking on her head. She said, "Let's call the mobile vet. Heave, I mean, have that . . . that creature put down. Quick and painless."

A hair-raising howl issued from inside followed by an outraged squawk. Em didn't know which came from Alphonse and which from Little Estelle.

Big Estelle argued, "You can't ask that, Kiki, just because you and Alphonse never hit it off."

"Never hit it off? That thing tried to kill me!" Kiki started shaking. She missed her forehead and rapped herself on the nose and winced. At this rate they'd never get her off the floor of the *lanai*.

Em shot Big Estelle a silent plea for help.

Big Estelle said, "Listen, Kiki, until today there's been no problem with him. We have really been working with him, and we found someone who gives anger management therapy sessions to animals. If you hadn't surprised us like that, you'd still be in the dark about Alphonse's whereabouts."

"Well, now I know. I refuse to live in fear for the rest of my life." She started tapping her temple. "I want him off this island."

"The other girls know too," Big Estelle confessed.

"What?" Kiki's eyes bulged. "What did you just say?"

"The Hula Maidens all know. They worked hard to keep from upsetting you while you were healing. We thought we'd have time to help you get accustomed to the idea of having Alphonse here on Kauai. We never meant to surprise you this way."

Em suggested, "What if the Estelles promise to keep Alphonse away from you, and you promise to call and warn them to lock him up before you come over?"

"I'm *never* coming over here again."

"Good riddance!" The door was closed, but Little Estelle's opinion came through loud and clear.

So did some distinctly cheerful monkey chattering.

# 24

SEATED AT THE kitchen counter sipping her morning coffee, Em watched her uncle pour a shot of his latest trial batch of Thriller into a small drinking cup attached to the bars of David Letterman's cage.

At the prospect of another taste, the parrot bobbed his head and did a happy dance. She'd never known anyone who took a job as seriously as her uncle's fine-feathered taste-tester.

"How's Kiki doing?" Louie watched Dave dip his beak into the fresh sample.

"Kimo said not good. She's been lying around the house for forty-eight hours straight, which is about forty-seven hours longer than the old Kiki could have ever stood it."

Em turned on her notepad and checked her emails as she always did before dressing and heading over to the bar. It was gray and raining off and on as trade showers blew through. She wished she could laze around for another hour or two, but that was impossible.

"Do you think she'll ever forgive the Estelles?" Louie asked.

"She's not just mad at them. She's furious at the whole squad for keeping the monkey's whereabouts a secret. She feels the Hula Maidens betrayed her, so I suspect she's deeply hurt."

Letterman was still drinking and making smacking sounds with his tongue. Usually if he hated a recipe he'd take one sip and squawk, "Yuck! Yuck! Patooie!"

So far this latest version of the Thriller seemed to be going down without a hitch.

"I think he likes it," Em said.

Louie made a few notations in the thick three-ring binder he called his Booze Bible.

"Now all you have to do is come up with a tall tale to go with the recipe," Em said. "Then we can introduce it one night next week maybe."

"Tall tale? All my stories are true." He winked and then added, "How about we premiere it at the first *luau* of the season? Maybe we can get the Maidens to come up with a Zombie Headhunter outfit and choreograph a dance to 'Going Out of My Head.'"

Em tried to imagine what the Maidens would consider proper headhunting attire. The very idea boggled her mind. "Do headhunters wear clothes?"

"Holy moly, I hope so," Uncle Louie said. "If they don't, please forget I said anything about asking the gals to dress like one."

Em looked over at the birdcage and noticed Dave had cleaned out the drink cup and was leaning against the bars with his gaze trained on Louie. His eyes appeared to be unfocused.

"Yo, ho, ho." His usual enthusiastic squawk came out more like a mumble.

Louie reached for the jigger again, and Dave's head slowly bobbed up and down.

"Okay, but this is the last one until you sleep these off, Little Buddy."

Em opened her email inbox and waited for the new mail to download, then immediately clicked on one from Burney Industries.

"I think I've finally heard from someone in Buzzy's family," she told Louie.

"Good. It's about time. He's been sitting in jail for nothing, poor guy. I took him some of Kimo's wontons yesterday."

"I hope they didn't get lost in the system."

She scanned the email and then went through it again slowly. Disappointment washed over her, making the gray day even more dismal.

"Bad news?"

Em looked up and found Louie watching her, so she read the email aloud.

"Ms. Johnson. Cease and desist contacting the Burney family as well as the various board members of companies and corporations or any subsidiaries owned by the Burney Family Trust. Buford Archer Burney the Third has not been recognized as a member of the Burney family or by any of its holdings since 1972. Should you not stop all communications upon receipt of this email, you will be contacted by our lawyers."

"Gosh, you'd think they'd be a little clearer," Louie joked.

Em stared at the tablet screen. "Kiki was right. Why would Buzzy be living in a tree and doing odd jobs if he was getting any support at all from his family?"

"Why indeed." Louie used a three-hole punch to get a new Booze

Bible page ready for the Thriller recipe. He inserted the blank paper into the binder and then started sketching a jungle scene along the bottom border.

"Maybe you should call Kiki and tell her she was right about Buzzy. Working on a fundraiser again might get her out of the doldrums," he said.

"You're right." Em picked up her cell and slid off the barstool. She started rinsing out their coffee mugs.

"I'll get the dishes," Louie said. "Maybe my mind will come up with a story if I keep my hands busy."

"Thanks. I'll go out on the *lanai* and call Kiki."

There were assorted cushy chairs to lounge in on the screened-in front porch. It was one of her favorite places to spend a rainy day. As Em passed Letterman's cage, she paused. The sight of the multi-hued parrot lying feet up on the floor of the cage never failed to startle her. She watched to make sure he was breathing before she stepped into the outdoor room.

"Dave's passed out," she told her uncle. "Looks like you have a winner."

# 25

DRESSED IN BLACK yoga pants under a lime-green print *pareau* topped with an old plaid flannel shirt of Kimo's, Kiki sat on the sofa in her semi-dark great room. The rattan shades were down, filtering out most of the overcast daylight that slipped through the clouds. The sound of the rain spattering the banana leaves outside the window matched the lethargic beat of her heart.

Two days. She'd lost two whole days of her life hiding out in her own home. Except for her stint in the booby hatch, she'd never felt this low, not even when she'd been suspected of murdering Louie's fiancée and had to hide out up on the mountain in Kokee. She stared at the coffee table and told herself she needed to get it together and keep it together, but she had no idea how to start.

After Em brought her home from the Estelles', Kimo was so worried he sat her down and had a heart-to-heart with her about how he feared she wasn't going to make it if she didn't overcome her PTMD, her post traumatic monkey disorder.

At the rate she was going, Kimo said he was going to be forced to take her back to Kukuoloko where they could seriously medicate her. He loved her too much to have her stroke out over a little monkey business.

She started to tell him she'd suffered a bit more than a *little* monkey business, but she knew she'd be wasting her breath. How could anyone who hadn't been nearly scalped by the devil incarnate possibly understand?

All anyone else saw when they first laid eyes on Alphonse was an adorable, furry little creature who liked to wear a red fez and perform mischievous antics. She knew better. Alphonse was not cute nor cuddly. He was a menace to society.

She tossed aside an empty jar that once held olives she'd marinated in vodka and wandered into the kitchen. The message light was blinking on her landline answering machine. She had turned off the ringer and hadn't looked at it since the latest incident. There were ten messages waiting.

Kiki pushed the play button on the recorder and folded her arms while she stared down at the machine.

"Aloha, Kiki. This is Trish. I heard what happened. Please call me back. *Please.*"

*Beep.*

"Hi, Kiki. This is Precious. Please forgive us. We were only trying to help both you and Little Estelle. Call me back. I hope you don't kick me out of the group."

*Beep.*

"Kiki? Dis is Flora. Get over it, okay? *Kala mai.*"

*Beep.*

"Kiki, Suzi here. For Pete's sake. We love you. You know that. Call me."

*Beep.*

"Hello? Hello? Is this Kiki's Kreative Events? Hello? My fiancé and I just decided to get married here on Kauai. I hope you can help us. Would you please call me back?"

*Beep.*

"Kiki? Hi! It's Big Estelle. I'm so sorry." There was an audible gasp and then a hang-up.

The next call was nothing but unintelligible sobbing. Kiki recognized the number on the caller ID as Lillian's and thought, *of course.*

*Beep.*

"I'm calling Kiki's Kreative Events for some information. I'm looking for a simple vow renewal on the beach. Do you have *kama'aina* discounts? I've lived here for two weeks every September for the past five years. Am I local? Does that count? Call me back if I can get a discount."

*Beep.*

"Kiki, this is Em. I know you're in there. I really need to talk to you about Buzzy. Call me when you feel up to it. Hopefully that will be sooner than later. Take care."

*Beep.*

Tempted to call Em back, Kiki let the notion fade and went to the refrigerator instead. She cared about Buzzy, she truly did, but she cared about her hula sisters, too, and they had all betrayed her over a monkey.

She scanned the contents of the fridge. Kimo had left her some of her favorite nibbles: cold teri-garlic chicken wings, assorted cheeses, flax seed crackers, and some of his famous artichoke dip.

She reached for a jar of Mandarin orange slices marinating in rum and headed back to the sofa. Buzzy and the rest of them could sprout gills and swim to the mainland for all she cared.

She sat down on the sofa and picked up the TV remote. Surfing the channels, she stopped to watch some wafer-thin *haole* girls twist themselves into pretzels doing yoga on a beach somewhere while she alternately munched on marinated orange slices and sipped rum out of the jar.

When she thought she heard someone call, "Hoo-ee!" she turned off the TV and listened.

There it was again. Someone had made the climb up her twenty feet of stairs to breach the upper *lanai* and was calling out to her.

"Hoo-ee! Kiki! It's Trish. Let me in, okay? I called Kimo, and so I know you're in there. I'm not leaving until we talk."

Kiki heard footsteps as Trish moved around to the window. Thankfully the shades were down, but that didn't keep Trish from rapping on the glass.

"Kiki Godwin, open up. If you don't, I'll call the police and tell them I'm afraid you might hurt yourself."

Kiki sighed. No way could she hurt herself any worse than the Maidens had already. She closed her eyes. Her forehead was too bruised to take even one single therapeutic tap.

"Hoo-ee! I'm going to count to ten," Trish yelled. "One."

Kiki stood up. She took a sip of orange-flavored rum from the jar.

"Two!"

The best she could do to make herself more presentable was to toss her hair over her shoulder as she padded to the door. She flung it wide open just as Trish hollered, "Three!"

Trish took one look at Kiki and reeled backward, nearly tumbling down the long flight of stairs to the ground below.

"That bad?" Kiki held the door open but didn't ask Trish in.

There was a long pause before the photographer answered.

"I . . ." Trish swallowed and looked everywhere but at Kiki. "You don't look that bad."

"Liar."

"I have to admit I've never seen you without makeup. Not even when we stay somewhere overnight as a group."

Kiki shrugged. "This is the new me. Casual Kiki."

"More like Rummage Sale Kiki."

"Want some?" She held out the jar.

Trish stared at the mini-orange slices floating in liquor.

"No, thanks. I want to come in. I've got something really important to talk to you about."

"I've got to take a nap," Kiki said.

"You need to hear me out. Please."

"If it's about the Maidens, forget it." Kiki blinked her eyes, bound and determined not to start crying.

"Actually, I'm here representing all of us."

"Then thanks, but no thanks." Kiki started to close the door.

"Hold it!" Trish pushed back. "We've all come too far, and we've been together too long for you not to at least hear me out."

"Right. We've been together for a long time, which is exactly why all of you should have considered my feelings *before* you decided to participate in the great monkey cover-up."

Trish had one foot over the threshold. Kiki pretended not to notice. Trish didn't back down.

"We're a sisterhood. We're the Hula Maidens. We were thinking of you, trying to protect you until you were stronger, but we had to think of Little Estelle, too. As miserable as Alphonse is, she loves that darn monkey to bits. He's the light of her life, and you have to remember, she's old, Kiki. She's never going to see ninety-one again. Who knows how much time she has left?"

"At the rate that woman is going, she'll outlive me, especially if she insists on keeping that thing on this island."

Just then a cloud heavy with rain drifted over the house and started dumping. Mist blew in the front door.

"Oh, poop. Come on in," Kiki grumbled. She stepped aside and let Trish walk in, closed the door behind her, and then led her through the shadowy interior to the main room.

"If you want something to eat or drink you'll have to help yourself."

"No, thanks. I just came to talk."

"You sure you don't want anything?" Kiki asked.

Trish shook her head no. "The Maidens all got together and came up with an idea."

"Nice. Now you're having meetings without me."

"Would you have come?"

"No," Kiki admitted.

"Okay then. Anyway, it goes without saying that everyone feels just terrible about what's happened. We should have told you that Alphonse was still on Kauai, but watching you jump at loud noises and duck for cover at the slightest provocation made us think we were right to wait."

"So you waited until that thing could scare the life out of me again."

"You weren't supposed to show up at Big Estelle's unannounced the other day."

Kiki sniffed. "Had I *known*, had any of you seen fit to warn me that monkey was there, I wouldn't have 'shown up' there at all."

"That's all water under the bridge now." Trish shrugged. "The bottom line is we all feel terrible."

"So you've said. Are you finished?"

"No." Trish walked over and plunked herself down on the sofa, pulled a colorful rack card out of her bag, and handed it over to Kiki. As she looked it over, Kiki sank into a deep chair.

"Full Moon Therapy Retreat by Andromeda Galaxy FMDT? Fumdut? What the heck does that mean? What's a FMDT?"

Trish took a deep breath and slowly released it. Kiki rolled her eyes.

"It means she's a Full Moon Drumming Therapist," Trish said.

"Someone named Andromeda Galaxy has a degree in full moon drumming? Seriously?" Kiki started humming the theme from *The Twilight Zone*.

"She's a very, very nice woman. I met with her at Mermaids in Kapa'a. We had lunch."

"The healthy sandwich place? I don't call nuts and grains lunch."

"Please, hear me out. Andromeda is a licensed full moon drumming therapist, and it just so happens the full moon is tomorrow night. She can help you, Kiki, I'm convinced of it and so are the other gals."

"Help me what? Sleep? The moon is already so full it's been keeping me up all night. That and, well, you know. Thinking about that *thing*. What if it escapes the Estelles' and tracks me down? I have nightmares about that thing swinging its way through the trees all the way from Princeville to finish what he started. He wants to kill me."

"He's a monkey. Why would he want to kill you? What's really keeping you up is your anxiety, your anger, and your fear. How about you let Andromeda give this a try? We'll all be there to help you."

"I think you've all helped enough. What is the *this* she wants to try?"

Trish leaned toward Kiki. Her face took on a hopeful expression. She started to sound like an infomercial host. "It will be a wonderful night out under the full moon. Andromeda says if you bathe in the moon's light, if you let it shine on you, let it pour over you like warm milk, you'll be able to focus your energy. Your troubles will be washed away as you turn them over to the moon goddess."

"Oh, poop." Kiki snorted.

"Kiki, at least open your mind to the possibility that it might help.

Your hula sisters are all excited about getting together and being there to help share the magical healing experience with you."

Kiki stared at the card. *Intensely Healing Experiences* it claimed in huge, silvery moon foil letters. *Only* four hundred dollars.

"Four hundred dollars?" Kiki tossed the card back. "Bathing in moonlight, which I can do in the back yard absolutely free, costs four hundred dollars?"

Trish's smiled widened. "Nope. Andromeda's given us a group rate, and we all chipped in for you, so you don't have to pay a thing."

Kiki wondered who was crazier, her or the rest of the Maidens.

"Where is this miraculous healing supposed to happen?"

"We'll be camping at Haena Beach Park."

"I don't camp."

"None of us has camped in years, but that doesn't mean we can't. And there's the drumming, don't forget," Trish added.

"What drumming?"

"Andromeda brings handmade especially-blessed drums for all of us. She is convinced that pounding on drums releases negative feelings and emotions and reduces stress. It also increases alpha waves. Wouldn't you like your alpha waves increased?"

"No, but I'd like hair to grow back on my bald spots. Can she manage that? I'd like to believe my best friends didn't keep secrets from me. I'd like that monkey to be launched on the next space shuttle to Mars, but none of that is going to happen, is it?"

Trish shrugged, but her enthusiasm never wavered. "Probably not, but maybe you'll finally be at peace with things you can't control. Maybe you won't be terrified of loud noises. Maybe you'll be able to forgive the Estelles. Maybe you and Alphonse will find a way to get along."

Kiki stopped fingering the rack card and tossed it onto the coffee table.

"I'll never be at peace with that monkey."

"But maybe you can learn how to live in the same universe," Trish said.

"Universe, maybe. But not on the same island. That's too close for comfort."

The rain had finally stopped. Sunlight was beginning to filter into the room through the bamboo shades. Kiki pulled her flannel shirt closer and ran her tongue over her teeth. They felt like they had little sweaters on them. She hadn't been out in two days. She'd purposely stayed away from the Goddess, willing to let the Maidens fend for themselves. No way was she going tonight either.

"You can sit here and sulk, or you can join the living," Trish said. "That hospital stay wasn't much help. Why not try alternative therapy?"

Kiki pouted in silence.

Trish picked up her straw bag. "We've already signed up and paid, and so we're going whether you join us or not. We're hula sisters, one for all and all for one, remember?"

"Are the Estelles going?"

"Yes. That's the point. It's a healing session for all of us."

"What about that *thing*?"

"Alphonse? Of course not, so please, say you'll go."

"Sorry, I'm not into hunching over a fire pit eating beans out of a can like a bum."

"We're having it catered."

"Nuts and grains by Andromeda Galaxy?"

"No, real food from the Goddess. Kimo's making all of your favorites. He's all for you trying this. The man is beside himself, you know. He's heartbroken seeing you so down. So, Kiki, do it for Kimo and for the sake of keeping the Maidens together."

Kiki gently tapped the spot above the bridge of her nose with her middle finger. Tap. Tap. Tap. She wasn't even aware she was doing it until Trish commented.

"That tapping is alternative therapy, isn't it? It must help."

"It keeps me busy." Kiki dropped her hand.

"Imagine beating on a drum as hard as you can, venting your frustration and anger. The full moon will be shining, the ocean beating against the shoreline. Your hula sisters will all be there to support you. The moon will be pouring her healing light down on all of us."

"All right, already." Kiki flung her hands in the air. "Stop. Enough. I'll go. I'll try it."

Trish jumped up so fast Kiki flinched.

"Sorry," Trish said.

"It's okay." Kiki was too exhausted by the conversation to get up. "Mind letting yourself out?"

"Of course not. Suzi and I will pick you up tomorrow around four. All you need are your toiletries. We'll bring your tent and bedding." Trish walked over to the door.

"Just one other thing," Kiki said.

Trish paused with her hand on the doorknob. "What?"

"I'll sleep in a tent, but I'm *not* pooping in a bucket."

# 26

EM UNLOCKED THE front door to the bar and began to arrange the chairs and tables on the *lanai* when a sleek black limo pulled into the parking lot. Since she could count the island's limos on one hand, it certainly wasn't the norm. She watched the front passenger door open. A beefy black man wearing aviator sunglasses, a tight black T-shirt, and black slacks opened the back door. Keeping one hand on the doorframe, he slowly scanned the parking lot.

A woman emerged from the backseat. She swung her long, shapely legs out first and stood on black stilettos. Like the bodyguard, she wore all black. She smoothed down a knit sleeveless dress that fit like a second skin. Her hair was long and dark and pulled back into a glossy ponytail. Her eyes were hidden behind Jackie-O sunglasses. A single strand of thick white pearls wreathed her neck.

The woman's skin glowed bronze, the color so even it had to have been applied. She was thin, too thin, but her muscles were toned. As the brunette's gaze turned to the *lanai*, Em recognized her immediately.

It was Alanna Grant, the film star and ex-wife of Cameron Delacruz.

If she noticed Em in the shadows of the *lanai*, the woman didn't show it as she walked up the path with purpose in each step. The bodyguard trailed close behind.

*A bodyguard on Kauai? Seriously?* Em thought.

When she reached the steps, Em stepped forward and greeted her with a cheerful, "Aloha."

The woman slipped off her sunglasses, smiled, and offered her hand.

"I'm Alanna Grant. Are you Em Johnson?"

The celebrity's manner was so unassuming, so open and friendly that Em almost forgot about the bodyguard hovering not far away and the limo in the parking lot.

"I'm Em," she said. "We're just opening up. Come on in. *E komo mai.*"

Alanna walked up onto the *lanai* and followed Em inside.

"Would you like a table near a window or somewhere in back?" Em wondered if the bodyguard was going to sit down too until he walked over to a corner facing the door, stopped, and crossed his arms. He'd kept his sunglasses on.

"Oh, I'm not here to eat. Some other time, maybe." Alanna looked around. "The bar is fine. I'd like to talk to you if you have a minute."

"Of course." Em motioned toward the barstools.

Alanna stood back, looked at the intricate tiki carvings on the bases, each of them with a different expression. Some of the tiki were fierce, some smiling, some grimaced, and a couple were sticking out smoothly carved tongues.

"Cute," she said. She studied the room. "I like this place."

"*Mahalo*," Em said. "My uncle is the owner."

Studying the tiki masks and other carvings on the walls along with all the photos of Louie and VIP visitors who'd come in over the years, Alanna said, "Lots of history here."

"You bet," Em said as Alanna slid onto a stool. "Would you like something to drink?"

"Club soda with lime, please."

Em stepped behind the bar. "You wanted to talk. How can I help you?"

"I understand you were there the night my ex-husband's Pollocks were stolen."

Em set the club soda on the bar. "That's right. We catered the event. The party was actually next door at Wally Williams's estate."

Alanna ran a long crimson nail around the rim of the glass but didn't pick it up.

"Yes, I know," she said. "I wanted to hear what happened from someone other than Cameron. He tends to become borderline hysterical and dramatizes the smallest incident so at this point you can imagine he's overly worked up."

Alanna finally took a sip of soda, then set it down again. "So how would you describe what happened that night, Em? Do you mind if I call you Em?"

"Of course not." Em never considered herself capable of being starstruck with any celebrity. They came in the bar all the time. But there was something so gracious and down to earth about Alanna Grant that it was easy to see how she had such a huge following.

"I really have no idea what happened at Delacruz's that night. The *Mahalo* Security guard in charge, Leo Kekina, came over to the party and said he couldn't locate his uncle, another guard.

"I walked back over there with Mr. Delacruz."

"And Cameron's latest arm candy?" Alanna asked.

"Jasmine. She stayed at the party." Em thought back and remembered Jasmine had stayed at the party, then she'd walked over alone once, but it was after the robbery.

"Ah. Still Jasmine. She's lasted longer than the others." Alanna sipped her club soda. "So you walked over to Cameron's with him."

Em nodded. "Yes, and the guard. We discovered empty frames. The walls were bare, the paintings gone."

Alanna finished the club soda and set down the glass.

"Over twenty million, you know? Half of that was mine once."

Em did know and could commiserate. It wasn't until she and her own late ex divorced that she learned he'd refinanced their house and was in so much debt they were penniless. She'd been awarded half of nothing. Luckily she'd ended up on Kauai with her uncle.

Alanna hadn't expected an answer. She went on to add, "I turned the Pollocks over to him in exchange for future movie contracts. If I'd known he was going to ship them over here and keep them in this environment with all the mildew and humidity, I'd have fought harder. If I'd been awarded my share, at least one of them would still be safe."

There wasn't much Em could do but nod.

"What was he thinking?" Alanna mused aloud.

"Another soda?" Em asked.

"No. Thank you. So, am I to understand there were no clues, no hint of anything left behind that would point to the thieves?"

"There wasn't any sign of a break-in. Whoever it was had to have the security code. The police have no idea how or where they slipped in and out undetected."

"What about the security cameras? I thought there is one in each room?"

"Whoever broke in had them all turned off."

"So much for smart house technology," Alanna said. "Cameron bragged the system was foolproof."

"I always figure if people want in, they can get in."

Alanna smiled. "This almost sounds like something out of one of our Cat Woman movies." She looked off in the distance, remembering. "Those were fun, not to mention box-office knockouts. Cameron should have stuck to making more of those." She leaned on the bar toward Em. "Let me give you a piece of advice. Never dangle from a two-story building in a skintight latex body suit."

"I'll remember," Em laughed.

"Do you know anything about the man they arrested? If there were no clues, why is he still in jail?"

"Yes. Buzzy works for us. He was at the party that night to bus tables and keep party crashers out. He wandered over to Mr. Delacruz's property; Buzzy tends to wander. The police found out after the robbery that he'd been put on an FBI watch list over forty years ago. Being in the wrong place at the wrong time didn't help. I believe he's innocent. He couldn't have done it."

"You sound very certain."

"I am. He's just not the type. There's not an evil bone in his body."

"So the local police have nothing else? No clues, no suspects other than this Buzzy guy?"

Em nodded. Certain she wasn't giving away classified information, she said, "There was another art theft the night before in Po'ipu. Nothing as rare or expensive was taken. Not by far."

"I'll bet Cameron is furious. I haven't seen him yet, and I'm dreading it. I just flew in from Maui."

Em nodded. She could picture someone like Alanna enjoying Maui far more than Kauai.

Alanna lifted her hand, and the bodyguard detached himself from the corner.

"A card for Ms. Johnson," she said.

He reached into the pocket on his T-shirt, flicked a business card toward Em. It contained a cell number and nothing more.

"If you hear anything else, you can reach me there," Alanna said. "As far as I know I'll be staying in one of the guest houses at Cameron's. He'd better extend an invite. My money paid for half the place."

Alanna Grant stood and smiled at Em.

"Thank you so much for your time."

"Of course," Em said. Alanna turned to go.

The bodyguard set a ten-dollar bill on the bar.

"On the house," Em said. He ignored her and left the bill there.

Alanna had to pause to let a tourist couple in their sixties accompanied by two teens, a girl and a boy, enter and head for a table. The girl elbowed the boy. They stared at Alanna.

"Grandma, Janet! That's Cat Woman!" The boy hopped around on the balls of his feet.

"I gotta get a picture." The grandma started rummaging in her oversized tote. "Nobody in Marshall's gonna believe we saw Cat Woman!"

By the time the grandmother found her phone, Alanna Grant had already slipped into the limo, and it was pulling onto the highway headed north.

# 27

TRISH AND SUZI picked up Kiki on time the next afternoon. When they drove into the gravel parking lot at Haena Beach Park, they were lucky enough to find a place to park. They had to sidestep potholes deep enough to drown a wild pig in.

The Maidens' campsite was easy to spot on the grassy area above the beach. Someone had set up a huge white tent with rolled-up sides. It looked like a something from *Out of Africa*. Beneath it, a long dining table was covered with a white linen cloth, crystal goblets, lovely Asian blue and white china, linen napkins, and hurricane lamps.

Five smaller tents with a just-out-of-the-bag spanking-clean newness about them were lined up in a semicircle facing the water. The Maidens' campsite was the opposite of all the worn and faded tents scattered here on the grass, beneath the trees, near the stream, and close to the bushes near the bathrooms.

Kiki's spirit was still low, and she wished she'd stayed home. She certainly wasn't ready to face the Estelles yet knowing Big Estelle would be groveling and Little Estelle smart-mouthing. She took a deep breath and told herself to get a grip. Seeing all the trouble the Maidens had gone to on her behalf, she felt obliged to stay.

"I'll admit I'm impressed. What a campsite," she said.

"Hey, we're a class act. You know that." Suzi checked the cell phone in her hand and apologized. "That's the last time I look at this thing until tomorrow morning. I promise. I have an escrow about to close." She tucked her phone away, and they walked over to the dining tent. Precious was there sitting in the shade in an oversized tie-dyed T-shirt that fit her like a maxi dress.

"I'm tenting with Lillian," she announced with a smile when they joined her.

"What?" Kiki frowned. "No MyBob?" Bob Smith was a shadow affixed to his wife.

"Nope. Just Lillian and me. We started calling ourselves the new-bies."

"I'm staying with Trish," Suzi said. "Flora and Pat are sharing a tent, and the Estelles will bunk together."

"What about me?" Kiki tried to tamp down a wave of nervousness. Would she have to pretend to be upbeat all night long?

"Your tent is right beside ours," Trish said. "We thought you might need some time alone as you ease your way back into the world."

"Where's Andromeda staying?" Suzi looked around.

"She should be here by now," Trish said. "She doesn't use a tent. She sleeps under the stars, if she sleeps."

"Does she realize this is Haena?" Kiki said. "I don't mean to be Debbie Downer, but it'll most likely pour rain at some point."

"It looks pretty clear right now," Precious said. "Oh! There she is." She pointed across the beach.

Kiki looked toward the water and spotted Andromeda Galaxy in flowing white linen pants, a sleeveless white shirt, and a long white scarf tied around her head turban style. Her neck was wreathed with strings of seeds and shells. Her long blond hair hung in loose ripples past her hips. She appeared to be in her mid-forties with a celestial smile on her face. Kiki watched Andromeda thread her way through the semicircle of tents headed straight for the group.

"You must be Kiki." She clasped both of Kiki's hands in her own. Andromeda's voice had a breathy, hushed quality, a cross between a sigh and a whisper.

"Yessss." Kiki tried to mimic the sound but reminded herself of the snake in *The Jungle Book*. "How did you recognize me? The *pupule* look in my eyes?" Kiki rolled her eyes around.

"Actually, Trish described you perfectly: long hair, colorful *pareau*, a bright aura around you. You're a hula celebrity, I hear."

Kiki didn't want to fall for flattery but then suddenly realized she was almost smiling.

"Really? Where did you hear that? You must have seen *Trouble in Paradise*, the reality show based on the Tiki Goddess Bar and Restaurant. We were all featured."

Andromeda blinked a couple of times, her expression blank. "Oh, no. Sorry. I don't have a television, of course."

"Of course? I didn't know there was anyone left on the planet without a TV," Kiki said.

Andromeda merely smiled.

"When do we start the therapy? I'll go get Lil," Precious offered.

"Not until well after sunset and the full moon has risen."

"What'll we do until then?"

"We eat and drink!" Flora walked up wearing a huge *pareau* tied over her swimsuit. "What else?"

# 28

IT WAS A SLOW afternoon at the Goddess. Em expected the evening crowd to be light, too, because word was out the Maidens wouldn't be dancing that night. So when Roland called and said he was on the North Shore and asked if she'd meet him for a late lunch/early dinner, she agreed. He'd been on duty so much lately that she wasn't about to pass up a chance to see him.

He was in Princeville, so she suggested they meet at Tiki Iniki, a newer but successful restaurant and bar in the Princeville Center.

"It won't hurt to scope out the competition," Sophie said when Em told her she was leaving to meet Roland and where.

"Uncle says there's never enough tiki to go around," Em laughed. "Besides, we're down here, and they're up there. We've got different menus, and they don't have Louie's legendary concoctions."

"They don't have Louie either," Sophie reminded her.

"That's for sure."

Em found a place to park behind the Bank of Hawaii and walked around to Tiki Iniki where she found Roland already seated at a table in the corner near the bar. Owners Michele and Todd Rundgren had totally tricked out the place with hip tiki collectibles. Em had heard Bamboo Ben, one of the Tiki world's foremost bamboo and tiki décor masters, created the interior. Stepping into Tiki Iniki was like stepping into an exotic oasis.

Roland stood when Em walked in, and she found herself blushing as he pulled out her chair and waited for her to sit down.

"Have you ordered?" She knew he was always pressed for time.

"Not yet. I just got here."

A waitress in a tight miniskirt and tank top brought them menus and asked what they'd like to drink. As much as Em wanted to sample one of their specialty cocktails, either a Hanalei Sling or The Iniki, she still had to work later, so she ordered an ice tea. Roland ordered a diet soda.

"Diet?" Em asked. "Since when do you drink diet?"

"Gotta stay in shape, you know."

"Oh, that's right. You need to stay trim for whenever you strip down and dance around half naked waving flaming swords."

"They're fire knives. Half naked?"

"Oh, I forgot. Half dressed."

He smiled.

She melted and laughed. It felt good to be away from the Goddess, even if she hadn't escaped the tiki atmosphere, and great to put this latest mess with Buzzy, Kiki, and Delacruz behind her for a while.

"What brought you up to Princeville?"

Their drinks arrived before he could answer. He quickly glanced at the menu and ordered an Iniki Burger and fries.

"Nothing for me," Em said. She'd had a late lunch. After the waitress left she said, "You know that burger has Spam mixed in the meat?"

"Yep. That's what makes it good."

"What about your waistline?"

He held up the diet soda. "Besides, if I get too skinny my *malo* might fall off in the middle of a performance."

"So what's going on in Princeville?"

"Been some break-ins at the Pali condos," he said.

The Pali was an older condo development, one of the first built in the Princeville resort community. Perched on the edge of the bluff overlooking the wide Pacific, it was the perfect spot to watch the sunset or the passing parade of whales when they migrated past in the winter.

"Art thieves?"

He shook his head no. "Small *kine* stuff. Cell phones, cameras, tablets, jewelry. Grab-and-go stuff. Probably kids."

"Kids? Really?"

"Visitors believe nothing bad happens in paradise, so they're too lax. They leave their doors unlocked and valuables lying around in their vacation rentals. Older guys get the kids to do their dirty work because the kids won't do hard time."

"Sad."

"But true." He lowered his voice and leaned across the table. "Pali security and the homeowners association are up in arms. They're setting up security cameras as we speak, hoping to catch the thieves in the act. The cameras should be up and running by sundown."

"You think they'll hit again so soon?"

"We hope they're short on brains."

"Alanna Grant came by the Goddess yesterday."

"The actress?"

Em nodded. "She's Cameron Delacruz's ex-wife. She wanted my take on the break-in since I was there that night. She's upset about the Pollocks being stolen. She told me she gave Cameron her painting in the divorce, and she asked about Buzzy. I told her I didn't think he could ever do something like that. I can't believe he's still sitting in jail, Roland."

"He hasn't asked for a lawyer."

"He probably can't afford a lawyer. The Maidens haven't had time to hold a fundraiser. Kiki's not up to it. In fact, I'm surprised she's not back in Kukuoloko."

"What happened?"

She told him about Kiki's shocking face-to-face with Alphonse.

"Alphonse who?"

"You know, the cavorting capuchin monkey that was such a pest on Oahu."

"I thought they shipped that stowaway back."

"Unfortunately, no. The Estelles have had him at their place, and the Maidens all kept the secret from Kiki."

"Where is she now?"

"Camping at Haena Beach Park. The Maidens thought she needed a full moon therapy session." She watched him polish off the last bite of the Iniki Burger and could tell he was thinking about what she'd said.

"Did you say *full* moon or *fool* moon therapy?"

"Very funny. At this point anything is worth a try. At least that's what Suzi and Trish think."

"I just hope no one ends up dead."

"Don't even whisper it." She fiddled with her drink coaster. "You know, I googled Buzzy and found out his family is really, really wealthy. As in *really* wealthy, but they disowned him years ago."

"That was on the Internet?"

She shook her head. "No. I tried to contact them though their holdings and was told they didn't want anything to do with him. What exactly did he do to end up on an FBI list?"

"He was an art major at Berkeley, a leading peacenik protester during the Vietnam War. That was enough to get him on the FBI watch list. Then he started forging draft cards to keep guys out of the service, and then when they were on to him, he disappeared."

"That totally explains his family disowning him. He was into flower power in the seventies, but he is from one of the wealthiest families dealing in military industrial contracts."

"He was a draft dodger, too."

"So he was never caught or arrested back then?"

Roland shook his head. "He disappeared totally off the grid. It wasn't until we ran his prints that he popped up in the system again. He was at the Delacruz property the night of the break-in. You add that to his being an art major, plus forgery, plus stolen Jackson Pollocks." Roland shrugged. "Adds up."

"Very conveniently. Good thing too, because you don't have any other leads."

"He'd know the value of the Pollocks. There aren't that many people around here who would see those paintings as anything more than paint splatters on canvas."

"The Delacruz divorce was so highly publicized that their fight over the paintings would have been noted by high-end art thieves. Whoever took the Pollocks was probably watching Delacruz and knew when he'd shipped the paintings over here. They could have followed the loot over, found the house, fooled around with the security system. *That* adds up to me."

"So if professional art thieves stole them, the paintings are probably already off the island."

"That makes way more sense to me than blaming poor Buzzy for doing more than bumbling around in the dark that night."

"If that's what happened, Delacruz is out a lot of money."

"And his ex will be even more pissed off than she is right now."

He caught the waitress's eye. She gave him a nod that she'd be right over.

"Delacruz's insurance company contacted me today. If or when we recover the paintings I have to let them know, and they'll fly an agent over. They said not to turn them over to the owner until they can evaluate them. I'll have to hold the art as evidence anyway."

When the waitress walked over, Roland asked Em if she wanted to share a dessert.

"Is it diet dessert?" She pretended to be checking out his waistline.

"Okay, I guess not." He sounded disappointed. When the waitress walked away he leaned back in his chair. "I showed Buzzy's photo around the Pali complex earlier."

"He couldn't be responsible for any break-ins while he's been in jail," Em noted.

"I was just thinking I'd get a hit. The trouble is, a lot of folks up here know him from his handyman business. No one claims to have seen him acting suspicious. They read about his arrest in the paper, and I got an earful of complaints. Most of them are as certain as you are that he's innocent, and they're all hyped up about attending some fundraiser to help pay his legal fees."

"The Maidens are planning one, at least they were. That's how Kiki ended up at the Estelles' and suffered the monkey sighting." The ice in Em's tea was long gone. She finished the lukewarm drink. "Why not let Buzzy go, Roland? He's not going anywhere."

"Look, Em, he was the only one besides the security guard going back and forth between the houses during the party. He could have gotten in, taken the paintings, and hidden them anywhere."

"He'd have only had time to hide them in the bushes on the property or the jungle behind it. *If* he moved fast enough. I've never seen him do more than shuffle."

"We searched the area and came up with nothing. Besides, I'm not letting our one and only suspect go. Uncle Bass is dead, and somebody has to pay for it."

# 29

SUNSET VIEWED from Haena Beach was stunning, but Kiki missed it while hiding out in her private tent. She'd been semi-okay until she saw Little Estelle, which triggered images of that *thing* again.

"Kiki, please come out," Trish called from outside the tent flap.

Kiki was lying atop her sleeping bag, her eyes covered by the crook of her arm. She moved her arm and stared at the top of the tent. Outside, it sounded like the park was filling up with full moon devotees.

Dinner was delicious, but she didn't eat much because of Little Estelle. When no one else was looking, the old reprobate would pull on her ears and make monkey faces at her. Kiki didn't tell anyone, but she couldn't get away fast enough and retreated to her tent before dessert.

Now Trish was badgering her, and obviously, the woman's patience was slipping. "Kiki, please!"

"I don't want to."

"It's not about what you want anymore. We're all here for you at our own expense because we love you. The least you can do is join us. Please."

Kiki sat up with a groan and crawled to the tent flap. She lifted a corner and peered outside. A virtual tent and tarp city full of la-la-land hippie types had sprung up outside. Low fires glowed all around. The sound of flutes, finger cymbals, and rattles filled the evening air.

The Maidens' dining tent was gone, and it left behind a clearing on the edge of the grass where the beach sloped toward the water.

All of the Maidens were there seated in a semicircle facing the ocean. Twilight stained the sky deep violet, and far off to the west there was still the faint fiery glow of the setting sun. The moon had made her appearance too and was rising slowly.

"Everyone's ready. Andromeda is about to begin. Pat is lighting the fire."

Pat was indeed lighting a fire just beyond the ring of Maidens.

Kiki let Trish take her hand and pull her to her feet.

"Remind me. I'm doing this why?" Kiki asked.

"Mainly to release your negative feelings toward Alphonse and the Estelles, but it will help you in so many other ways. Come out of there and let the moon shine on your true self."

"I could use a little moonshine of the liquid variety right now," Kiki mumbled.

What about the damn monkey's true self? As far as she was concerned, he was the one who needed help.

Trish was already walking toward the drum circle, so Kiki fell into step behind her and whispered, "Here goes nothing."

As she approached, all the Maidens smiled and waved to her, all but Little Estelle who was seated on her Gadabout with a drum balanced in front of her. Kiki had to lower herself to her hands and knees and then roll around in order to sit on the grass. Pat was able to sit cross-legged. The others were straight-legged with their drums in front of them.

Andromeda stood before the group with a drum cradled in the crook of her arm. Her flowing white outfit luffed on the gentle breeze. The moon was rising and so bright there were almost no stars visible. The palm trees were black silhouettes against the night sky, their fronds occasionally glistening silver.

Andromeda waited until they were all watching in anticipation before she started in her hushed voice. "Each of you has chosen the drum that spoke to you personally. All of them were made with care." She stepped toward Kiki and extended a drum. "I chose this one for you, Kiki, because it's a special drum inspired by Yogi Pandarandarum, my spirit guide and teacher on the other side."

"The other side of what?" Pat poked the fire with a long stick.

"The other side of the veil. The great beyond," Andromeda said.

Kiki accepted the drum and nestled it on the ground between her legs. Somewhere off in the maze of false *kamani* trees along the nearby stream, a rooster crowed.

"That moon's so bright them damn roosters think it's mornin' already," Pat laughed.

Andromeda ignored her. "I'm going to clap my hands slowly, very slowly at first," she said. "When I do, you follow the beat and stay together."

She began to clap her hands. Clap, hold, clap, hold.

"That's it. It's the beat of your heart, the beat of the waves of Mother Ocean. Close your eyes now, ladies. That's it. Keep them closed and keep drumming. Keep it all together."

Once in a while someone hit an off-beat. Kiki squinted around through her eyelashes until she found Lillian. Sure enough, she was offbeat as usual. Feeling woozy, Kiki kept her eyes open.

"Faster." Andromeda's eyes were closed as were all the others. The FMDT was swaying to the beat, urging them on. "Faster, ladies. Faster."

The drumming sped up. All of the Maidens pounded harder and faster.

"That's it!" Andromeda's whisper was gone. She was bouncing from side to side on her toes and clapping maniacally. "Keep going! Keep it going! Be *one* with the drum. Be *one* with the sea. *Feel* the light of the moon pouring into you! *Feel* its healing power. *Feel* it release your fears, your worries, your cares. A new *you* is being born tonight!"

All over the park the hippies and campers joined in with the rhythm of their drums. The flautists flauted. The cymbals chimed. One group had taken up pot and pan lids and was clanging them together. Three young women began to chant indecipherable words. Little Estelle threw back her head, tossed her drum aside, and started tooting the Gadabout horn in time to the drumming.

Suddenly a young male hippie came bounding out of the *kamani* trees. He threw his head back and yowled at the moon.

Kiki's hands froze on the drum. She started to shake harder than a palm tree in a hurricane. The man bared his teeth and beat his chest with all the abandon of King Kong. Lost in their frantic drumming, eyes closed, Andromeda and all the Maidens were oblivious to the threat.

Before Kiki had time to react, the hippie howled again and ripped off all his clothes. His knuckles grazed the ground gorilla-style as he loped straight toward the Maidens' drum circle.

There was no time for Kiki to cower, to run, or to duck and cover. There in the moonlit night something inside her snapped. A voice inside her mind, *her* voice, screamed louder than the drums. The message was clearer than the sky around the full moon.

*No more monkey business!*

The crazed hippie ran straight into the circle of Maidens. Kiki levitated to her feet, pulled her arm back, and heaved the special edition Yogi Pandarandarum drum at his head and roared, "This stops here, sucker! This stops here!"

# 30

WHEN THE SUN rose the next morning, Kiki was back in charge not only of the Maidens but her life.

"Get these tents down, ladies. We've got crimes to solve and dances to learn." Feeling her old self for the first time in months, she marched around the campground issuing orders. Finally, she paused to take a deep breath.

"You need to be careful, Kiki."

Kiki turned around and found the full moon therapist at her elbow. Andromeda's arms were filled with drums.

"I feel great," Kiki said. "The only thing that would make this moment perfection is having a double of one of Louie's Blood on the Beach cocktails in my hand."

"You could have a relapse," Andromeda warned.

"I don't think so. I've taken back my power. No one's taking it from me again. Not even that furry little Alphonse."

"You've made an incredible recovery. I've never seen anything like it." Andromeda was all smiles. Precious walked by them carrying so many drums her head and shoulders were out of sight.

"Am I headed toward the parking lot?" she yelled.

"Straight ahead," Kiki directed.

"I'd better follow her over to my car," Andromeda said. "I've got to get going. I'm holding a post-full moon event at my home in Lawai. You're welcome to join us. No charge, of course."

"Oh, I've got plenty of catching up to do. Thanks anyway," Kiki said.

"Don't forget to thank the full moon goddess once a month." Andromeda leaned close as if expecting an embrace.

"Sure thing. Have a great post therapy." Kiki sidestepped Andromeda when she saw one of the hippies across the park holding a plastic bag full of ice against his head. In broad daylight the skinny hippie King Kong was even less of a threat than he turned out to be.

She crossed the park to speak to him, and when he looked up and shifted the ice pack, she got a good look at the cut on top of a huge lump on his forehead.

"I'm really sorry," she said, meaning it. "You were pulling that gorilla stunt and headed for my friends, and I snapped."

His smile was lopsided, his eyes as red as meatballs on a bed of spaghetti. "It's all good, auntie. All good. No worries. Like, that was some really powerful moon last night. Like, no way to control ourselves."

"For sure, dude." Kiki watched him wander off toward the water to join his own kind. The Maidens were scurrying around, packing up their sleeping bags and tents. Pat had already taken care of her own and Kiki's.

"Where are the Estelles?" Kiki asked her.

"They had to get home to see to Alphonse." The minute the monkey's name passed her lips, Pat covered her mouth with her hand. "I'm so sorry."

"Not to worry." Kiki smiled. "I talked to Little Estelle earlier and told her I had my mojo back, and from now on she'd better keep an eye on that furry maggot."

"What'd she say?"

"Well, she didn't crack any jokes, that's for sure."

"Nobody's gonna mess with you after seeing the way you laid that hippie out in the middle of the drum circle last night." Pat nodded. "I thought he'd never stop bleedin' like a stuck pig."

Kiki's hippie takedown had shaken them all out of their drum chant trance and sent them running for cover. Little Estelle roared off on her Gadabout, and Big Estelle didn't find her until morning.

"So what's up now, boss? I took the whole day off." Pat dug through a pile of her things that was nearby and came up with a clipboard.

"First, we need to get back to Delacruz's place. We never talked to him personally."

"Delacruz." Pat started a list.

"We have to finalize the Free Buzzy Fundraiser."

"Buzzy money," Pat said, writing. "What about dancin' at the Goddess?"

"If we get there, we get there," Kiki said. Feeling whole and free, she wanted to ride the wave of euphoria as long as it lasted.

Suzi and Pat were the only Maidens available to go with Kiki to Cameron Delacruz's compound. Everyone else had obligations at work, not that Kiki cared. There would be fewer of them to wrangle.

Getting into the estate was as easy as before since Jasmine answered the intercom at the front gate and buzzed them in. They drove up the long drive, and when they reached the house, Delacruz himself was pacing the *lanai*. His wasn't the warmest of welcomes.

"Who did you say you were again?" He stood at the edge of the *lanai*, blocking their way up the stairs. Jasmine hovered behind him.

"Those are the ladies who danced at Wally's party, babe," Jasmine reminded him.

"So, what do you need?" It was obvious he didn't care if he insulted them or not.

"We came by before to welcome you to the neighborhood. Naturally, we're concerned about your break-in. We're well-known around here for solving murder cases. Compared to some of the crimes we've solved, tracking art thieves should be pretty simple."

"Yeah? Apparently not for the KPD," Cameron said. "They haven't gotten a confession out of that damn hippie they have in jail, and they haven't recovered my paintings yet, either."

"Would you ladies like to come in and have a drink?" Jasmine asked.

Delacruz piped up, "I'm sure they're in a hurry."

His cool reception didn't faze Kiki. Not only did she feel invincible after her full moon transformation, but during their trip to Oahu she'd honed her skill at barging into places she wasn't wanted or expected.

"We'd love a drink," Kiki said.

"Darn tootin'! I'm thirstier than a cured ham," Pat said.

Jasmine ignored Delacruz's obvious displeasure and ushered them inside. She made them a round of gin and tonics.

"Because it's so humid," she added.

Kiki, Suzi, and Pat toasted Jasmine who, unlike Delacruz, was having a cocktail with them.

Kiki wandered around the austerely white room, hoping she looked like she was casually looking around and not snooping.

"So do you know how the thieves broke in yet?" she asked.

Delacruz was trying to ignore the women but had overheard. "By tripping up that overpriced, overrated security system, that's how."

Across the room, Suzi drew herself up. "I'm a realtor. I have recommended Hale Akamai Security to all of my clients, and there's never been a breach in their system before."

"There's a first time for everything." Delacruz eyed her speculatively. "Did you happen to recommend them to the first owners who originally built this place? I'm suing Hale Akamai and my contractor and maybe the previous owners, too. Why not?"

"I didn't sell this house to the original homeowners of this property," Suzi said, bristling.

"Do you have a card?" he asked.

Suzi didn't hesitate. "Nope, fresh out. Been meaning to get some."

Kiki stared at her hula sister. Suzi was never out of cards, never unprepared. Kiki quickly changed the subject.

"I need to call my lawyer." Delacruz disappeared down the hall without a goodbye.

Kiki pulled a plastic container out of her straw bag and turned to Jasmine.

"I almost forgot. We brought you a tub of Hanalei *poi*. Better put it in the refrigerator. It's so *ono*."

Jasmine reached for it. "That means delicious, right?"

"The best." Kiki nodded.

Jasmine carried it to the huge stainless refrigerator so far across the room she had to raise her voice to call out to them. "I read somewhere that *poi* is the perfect food."

Pat was standing on the edge of the room where the wide glass sliding doors had been pushed open to give the place an indoor, outdoor feel along with a view of the expansive pool, guest houses, and garden.

"Is that Alanna Grant? Holy cow!" Pat shouted.

"Yes. She's Cameron's ex," Jasmine said.

"What's she doing here?" Kiki polished off her gin and tonic and sucked on a piece of ice.

Jasmine shrugged. "Her money helped pay for the place before their divorce. She said she has a right to at least hang out, and Cameron thought it was easier to let her stay a few days than fight it."

"Who cares why she's here?" Pat said.

"Stop ogling," Suzi told her. She finished her drink and set the glass on a side table.

"I'll ogle all I want. That's Cat Woman! In a thong!"

Jasmine walked over to join them again and in a voice barely above a whisper said, "I personally think she came to rub the robbery in Cameron's face."

"She can rub anything she wants anywhere on me," Pat said and sighed.

"We'd better go, Kiki." Suzi was next to the front door, giving Kiki a let's-get-out-of-here look. She glanced at her watch. "We have that appointment in town, remember?"

"We? You never said nothing about an appointment in town." Pat refused to turn around. She kept her gaze locked on Alanna.

"I just remembered it," Suzi said.

"Well"—Kiki turned to Jasmine—"thanks for letting us stop by."

Jasmine asked the one thing sure to win over Kiki's heart. "When are you ladies dancing at the Goddess again?"

Kiki looked over at Suzi, still not certain what was going on. Her friend looked like she was going to hyperventilate at any minute. Pat was watching Alanna Grant apply suntan lotion to her over-exposed rear end. It was one of the first times Kiki had seen Pat speechless.

"We'll probably be dancing again tomorrow night," Kiki said.

"If I can talk Cameron into it, maybe we'll stop by."

"Feel free to bring Alanna," Pat said.

Jasmine's smile faltered. "I don't think so."

# 31

THE THREE MAIDENS piled back into Suzi's car. She made a phone call, asked if her brother was in, snapped off her phone, and then hit the ignition. Once she was off Delacruz's property and on the highway, she stepped on the gas.

"What's wrong? Where are we going in such a rush?" Kiki hated being in the dark.

"We've gotta get to Lihue *wikiwiki*. Gotta get to Sundowners."

"The bar? Why not just stop at the Goddess if you need another drink so bad?"

"Because my brother's at Sundowners karaoke happy hour, and he's not gonna pick up his phone, that's why."

"And you suddenly need to see your brother why?" Pat had spread out, arms stretched wide across the back seat.

"Because he owns Hale Akamai Security Systems, that's why. I get a kickback for every referral. If Delacruz is going to sue him, my brother needs to know now."

"So text him," Pat said.

"Did you not hear me say he was at karaoke happy hour? No way will he be picking up his phone for hours." Suzi slowed down as they cruised through Hanalei town and then hit the gas when she passed the Dolphin restaurant, the last building before the *taro* fields.

"You sure this can't wait until tomorrow?"

"I cannot stress the seriousness of this situation. A lawsuit, especially one pursued by a man as wealthy as Cameron Delacruz, is nothing to ignore. You heard the man, he was going to call his lawyer right then and there."

"Did you lie? Were you the one who recommended Hale Akamai to the folks who originally built the house?"

"No. That's the truth, but I did stop by and mention my brother's company to the contractor Delacruz hired to do some renovations before he moved in. I have a feeling Delacruz is going to backtrack that system all the way from the manufacturer to my brother, the contractor, and then to me. We could all go belly-up."

"So you're not out of business cards?" Pat asked.

"Of course not. I'm a realtor. I've got more business cards than a fish has scales."

Thankfully, traffic was somewhat light, and there were no road crews out trimming trees or filling potholes, so they made it to Lihue in forty-five minutes and pulled into the Sundowners Sports Bar parking lot.

The dark, crowded room reverberated with sound. Four flat screens were on—two over the bar, and two flanked the stage high on the wall. A different sports event played out on each. Patrons were squeezed together into high-backed wooden booths; others lined the long bar.

Pat scooted past a huddle around a pool table and made a beeline toward the bar while Kiki and Suzi staked out a free booth.

"I can barely see," Kiki groused. "If it wasn't for the neon beer signs around the room and the glow from the televisions, we'd need flashlights. Do you see your brother?"

"He's the guy on stage," Suzi said.

KIKI STUDIED THE man holding a mic. He was talking to a DJ seated at a table stacked with ring binders full of song choices.

"What's his name?"

"Earlbert."

"Albert?"

"Earlbert. Earl-bert."

"You gonna wave him down?" Kiki asked.

"Nah. Better let him sing his song."

The music began, and Kiki recognized the tune "Happy." Earlbert started singing just as Pat walked up to the table carrying a vodka martini for Kiki, another gin and tonic for Suzi, and a Hinano beer for herself. She slid into the booth they'd chosen, leaned across the table toward them, and yelled over the music.

"I don't get this song. What does feeling like a room have to do with being happy? Why would that make somebody happy? Wouldn't you want a room with a view?"

"I thought they were saying I feel like a room without a tooth." Kiki slid her olives off a plastic sword. They plopped into the drink to marinate.

"It's room without a *roof.*" Suzi rolled her eyes.

"Even stranger," Pat decided.

"Now I don't get it." Kiki carefully sloshed her drink around the glass.

Suzi leaned toward the middle of the table. "The guy who wrote it was trying to say he was as happy as a room without a roof. In other words, he's so happy there's no lid on it. The sky is the limit. I think that's what he was trying to say. Otherwise it doesn't make much sense."

"Well it sounds just plain weird." Pat took a long swig from the beer bottle.

Rather than shout over the music, the three sipped their drinks. As the song ended, Suzi waved to Earlbert, who acknowledged her with a lift of his chin.

Kiki watched Earlbert give up the mic with regret, grab a beer bottle off a nearby table, and head their way.

"Hey, Sis," he said. "What's up? You got an appointment with a client?"

"I wish." Suzi slid over to make room for him in the booth.

"Got a referral for me?"

She shook her head. "You read about the break-in and stolen art on the North Shore at the Delacruz place?"

He finished his beer. "Read about it? The police already been by Hale Akamai to talk to me and everybody else because we put in the system. I told them that had to be an inside job. I stand by my installation and the product."

"No matter that you do." Suzi pulled the lime slice out of her gin and tonic and took a bite out of it. "Mr. Delacruz is going to sue anyone and everyone connected with the smart house system. That means the manufacturer, you, his contractor, and even me when he finds out I recommended you to the guy."

"Let 'um. Not gonna find nut'tin."

"Nut'tun." Pat nodded her head.

"He's got deep pockets, Earlbert," Suzi said. "And he's majorly steamed."

"I would be too in his position, but I'm not worried. We've never, ever had a breach or override incident. I told the police it had to be an inside job. Maybe he didn't tell anyone the code, but someone on his staff got a hold of it somehow."

"What about his contractor? I don't really know him," Suzi said.

Earlbert said, "He had to sign a disclaimer. I make the workers sign one every time some bigwig is involved. Gotta cover all the bases. Besides, like I just said, this Delacruz guy set his own code, so he's the only one that knew it unless he told somebody."

Kiki finished her martini and slid the glass toward Pat, who got up for another. She turned to Earlbert.

"Delacruz isn't about to confess to giving the code to you or anyone else. How can you be certain it wasn't someone who works for you?"

Earlbert and Suzi both turned to stare at Kiki.

"Everyone who works for me is in our family," he said.

"Everyone," Suzi assured her.

# 32

AN HOUR BEFORE closing down the kitchen, Em ushered a party of four to a table in the center of the room. She handed them a menu and then told them about the specials. She'd just turned around when she saw Kiki walk in and grab the only free barstool. Em stopped by the various tables to make sure everyone had all they needed. When she finally got back to the bar, Sophie was shaking Kiki's martini.

"How was the campout?" Em asked Kiki.

"Exhausting."

"Anything solved? Are you speaking to the Estelles again?" She hoped the ladies got something for the exorbitant amount they'd paid for the full moon experience.

"I'm speaking to them." Kiki took the martini Sophie set before her, closed her eyes, and smacked her lips.

"So it worked? I'm amazed."

"Let's just say it shifted my focus. I'm not afraid anymore. Not that I look forward to seeing that furry, limp-dicked you-know-what any time soon," she added quickly. "But surviving a primal primate attack at Haena did the trick."

"What? They brought Alphonse to the campout?"

"No, the park was full of hippies, not just us. One of them gave in to his primal urges and started howling and pounding his chest. I was the only one watching and saw him when he hunched over like a gorilla and charged toward our drum circle." She drank half the martini, set the glass down. Both Em and Sophie hung on every word.

"So what happened?" Sophie wanted to know.

"So something came over me. I'm not kidding. A power whooshed through me. I'm not saying it was the moon or all that infernal drum pounding, but when I saw what looked for all the world like a blown-up version of Alphonse loping toward us, something in me snapped. I was back in control. I wasn't afraid. I hurled my drum at his head and knocked him out cold. I've taken my power back, girls. Taken it back. I'm not going to wallow in fear anymore."

She polished off the martini and handed Sophie the glass.

"I'm not driving, so I'll have another. Suzi dropped me off. I'll ride home with Kimo."

"So do you feel like your old self?" Em asked.

"No. I feel even better. Nothing can stop me now. I've been rejuvenated. My alpha waves must have been reloaded."

Em wasn't sure if that was a good or bad thing. Kiki was a power to be reckoned with before she found her new *mana*.

"I'll be perfectly honest," Kiki said. "I don't know if it was the full moon or the drum ceremony or just the fact that I was sick of feeling helpless, but something worked out there under the moon. Something big happened. I met with the Estelles and said I'd forgive them if they promised to keep that monkey under lock and key and never let him near me again."

"Sounds like a step in the right direction."

Kiki was scanning the bar. "Looks like a good night."

Em nodded. Every night was a moneymaker. "We do even better when you girls are dancing."

"We do draw a crowd." Kiki smiled.

*One way or another*, Em thought.

"How come you don't have karaoke night anymore?" Kiki asked.

"Too many bar fights over the mic. Hard to get some people to give it up."

"Everyone wants to be a star, that's for sure. Suzi and Pat and I went to Sundowners Sports Bar earlier. There was huge crowd there for happy hour karaoke."

"You drove all the way to Lihue for karaoke?"

"We drove in to talk to Suzi's brother Earlbert. He owns Hale Akamai and put in the security system at the Delacruz house. He swears by his product, employees, and workmanship and doesn't seem in the least concerned. He claims it had to be an inside job and said that it had to be someone who works for Delacruz.

"I've been trying to talk to Roland about it, tell him what Earlbert said, but he won't call me back."

"I'm sure by now he's talked to Hale Akamai and the mainland manufacturer of the system. He's been busy with some break-ins up at the Pali condos in Princeville."

"More art theft?"

"No, grab-and-go small stuff. Kids, he thinks."

Sophie walked back to Em. "I'm off now," she said. Em glanced at the clock, surprised it was so late. Time had flown by.

"Head on out," Em said. "I've got it from here. Uncle Louie should be walking over soon for final rounds."

"I'm going out to the kitchen to talk to Kimo," Kiki said.

"I'll have Roland call you if I hear from him," Em promised.

# 33

THE NEXT MORNING after a long swim, Em walked into the Goddess office through the back door. She heard Kiki and the Maidens already there.

Em fluffed her still-wet hair with her fingers and stuck her head into the main room intending to just say hello. When Kiki saw Em, she left Pat inside and walked into Louie's office.

"I am so furious." Kiki perched on the corner of the old, scarred wooden desk.

Before Em could respond, the lead Hula Maiden went on. "Roland finally called me early this morning. He brushed me off when I told him that Suzi's brother said it had to be an inside case. Said he can't say anything about an ongoing investigation. I just hate being in the dark."

Em could tell Kiki was full of piss and vinegar this morning. She *harrumphed* and sighed and tossed her hair back over her shoulder, going for high drama.

"And he went on and on about how maybe we should focus on Buzzy's fundraiser instead." Kiki paced to the door and back.

"So he's not getting out anytime soon," Em said.

Kiki shrugged. "I guess the FBI wants him held indefinitely. What do they think? Just because he led Vietnam War protests that he's turning into one of those homegrown terrorists, for Pete's sake?"

Thankfully, the phone rang, and Em signaled that she needed to answer, so Kiki marched back into the bar.

"Tiki Goddess," Em said.

It turned out to be Wally Williams. He sounded panicked, more so than usual.

"Oh, Em! I'm so thrilled you answered. I just got an emergency call from Cameron Delacruz. He's on Oahu doing another interview show, and the KPD called and wanted to see him in person immediately. He called and asked me to go represent him."

"Can you get there?" Em wondered if he'd called to ask her to go instead.

"Yes, but please, please go with me. I don't like going to police stations alone. Too many macho men around giving me—how do they say it here? Giving me stink eye and making fun of me."

No one was going to make fun of Wally or give stink eye if she could help it.

"Of course I'll go." Louie could cover for her until they got back.

"Wonderful. I'll drive. Be there in a few."

"Wally?"

"Yes?"

"Better leave the boa home."

"Right. Don't wear the boa. Got it."


IN UNDER AN hour they made it to police headquarters in Lihue. Wally told the receptionist why he was there, and soon Roland walked out to greet them. He shook hands with Wally and looked surprised to see Em. Wally told him he was there representing Cameron Delacruz and had asked her to come with him.

"I'm sorry you both had to make the drive. I need to speak to Mr. Delacruz personally."

Wally visibly wilted.

"Wally's his appointed representative," Em said.

"Cameron's on Oahu doing another television news show interview," Wally added.

"I need personal confirmation on the paintings," Roland said.

"How about phoning him?" Wally suggested. "I hate to have to tell him I left if there's anything he can say to convince you."

They followed Roland into an inner office. Wally gave him a phone number, and Roland placed the call. Delacruz's voice came on over the speakerphone.

"We'll be here on Oahu until tomorrow morning," he said when Roland explained why he needed to see him personally. "I sent Wally Williams in to represent me. What's up? Did you finally come up with something that will solve this thing? Any proof that damn hippie did it? Or are you clowns still shooting in the dark blindfolded?"

Em wondered how Roland kept his cool. His expression never changed.

"We recovered your missing art, Mr. Delacruz. I'd like you to verify that the paintings are yours."

Both Wally and Em gasped.

"Oh my stars and garters! That's fabulous. Isn't that fabulous, Cameron?" Wally leaned over and yelled into the speakerphone.

"Thank God!" Delacruz hollered. "I'll try to get back to Kauai tonight. Maybe get on standby. Maybe I'll rent a private jet. Somehow I'll get there. In the meantime, you have my permission to give the artwork to Wally. Oh, they're calling me. I'm up for the next interview. Gotta go."

The line went dead.

"Wait." Roland looked at the phone. He tried dialing back, but Delacruz's voice mail answered, and he punched the call off.

"You found the paintings? How? Who stole them? Did you catch the thieves?" Wally was ecstatic.

"The paintings were stashed in one of the condos at the Pali complex along with the painting stolen from the Po'ipu gallery. It was the grab-and-go kids who broke in again, but this time all they found were the paintings. They'd heard their parents talking about the big robbery and decided to turn them into us for the reward."

Em couldn't believe it. "Surely not."

"Oh, yeah. As I said before, short on brains."

"What a relief." Wally was fanning himself with both hands until Roland picked up a Kauai Activities League pamphlet and handed it to him. The makeshift fan worked. "Where are they?"

"The boys? Juvenile detention," Roland said.

"No, the paintings," Wally said. "I can't wait to see them."

"I'm sorry, Mr. Williams, but I can't hand them over to you. As soon as we have visual verification, Mr. Delacruz's insurance company is sending an art expert over from the mainland to confirm their condition, authenticity, and current value. It's standard procedure."

"But Cameron will be furious if I leave without them."

Roland shrugged. "Nothing I can do about it."

Wally was on his cell in an instant. Roland flashed Em a *"Who is he calling?"* look.

She shrugged.

"Alanna, this is Wally. BNE, darling. Best news ever! The paintings have been found. Yes. It's true. I'm right here at the police station with Em Johnson from the Goddess and Detective Sharpe. Yes. In Lihue. You are?" Wally spoke over the phone to Em and Roland. "She's here in town. At Kauai Pasta. She'll be right here. She can certainly identify the paintings."

Wally told Alanna goodbye and sat back with a smile.

"Ms. Grant is no longer the owner of the artwork, is that correct?" Roland asked him.

"Right." Wally's smile faded. "Surely she can tell you if they were Cameron's. She was half owner once, and she loves those paintings so."

Em nodded. "What's the harm in letting her see them, Roland? Plus, I'd like to hear more of the details myself."

Just then a uniformed officer walked in with a takeout box for Roland, nodded, and set it on his desk. "I'll be happy to accommodate Cat Woman," Roland said. "As long as I can eat."

He offered Em half his hamburger. She declined and so did Wally. Roland polished the burger off by the time Alanna Grant breezed in. Before the door to the private office closed behind her, Em glanced out and saw the lobby swarming with blue uniformed lookie-loos. Alanna's bodyguard had waited for her there.

Looking sleek and glamorous despite the fact that she was wearing a simple black tank top and long black knit skirt, Alanna pulled off her sunglasses and introduced herself to Roland.

"You recovered the artwork," she said, smiling. "*Mahalo.* May I at least see them?"

She asked in the way someone who wants to visit a loved one in the ICU might inquire. Until she spotted the canvases spread on the table, and her hands went to her heart.

"Oh, I'm so happy they're safe and sound." She cried out with the relief of a mother reunited with a lost child.

"Are those the paintings you once owned with your husband?"

She gingerly fingered the edge of the canvas where it had been ripped away from the frame and nodded. "They are."

He picked up an empty folding chair and moved it next to Wally's. "Please, have a seat."

"Did you catch the thieves?"

"The paintings were discovered by some kids in the closet of an empty condo at the Pali resort in Princeville. Someone recently rented the place long-term, but it was obvious once we went over the unit that no one was actually living there. The refrigerator and closets were empty. There was nothing personal in the condo at all, just the rental furniture. Whoever stole the paintings and artwork was using it as a place to stash them."

"Did Buford Burney confess?"

"Actually, he didn't. The kids saw the paintings, and luckily they'd heard folks talking about the reward, so they decided to try and collect."

"Very enterprising kids." She leaned forward. "May we take the paintings back to Cameron's?"

Roland shook his head. "Sorry. Mr. Williams already volunteered, and Mr. Delacruz was good with entrusting them to him, but I can't release them to anyone. Not only do we have to hold them as evidence, but Mr. Delacruz's insurance company is sending over someone to check on the condition and appraise them at their current value. They'll be well taken care of until then."

"So do you have any leads?" She ran her hand over her perfectly combed-back hair. "Was anyone spotted going in or out?"

"An offsite agency rented out the condo over the phone, which is typical with vacation rentals."

"That's too bad. I know Cameron will want the thieves caught as much as he wants the paintings back."

"Without a confession from Buzzy, I mean Buford, we still have nothing. If we could keep the discovery quiet, the thieves would be shocked when they think the heat is off and show up to collect the paintings," Roland said.

"So will this finally prove Buzzy's innocence?" Em hoped.

"Not necessarily, especially since he was always in and out of the units doing repair work. No one would think anything of seeing him hanging around any of the condos. He could have stashed them himself. We're just lucky they were found at all."

"So I guess that's it," Wally said.

"Sorry I can't turn over the paintings to you," Roland apologized again.

"No apologies necessary," Alanna said. "I don't care who found them or how you retrieved the paintings as long as they're safe and sound. Those pieces are like the children Cameron and I never had."

Alanna stood, thanked Roland again, shook his hand, told Em and Wally goodbye, and left.

"Time for me to get back to the Goddess," Em said.

"I'll call you," Roland told her.

She nodded. Wally said goodbye to Roland. Em and Wally walked back to his convertible BMW.

"Well, there are certainly going to be some very, very upset art thieves out there somewhere," Wally said. "The police may never catch them now that the paintings have been recovered."

"Don't bet on that," Em said. "Don't forget Uncle Bass Kekina died on the job during the heist. Roland won't be giving up on this one any time soon."

# 34

"THE WHOLE NORTH Shore is talking about the big find." Sophie and Em were side by side the next morning stocking the bar.

"A lucky break if you ask me," Em said. "Roland was pretty frustrated at getting nowhere."

"I'll bet Cameron Delacruz is stoked. Think he'll get a new attitude? I saw him on the news last night, and he was still crabbing about how slow the KPD works. He made it clear he was happy to announce the paintings had been found, but he wants the thieves held responsible."

"I doubt anything would make him happy," Em said.

Before Sophie could reply, Kiki came breezing into the bar through the kitchen.

"Not even a locked front door can keep her out," Sophie whispered.

"I've called a meeting of the Maidens," Kiki said as she slipped onto a barstool. "A top secret meeting." She looked around the bar. "Would you mind if I lower the window coverings? I'd hate for someone to get wind of what's going on."

"Yes, I'd mind. It's hot enough in here as it is," Em said. "What's going on?"

Kiki leaned her elbows on the bar. "May I have a Tiger Shark Attack?"

"We're not open yet," Em said.

"When did that ever stop me?" Kiki laughed.

Sophie grabbed a tall glass and started mixing up Uncle Louie's version of a Bloody Mary. "Are you all celebrating the return of the stolen goods?" she asked.

Kiki shook her head. "No. Not until the thieves are caught and Buzzy is out of the slammer."

"So what's the secret meeting about?" Em wanted to know. "Are all the girls coming?"

"They'd better. I don't want to say anything just yet, but the Estelles have come up with something that just might free Buzzy. For obvious reasons we won't be meeting there." Kiki's eyes never left Sophie's hands as she mixed the cocktail.

"Obvious reasons being your aversion to the monkey?"

"You got it." Kiki nodded.

Sophie slid a slice of lime onto the salted rim of the glass. "Here you go."

"I'm not sure we can secure this room," Kiki said after tasting the drink and looking around.

"Would you like to meet in the beach house? Louie won't mind," Em suggested.

Kiki took a deep breath. "No, I think we should meet here. This is home base for us."

There was a commotion on the front *lanai*. The door handle turned, and someone rattled the door back and forth.

"Coming! Don't break the door down," Em called out. The building was a hundred years old. The tropical weather, crowds, and the pace of island time kept the place in need of constant repair.

She walked out from behind the bar and crossed over to the front door. As soon as she swung it open, a contingent of Hula Maidens swarmed in. Trish, Suzi, and Flora headed for the bar. Kiki stood up and waved them over to a table in the middle of the room.

"Better pull some more tables together," Kiki directed. As the ladies did her bidding, Precious, Lillian, and Pat walked in.

"Got any breakfast beer?" Pat called out to Sophie then added, "Hey, I like the yellow hair."

"Mellow yellow." Sophie touched the spiked tips of her three-inch buzz cut.

Sophie set a cold bottle of Hinano on the bar. The other ladies all declined a drink.

"As soon as the Estelles arrive, I'll start the meeting," Kiki said. "In the meantime, did you all hear the stolen paintings were recovered in Princeville?"

"I can't believe it," Lillian's voice had reached a crescendo already. "Art thieves in Princeville. I told MyBob to hide our velvet Elvis."

"Always wanted a velvet Elvis," Pat said.

Big Estelle walked through the front door. Her mother followed on her motorized Gadabout. She gave the horn on the handlebars a couple of toots and pumped her fist in the air.

"Little Estelle in the house!" she shouted.

The Maidens made room for them at the table. Little Estelle parked at one end. Kiki and the girls on barstools went to join the others.

Sophie leaned close to Em and said, "Looks like they're not budging."

"No worries. We're not open to anyone else." Em went back to the front door and locked it.

"Pat," Kiki directed, "I'd like you to sit near the windows where you can see the parking lot. If anyone gets within two car lengths of the building, let me know and we'll stop talking. What you are going to hear, ladies, is all top secret. Tip top secret." She mimed locking her lips shut and tossing away the key.

Precious laughed. "As if, Kiki."

"No one breathes a word of this." Kiki wasn't smiling.

"Or you'll be fined," Pat added.

Kiki shook her head no. "Not fined. Out. Leak one word of this to anyone, and you'll no longer be a Hula Maiden."

A hush fell over the occupants of the table. None of them could contemplate such a terrible fate. They all mimed locking their lips and tossing away invisible keys.

"Big Estelle," Kiki said and motioned the stately senior to the head of the table. "Why don't you explain?"

Little Estelle tooted her scooter horn as her daughter took Kiki's place and Kiki sat down.

"As you know, all those expensive paintings have been recovered," she began, "but our Buzzy is still in the clink."

"The slammer."

"The calaboose."

"The pen."

"The joint."

"The farm."

"The pokey."

"Enough!" Kiki jumped up. "All right, you've all had your fun. Now let Big Estelle talk."

Sophie walked over to Em again and leaned close. "What are the chances this meeting will be *pau* by the time we open?"

"We unlock the doors at eleven no matter what," Em said.

"As I was saying, Buzzy is still incarcerated, and his family isn't going to do anything about it. So the Goddess family has to come together to help out. Kiki and I were working on a fundraiser before she found out . . ." Big Estelle paused and glanced over at Kiki, who nodded for her to proceed. "Anyway, before she found out that we'd adopted Alphonse."

Thankfully, Big Estelle didn't mention the second attack at her home. Kiki acted nonplussed as she stirred her Blood on the Beach with her straw.

"So I was thinking about what to do for a fundraiser yesterday and was surfing the Internet when I found this." Big Estelle reached into the bodice of her *muumuu* and pulled out a folded sheet of copy paper. She opened it and held it up so that the others could see. Most of them leaned forward, squinting at the page.

"So what does it say?" Precious asked.

Big Estelle pointed to the headline. "Monkey Art Hoax." Then she turned the page around and read, "Pierre Brassau was a chimpanzee and the subject of an elaborate art hoax."

She looked up from the page and paraphrased. "In 1964 a Swedish reporter decided to see if art critics could tell the difference between modern art painted by a human and paintings by a chimp. So he wrote a story about a virtually unknown French artist named Pierre Brassau. His art was put on display in a gallery alongside other modern artists. Sure enough, one critic claimed Brassau painted with 'determination, fastidiousness, and the delicacy of a ballet dancer.'"

Big Estelle looked around the table. The Maidens were staring up at her.

"Tell them the rest," Kiki urged.

Big Estelle nodded. "We enrolled Alphonse in an anger management class when we first sheltered him. One of his therapies involves painting."

"That explains the stains on your clothes," Trish said.

"And our draperies, what's left of them, and everything else in the house."

"Are you two thinkin' what I think you're thinkin'?" Pat leaned back in her chair and looked between Kiki and Big Estelle.

Little Estelle cackled. "My Alphonse is going to be famous!"

Kiki stood up. "We're thinking we'll hold a fundraiser for Buzzy, and since this thing started with stolen art, we decided to hold an art showing. A very 'high-end' art show. We'll sell tickets to folks, and they'll come and view the pieces."

"We'll price everything for at least a thousand dollars," Big Estelle said.

"Or more!" Little Estelle shouted.

"If we sell any pieces, the money will go to Buzzy's fund," Kiki added.

"Great idea," Trish said.

"Nobody'll know the stuff was painted by a monkey. That's rich," Pat said.

Kiki held up her finger. "And if we're lucky, the show will draw out the thieves."

"How do you figure?" Pat held up her beer bottle and checked the level. There was an inch left. She drank it.

Kiki said, "Well, whoever stole those paintings of Delacruz's has to be very daring or very stupid. They stole them right in the middle of his party when there was a houseful of people coming and going next door. The way I see it, they're probably pretty pissed now that the paintings were found in their stash house. Hopefully they'll be stupid enough to try again, but this time we'll be ready."

"*We?*" Lillian squeaked.

"Man up, Lillian. It's not the Hula Maidens' first takedown of a wanted criminal," Pat said.

"And it won't be our last." Kiki smiled. "Not by a long shot."

"So where we gonna have the showing?" Pat asked.

"How about the Princeville Community Center by the library?" Big Estelle suggested.

"How's a thief or thieves going to sneak in there? Windows all around, and the park is right outside the windows," Trish said.

"We'd better hold this shindig at night." Flora swatted at a mosquito.

"Night for sure," Kiki agreed.

"How about Princeville Library?" Lillian wondered. "MyBob and I are Friends."

"I thought you were married," Pat said.

"We are. We're in the Friends of the Princeville Library organization," Lillian explained.

"Not the library. We need something more upscale."

Em had been following the conversation. She volunteered, "How about holding it here at the Goddess?"

Kiki shook her head no. "Not classy enough."

"Not classy enough for *monkey* paintings?" Sophie said.

"How about Wally's?" Big Estelle suggested.

"No way," Suzi said. "The neighborhood's still up in arms about the last break-in. If it happens again, they'll come unhinged even though the monkey art isn't worth anything."

"It is to me," Little Estelle barked back. "Who do you know that owns paintings by a monkey?"

"Hell," Pat said. "I don't even know anybody else who has a paintin' monkey."

"We're getting off track," Kiki said.

"Going off the rails." Precious hopped off her chair. "Anyone else want some ice water?" She headed for the bar. A couple of the ladies raised their hands.

"What about that new community center at Waipa?" Flora asked.

"Possibility." Kiki scrunched up her eyes in thought. "Middle of nowhere, though. Good and bad access for thieves. They might be seen sneaking across the open ground."

"If they're fast, they could hide in the *taro* patch or all the bushes around there, and we'd never catch them."

Suzi waved her hand. "I have a huge beach house listed at Anini. I'll ask the owners if we can use that for the showing."

"Not enough parking," Trish said.

"Nighttime, dark beach out front. Easy in and out," Suzi added. "Perfect trap."

The group fell silent. Em studied their expressions. She could see they were all considering the realtor's suggestion. She glanced at the clock, hoping they'd make a decision in the next fifteen minutes. It was almost time to open.

"Call your clients," Kiki told Suzi. "If they agree, that'll be a good sign. We'll hold the showing at the Anini house. We can find someone to work valet parking. A volunteer, that is."

"We'll need pupus," Flora said.

"And wine, red and white," Trish added. "Maybe a special cocktail from Uncle Louie."

Relieved they wouldn't have to close down for a private party, not to mention dangle monkey art as bait for a break-in, Em volunteered, "We'll donate the pupus and a new cocktail," she said. "It's the least we can do for Buzzy."

# 35

PAT WAS STILL keeping an eye on the open windows over the parking lot. "The Movie Tour bus just pulled in," she yelled. "Cut the secret stuff."

Em glanced out the window. Sure enough, the fifteen-passenger van that hauled tourists from one famous film location on Kauai to another had pulled in. Tourists were beginning to unload, thrilled to be having lunch in the bar made famous by the reality show *Trouble in Paradise*.

"Sorry, ladies." Em walked over to the Maidens' tables. "It's time for us to open for lunch. You'll have to clear out."

"Almost *pau*, Em. Just have to give out assignments." Kiki snapped her fingers at Pat. "Take notes."

Pat reached into her back pocket for a small spiral notebook with a ballpoint pen attached. She flipped the notebook open, poised the pen over the paper, and nodded to Kiki. "Hit it," she said.

Kiki turned to Suzi. "Check with your Anini homeowner. Everyone else, keep your fingers crossed. We need that place."

Pat scribbled. The others nodded. Kiki went on.

"Flora, ask your grandsons if they'll be our valets. They gotta do it out of the goodness of their hearts. No pay."

"I can ask," she said.

"They gotta wear somethin' other than board shorts," Kiki added, though surf trunks were worn as both casual and formal wear most places on Kauai.

"Estelles." Kiki pointed at the two women. "Get that monkey to paint faster."

Big Estelle smoothed down the front of her *muumuu*. "We already have an extensive collection."

"Unfortunately, we can't display your draperies," Kiki quipped.

"Twenty-three masterpieces of all sizes in oil," Little Estelle added. Then she raised her fist and circled it over her head three times and shouted, "Whoot, whoot, whoot!"

"We'll need press," Kiki said. "Lots of press."

"Ladies, I'm going to have to unlock the front door," Em warned. "The tour bus folks are getting unruly out there. It's starting to sprinkle."

"Estelles, I'll call you, and we can write a bio for the *artist*," Trish said.

Lillian raised her hand. Kiki pointed to her.

"Should we change his name? Someone might recognize it."

Precious laughed. "Who's gonna recognize it? His monkey friends? Is he on Facebook or something?"

"We'll give him a last name. Say he's a recluse and rarely shows himself in public," Trish said.

"*Shh!*" Kiki waved her hands up and down as Em opened the front door. Tourists of all shapes and sizes began to stream in. "Ixnay on the unkymay," she said.

Pat dropped the pen and notebook and grabbed Kiki by the shoulders. "She's losing it again! She's speaking gibberish!"

"I am not!" Kiki shoved Pat away. "That's pig Latin."

"Well, how in the hell would I know that?" Pat bent over and picked up her notebook. "I never studied no foreign languages."

Kiki looked at each of them in turn. "Okay, ladies, most of you have assignments. Those who don't, help the others. Meeting adjourned."

Everyone picked up their purses and totes, grabbed their drink glasses, and bussed their own tables. Kiki was about to leave the table when her cell phone went off. Caller ID belonged to a number she didn't recognize, but she answered anyway, thinking someone might want to book an event.

Em worked around her, placing a basket with salt and pepper, *shoyu*, napkins, and other condiments in the center of the table. She waved four people off the tour bus over to the table. Kiki sidestepped her way around them and headed to the end of the bar while listening to the caller.

"That was Jasmine," she told Em when she hung up.

"Delacruz's Jasmine?" Em asked.

"Yep."

"I didn't know you two knew each other."

"I paid them a couple of welcome calls. Some of us chatted her up."

"Oh, right. When you all went snooping."

"We prefer to call it detecting. She said Cameron's back from Oahu, and he's gone crazy, yelling and screaming about the police holding his Pollocks hostage."

"According to Roland, it's evidence, and they can't release it. Not only that, but there's an insurance appraiser coming over from the mainland to take a look at the pieces."

"I guess he's really raving. It's so bad that Alanna moved out of the guest house. Jasmine wants me to get her out of there, too. She's gonna check into the St. Lexis."

"Cameron really must be on a tear," Em said.

"Sounds like it." Kiki's eyes widened. "You know, if the paintings *were* stolen by someone on the inside, it could have been Jasmine. She was there that night."

"But I don't remember her ever leaving the party or going off alone for any length of time by herself. She did walk from the party to the Delacruz house alone, but that was after the robbery."

"She still could have been in on it with someone else. Maybe she was keeping an eye on Delacruz for the thieves, distracting him."

Em shook her head. "I don't know. What about the Po'ipu break-in? You think she was in on that too?"

"Maybe it was just a coincidence," Kiki said.

"A very big coincidence. Roland said art theft is a pretty rare crime around here."

"Maybe the Po'ipu robbery was to throw the police off."

Kiki dug her keys out of her purse and then slipped the strap over her shoulder. "I'm leaving to pick up Jasmine at the end of her driveway. I'll tell her all about the big art show fundraiser. If she's the thief, it might get her all hot and bothered to try again."

"Really play it up," Em said. "When Delacruz calms down, Jasmine will surely tell him about it, too. Suggest this is a hot new artist, and he'd probably want to be the first to start collecting. Get in on the ground floor and make a lot of money later."

Kiki liked that idea. "For sure. If they are in cahoots and stole the Pollocks, then maybe we'll tempt them to try again. We'll be dangling the bait. But this time they won't be dealing with *Mahalo* Security. They'll be tangling with the Hula Maidens."

"Just be careful," Em warned. "Jasmine may not be the thief, but she could be connected. If she is guilty, she could be dangerous. So could Delacruz."

"Not to worry. I'm still charged with superpowers after my full moon bath."

# 36

SINCE EM HAD opened that day, she left early and let Tiko and Sophie close up. Louie walked over to the bar to lead the guests in the closing Tiki Goddess song, so Em relished a quiet moment at the beach house alone. She'd had relatively few quiet moments since she moved to Kauai.

David Letterman was on his perch enjoying a Discovery Channel marathon of *Winged Planet*. At the moment he was cawing at the screen, excited by an episode about pelicans and dolphins teaming up. He cheered every time a pelican dove into the water and came up with fish.

Earlier she had slipped into one of her favorite old *pareau*. Wrapped in the soft, light fabric covered with lime-green and pink floral print, Em was just pouring herself a glass of ice water flavored with mint and slices of lime when over the sound of the waves lapping the shore, she heard footsteps. Someone was on the path outside the cottage.

She turned down the sound on the television, annoying Letterman into frantic squawking. "Up!" the parrot screeched. "Up, up!"

A terror at best, he was surlier when he hadn't been drinking. Em ignored him and walked out to the screened-in front *lanai*.

"Hoo-ee," Roland called the familiar island greeting.

Em's heart skipped a beat. She opened the door and stood back as he walked in, filling the room with his tall, dark, and handsome presence.

"Anyone else here?" He looked toward the main room where a furious Letterman was trying to dismantle the bars of his cage with his beak.

"Nope, for the moment I'm home alone. Louie will be back soon, though."

Without another word Roland swept her into his arms for a long, slow kiss. When he finally raised his head, Em said, "Wow."

"Yeah. I've missed you."

"I've missed you, too," she whispered.

"Up! Up!" Letterman rattled his cage.

"Wanna go to Maui?" he asked.

"Tomorrow?"

He smiled, and she knew he was thinking of an old *hapa haole* song, "We're Going to Maui Tomorrow."

"The sooner the better," she added.

"Not tomorrow," he said. "But after this case wraps, for sure."

"You think it's ever going to wrap?"

"Eventually. We have the paintings. Now we just have to find out who stole them."

"Can you lift fingerprints off them?"

"We can't touch them yet. Not until the expert checks them out tomorrow. His flight was held up by mainland weather, and he's spending the night in Honolulu. He'll be here in the morning."

"Would you like something to drink?" she offered.

"What I'd like doesn't come in a glass." He kissed her again.

"Have a seat." She waved her hand toward one of the long, comfortable rattan sofas nearby. "I'll just go turn up the sound so Letterman will calm down."

Roland glanced into the main room at the flat screen television that took up most of one wall. "I thought his favorite show was *Survivor*."

Em shook her head as she walked into the other room, found the remote, and turned the sound up enough to silence the parrot.

"He used to love it, but now he enjoys *Winged Planet*, and he loves Tillman the skateboarding dog. Besides, this time of day he really needs a drink. Louie will take care of it when he gets back. He's closing up with the gals."

When she joined him on the *lanai*, he waited until she was comfortable on the sofa beside him before he looped his arm around her shoulders.

He frowned. "You know what Kiki wants? She's left me fifteen voice mails. Each one gets a little more frantic."

Em pulled back to look at him. "You know she hates it when people don't answer her messages. Why not get back to her and have it over with?"

"When I can make it an excuse to stop by and see if you know what's going on first? Besides, whenever she calls, it's because she's up to something and wants me involved."

Em sighed. "That's probably true." She wondered how much of the art show plan Kiki was going to divulge to Roland. Not certain, she only said, "The Maidens are planning a fundraiser for Buzzy's defense. Should he need it."

"As soon as the FBI says we can release him, we will. I think the fact that his family has money is holding all of this up. The FBI will think twice before charging him or making him disappear into the system. One way to look at it is that as long as we're holding him, he's not going to vanish."

"His family won't stand by him," Em said, sad for Buzzy.

"The FBI must not believe that. So tell me more about the fundraiser," he said.

"The Maidens came up with an idea for an art show, a gala displaying the work of a major up-and-coming contemporary artist."

"More of that modern stuff?"

"Yes. More plops and drips."

"They're not going to try to sell it, are they?"

"They're selling tickets to the cocktail party. They'll have overwhelming community support, of course. If anyone buys one of the paintings, that will be gravy money."

"Less the artist's take."

"Oh, I'm pretty sure he's donating them."

"Never heard of an artist who didn't need money. So why is Kiki so frantic to talk to me?"

Em avoided responding to his comment and said, "The art show is just a front to draw out the Pollock thieves. Kiki thinks if they really play up the art that the thieves will try to steal it, and they'll be caught in the act. That's where you come in, I guess."

"We're supposed to be there to catch them in the act?"

"I hope so. It's either that, or the Hula Maidens will be on their own."

Roland shook his head and stared up at the bamboo ceiling. "I hate to think of what could happen to the thieves if those women get their hands on them first."

"Me too. Kiki's a new woman since her full moon therapy. I'm afraid she's turned back into a take-no-prisoners gal."

"What if something goes wrong, and this new artist's work gets destroyed? Delacruz is already hysterical about any damage his pieces may have sustained when they were torn off the frames. What if that happens again?"

Em wasn't sure how much or whom Kiki was going to tell all about their "up-and-coming" artist, even Roland.

"You don't have to worry about it, really," Em said.

"I do have to worry about it. I'm here to serve and protect. Even ugly art falls under our protection."

They heard Louie coming up the path humming the Tiki Goddess song. He breezed through the door, his usual jovial self.

"Hi, Roland. Good to see you. Thriller?"

"I sure hope I thrill her," Roland said.

Em laughed. "He means would you like a Thriller? It's his newest cocktail."

David Letterman started squawking, "Dave! Dave! Dave wanna drink!"

"No thanks, Uncle Louie," Roland said. "I'm on duty."

"When you're wearing an Aloha shirt I can't tell," Louie said.

"Neither can the bad guys," Em said.

Roland drew his arm from around her shoulders. Em wished he could stay.

"I'd better get going." He stood up.

"Don't let me run you off." Louie paused between the *lanai* and the main room. "I'm going to turn in early."

"I just came by to say hello." Roland's voice held a tinge of regret.

He bid Uncle Louie goodbye, and Em walked him down the path that ended at the Goddess parking lot. The night was balmy. They were dusted with misty rain for a few seconds as a cloud passed by on the trade wind breeze. Overhead palm fronds softly rattled, the sound nearly overpowered by the lull of the surf.

"I'll tell Kiki that I let you in on the fundraiser details." Em glanced down at their clasped hands. "You can avoid calling her back right away."

"That would be great. If she asks about having officers on duty that night, tell her I'll look into it, but she shouldn't get her hopes up."

"How about if you're there as my date?" She fully expected him to turn her down.

"Sounds good."

"Really?"

"Let me know when and where right away."

"Okay. By the way, I'll be in Lihue day after tomorrow for supplies." She hoped the hint didn't make her sound needy.

"How about we meet for lunch?" he offered.

"If you're busy I can always just text you the fundraiser information."

He glanced around the nearly empty parking lot. The lights were still on in the Goddess. The only cars in the lot belonged to Kimo, Tiko, and Sophie. Roland pulled her close and kissed her again.

"Isn't that better than a text?"

# 37

A DAY AND A half later Em was in the office going over the list of supplies she was picking up at Costco when Kiki knocked on the door-frame before she walked in.

"I was just leaving for town," Em said. "Need anything?"

Since Lihue was an hour away on a good traffic day—good meaning there was no roadwork, tree trimming, or fatal accidents in the way—folks were in the habit of asking if friends needed any items picked up.

"Nothing I can think of." Kiki shook her head. The garden arrangement of greens and flowers pinned around her head started to vibrate. She pulled a large manila envelope out of her tote bag and set it on Louie's desk. "I stopped by to drop off the tickets for the fundraiser. They're all numbered, and there's an invoice. Just take the money, put it in the envelope, and write down the name of whoever bought the tickets."

"I'll tell Sophie and Louie so we're all on the same page," Em said. "How many sales do you anticipate? Are you cutting them off at some point? We need to know how many pupus to make."

"People may buy tickets and not even attend. I'd say plan on two hundred."

"Two hundred? Can the house handle that many?"

Kiki nodded. "They've had a lot of fundraisers, or so Suzi said. We've got valets coming, and they'll park cars at Anini Park. I can't tell you how exciting this is. It's all falling into place."

"That's great."

"I'm headed up to KKCR for an interview." The local public radio station located in Princeville was always great about helping groups with fundraising activities. "We've already had an incredible response, and we're only on our second day of sales. Trish submitted the *Garden Island* article with the *artist's* bio. She and the Estelles gave him a last name. Alphonse Cappucchino. It's a play on capuchin, since he's a capuchin monkey, get it?"

"I get it." Em found her purse, folded her shopping list, and slipped it inside.

"The bio is great. Alphonse Cappucchino is a new contemporary artist who creates abstract impressionism in the style of Mark Tobey, James Brooks, and Jackson Pollock. Alphonse is somewhat of a recluse who never makes public appearances. The artist claims his work speaks for itself."

"Too bad he won't be there to meet his admirers." Em pulled Louie's truck keys off a hook on the wall by the back door.

Kiki feigned a shiver. "Don't even whisper that."

Em was happy to see Kiki seemed to be recovered. Thinking of the broken, nervous wreck the woman had been a short time ago, she thought it was a miracle Kiki was now working with the Estelles and aware that her nemesis Alphonse was on Kauai. Maybe there was something to the full moon thing.

Before Em reminded Kiki she needed to get on the road, Kiki grabbed her tote bag, tugged her sarong up, tossed the ends of her hair over her shoulders, and walked over to the open door. She leaned against the doorframe in a pose reminiscent of Dorothy Lamour in *The Jungle Princess*: one arm raised, her hand behind her head, one leg pulled up seductively.

"Well, I've got to run." She moved her hand to her forehead and sighed dramatically. "So many places to be. So little time. Listen to KKCR while you're driving into town. I'll be on in thirty minutes."

Em did indeed listen and smiled as the miles from the North Shore to Lihue rolled by. Kiki pushed the fundraiser with every persuasive tool in her toolbox. She promised delicious Tiki Goddess pupus and fine wines along with a new cocktail by the famous mixologist Uncle Louie Marshall, sang a few lines of a song she was choreographing for the event, and described some of the paintings by the "soon-to-be-unaffordable" Alphonse Cappucchino that would be on display.

Em made a couple of quick stops and texted Roland. She was headed into the home improvement and garden supply store for some replacement palms when her cell rang.

"I was expecting a text," Em said.

"Thought you'd want to hear my voice," he said.

"I do." She smiled at nothing.

"Do you have time to stop by the station? The art expert just got here. Delacruz is here and so is the Po'ipu gallery owner. I thought you might like to be here to hear what he came up with after analyzing the paintings."

"I thought he was coming yesterday."

"So did we all, but it turns out he got hung up at a museum in Honolulu first."

"Are you sure it's all right? I don't want to be a lookie-loo." She didn't add that Delacruz wasn't one of her favorite people. The less time she spent around him the better. Still, she was curious about the stolen Pollocks and whether or not they'd sustained any horrific damage.

"I've asked you to be here, so it's all right. I've gotta go. You coming by?"

She nodded, smiling, then remembered he couldn't see her. "Yes. I'll be right there."

"I'll tell the front desk to let you through."

From the Home Depot she headed straight to the main police station across from the airport. Roland introduced her to Samuel Thurston, the expert from the mainland. He was not much taller than Em, dressed casually in khaki slacks and a light-blue golf shirt. A Betty Hutchens was there as well. Roland introduced Ms. Hutchens was the owner of the Po'ipu gallery.

Thurston said, "I was just explaining to Mr. Delacruz and Ms. Hutchens how I tested their paintings."

Em nodded to acknowledge Ms. Hutchens. The art dealer was dressed in a long batik skirt in rainbow colors and a flowing purple top. Her auburn hair was streaked with gray and twisted into a knot atop her head. She held it in place with an oversized shell-encrusted hair clip.

Delacruz paced near the back wall of the room that contained two long tables and six utilitarian chairs. "I have the papers right here." He waved some sheets of paper at Thurston. "Documentation that my paintings are authentic."

Thurston didn't respond to the comment. "Certificates of authentication are easier to fake than paintings. Most artists' styles are as familiar as fingerprints. Ms. Hutchens' painting is newer. In fact, it was very recently completed. I tested the paints used with a device referred to as an XRF, x-ray fluorescence gun. I studied other works by Ms. Hutchens's featured artist, and the brush strokes, gestures, and textures, as well as the signature and the element levels in the lead, iron, and zinc in the paints were all a match. Your piece is indeed the original." He turned to Betty Hutchens. "Except for the slight damage done when it was torn off the stretcher frame, I'd say it's barely suffered. I'd be happy to write up a report for your own insurance agent," he offered.

"Oh, *mahalo!*" Relief lit up her light blue eyes, and she smiled.

Thurston turned to Cameron Delacruz. "Now, on to your two huge works of abstract impressionism on canvas."

"Two huge *expensive* works," Delacruz mumbled.

Again, Thurston went on without acknowledging Delacruz. "The problem with authenticating Pollock's work is that there are few if any brush strokes for comparison. He rarely signed his paintings, so searching for a signature is often futile. A close examination of the photographs of the paintings you owned showed no signatures. He also painted in various sizes and formats. At times he used an electric mixer to broadcast paint on canvas. There are rarely patterns or stroke marks to help determine origin. At one time there was a Pollock authentication board, but they disbanded in 1996."

"So what's the bottom line?" Delacruz rubbed his palm over his glistening forehead.

"The police have recovered two good forgeries of the Pollocks you claimed to have owned. They're very well done, but they're fake nonetheless."

"What?" Delacruz shouted.

Em feared the producer's head was going to explode.

"How in the hell can you say that?" He waved his arms around. "You just went on and on about how it was impossible to tell if they were real or fake, and now you're telling me they're fake, just like that?"

"Jackson Pollock died in 1956. Many of the paints on both of your paintings were definitely produced years after the artist died."

"No." Delacruz looked mad enough to chew up a metal chair. "No, no, no. No fricking way."

"I'm *fricking* afraid so." Thurston nodded. "Definitely forgeries. Good ones, but not real."

Delacruz sank into a chair, shaking his head. "I can't believe it. I was taken by my art dealer." Frantically he grabbed his cell, punched in a number. He started screaming into the phone, leaving a message for his art dealer that even had Roland blushing. It was short, blunt, and crude and ended with, "I can have you arrested. Or worse. I'll ruin you. Or both."

When he ended the call he looked around the room. "What?" he said. "The guy took me for thirty million."

Em almost felt sorry for him. He was out the overly-inflated insurance money he'd been hoping to recoup. Roland was sitting on the corner of the table. He reached over and touched the underside of the corner of the canvas painting where it had been ripped off the frame.

"Where are the real paintings, Mr. Delacruz?" Roland asked him.

"What do you mean? Those *are* the real paintings! At least I thought so. Do you know what I paid for these? For nothing, apparently?"

"The whole world knows. You've been on the news more than POTUS lately, saying they were worth thirty million," Roland said.

"Our company insured for no more than twenty-five," Thurston said. "When they were believed to be genuine, that is."

Just then the door opened, and Alanna Grant walked in. Em wondered how anyone could look so put together all the time.

"Ms. Grant," Roland said. "You're here because?"

"I called her," Delacruz explained.

"I thought it would be all right to be here." She smiled at the insurance appraiser and then the gallery owner. "I'm Cameron's ex. I used to own the paintings with him."

"They're copies," Delacruz told her. "We were sold a bill of goods."

Alanna blanched. Her hand slipped to her throat; her eyes filled with tears. "What? How can that be?" She staggered over to a chair, turned to the expert. "Surely you're wrong." Thurston shook his head. "I'm afraid not. The paintings are imitation. Very good ones, but fake nonetheless. I can't insure these for the millions we were previously covering them for. I think your umbrella homeowners policy will do in this case."

Roland said, "It's possible whoever stole the originals smuggled them off the island and replaced them with these. They might have left them in the condo to throw us off, not thinking there would be an authentication."

Delacruz perked up immediately. "That's true." He nodded. "That's probably what happened. They took my paintings and replaced them with these." He turned to the art expert. "I should be compensated for the originals."

"Not until you can definitely prove you didn't buy forgeries in the first place." Thurston was packing papers into his briefcase.

"You insured them as originals," Delacruz said.

"You had receipts from a very reputable art broker. We had no reason to doubt."

"I still have the receipts." Cameron looked as if he was about to cry.

"But these are still forgeries," Thurston said. "There is some hope. If and when the real paintings come up for sale on the black market, word might get out. But don't count on them surfacing for years, though."

"I take it that it'll be all right for us to dust these for fingerprints now," Roland said.

"I've done what I came to do. You're free to dust them." Thurston was ready to leave.

Alanna's color slowly returned as she sat there listening to the exchange. The producer turned to Roland. "Do you need us?"

"No, you're free to go," Roland told Delacruz.

"Want a ride back to the compound?" Delacruz asked his ex.

"No, thank you." She stood up slowly and glanced over at the canvases with a wistful expression before she turned to glare at her ex. "Unbelievable," she said. "You bought fakes."

"Me? Me? You were just as excited as I was when we bought them." He held up both hands. "Look, I'm as shocked as you are. We've been made fools of."

"Where's your girlfriend?" Alanna asked.

Uncomfortable witnessing the exchange, Em turned to Roland. He watched the scene unfold as if he were viewing one of his favorite movies.

"Jasmine?" Delacruz studied his ex-wife for a moment. "She's staying at the St. Lexis. Why?"

"I'm wondering if she'd had brains enough to have forgeries made, steal the originals, and hide these, knowing eventually they'd be found, and the heat would be off. She couldn't have guessed there would be an appraisal and the switch would be discovered so soon."

Delacruz fell silent, the wheels of his mind obviously churning over what Alanna suggested.

"Who else could it be, Cam? You insisted this was an inside job," she said.

"Yes, someone inside the Hale Akamai security company, or those *Mahalo* Security people. Or the contractor."

"What about your mistress? I'd start there."

"Don't be ridiculous. She couldn't have done it."

"You'd better find out, Cameron, before I do." Alanna Grant stormed out without a backward glance.

Roland stood up, towered over Delacruz. "What do you think? Could Ms. Bishop have stolen the paintings? Could she have been in on it with someone?"

"No, not at all," Delacruz was quick to answer. "Then again, I can't be completely certain."

"You say she's staying at the St. Lexis?" Roland had his notebook out.

"Yes."

"Have a seat, Mr. Delacruz," he said. "I'm going to have Jasmine Bishop picked up for questioning."

Delacruz looked panicked. "Why do I have to stay? How long will I be here?"

"Until I'm sure you won't take matters into your own hands or call and let her know we're coming. Given your and your ex-wife's volatility, I'd like to have Jasmine Bishop in here for her own safety right now. Once she is with an officer, you'll be free to go." He asked Delacruz for his cell and promised he'd give it back as soon as Jasmine arrived at the station.

"Can you do that? Keep him here?" Em looked over her shoulder after they exited the room together.

"I can until he figures out I can't."

"He's furious about the fake paintings right now, but he'll calm down and start squawking, demanding a lawyer sooner than later. Not that anyone on Kauai would suit him."

"I'm banking on later."

Em thought about everything she'd heard in the last few minutes.

"Are you going to release Buzzy now?"

"How can I? You heard the appraiser say those were expert forgeries. Buzzy has an outstanding warrant for forgery."

"He forged draft cards, not Pollock paintings."

"He was an art major, remember."

"Oh, Roland."

"Sorry, Em. I can't do it. Not yet."

She paused, remembering her conversation with Kiki a couple of days before. "Alanna's not the only one. Kiki thinks Jasmine might have been in on the heist, too."

"You didn't tell me."

"I really didn't think she could have been. Jasmine was never out of sight the night of Wally's party. Not as far as I can recall. Maybe Alanna's suspicions aren't that farfetched."

"Questioning Jasmine is worth a shot."

"If you arrest Jasmine too, this place is going to get pretty crowded with everyone you suspect under lock and key."

"She may be a flight risk."

"Remind me not to become one of your suspects," she said.

"I'd like nothing better than to have you under lock and key, Ms. Johnson."

# 38

THE BEACH AT Anini, considered one of the safest on Kauai, was protected by the longest, widest coral reef in the island chain. The spacious, elegant homes hugging the shoreline were designed to take advantage of the view and featured the deep blue of the wide Pacific just a few steps away and the Kilauea lighthouse to the south.

As Kiki pulled into the driveway of Suzi's fourteen-million-dollar real-estate listing, she couldn't help but admire the lush, manicured garden full of flowering plants and trees. Taking it all in, she figured there had to be five thousand square feet in the two-story home.

Though the party wasn't to begin until just before sunset, Kiki had already dressed for the formal event in a solid black *pareau*. Her hair was adorned with white orchids and gardenia blossoms. She slipped out of her shoes in the outdoor foyer, the polished teak floor smooth beneath her bare feet. As she made her way into a kitchen any chef would die for, she was relieved to see most of the Hula Maidens already there, hard at work putting last-minute touches on flower arrangements, setting up easels and paintings, and fluffing designer pillows on the long bank of sofas and deep plush chairs.

Like her, the ladies all looked very formal trussed up in black *pareaus* with white flowers for their hair adornments. Multiple strands of long white shell necklaces were draped around their necks and hung down to their belly buttons. The strands of tiny shells whispered with every step.

Suzi was in the kitchen overseeing the two young servers in black when she spotted Kiki. "You're back. Good."

Kiki stood next to her and leaned close. "I'm glad I went home to shower and change. We've already put in a long day." She nodded to the young people and whispered, "Who are they?"

"Em sent them along to circulate the pupu platters." The twenty-somethings were busy laying out bits of rumaki made of bacon-wrapped dates and water chestnuts, shrimp wontons, teriyaki beef, and chicken skewers on trays. "They worked for her at Wally's big shindig."

"We're not paying them, are we?" Kiki was about to tell them they could leave and put the Maidens in charge of passing pupu platters.

"Em said they're on her. She and Louie have been so generous about this whole thing."

"For sure. Then again, we are their entertainment most nights."

Suzi nodded. "No one else will have us."

"I know. We owe the Goddess, for sure."

"I can't believe we sold out of tickets so fast."

"Too bad we couldn't have found a larger venue. We could have accommodated more people."

"But this is grand and intimate. What a house, huh? Want to make an offer?"

"It's fantastic. I wish Kimo could see this kitchen." Kiki shrugged. "I couldn't afford it even if I got everyone I know and all of their friends to kick in."

Lillian came running into the room. Her bouffant hairdo appeared to be a darker shade of pink against the white flowers in her hair.

"Guests are arriving. What should we do?"

"Greet them and steer them toward the living room where the paintings are on display." As Lillian ran back out, Kiki told the servers to wait five minutes and then start circulating trays. She went into the dining area where they'd set up the wine bar. Pat was manning the table.

"All set, chief." She saluted Kiki and clicked her bare feet together.

"Great. No full pours, remember."

"Got it. Half a glass."

"Maybe a little over half. We don't want to look stingy."

Kiki held her breath as two well-dressed couples strolled in. Lillian was babbling away, telling them about Alphonse Cappucchino as she led them into the expansive living room. Like Fernando's Hideaway, the glass walls here virtually slid out of sight to create an atmosphere of indoor-outdoor living. It hadn't dawned on Kiki until that very moment that a thief could grab a painting, step outside, and disappear into the foliage in an instant.

"What're you thinkin'?" Pat asked.

"Keep your eyes open. This place isn't all that secure. That's good and bad. We've got the bait dangling. If we're going to catch a thief, we've got to be ready."

Kiki watched the couples saunter over to one of the larger paintings on an easel set up between two potted palms. They were holding the small brochures Trish and Big Estelle had printed up for handouts. The four of them stood back a few feet and studied the canvas.

"Incredible," one of the women said as she fingered a strand of pearls. "So lively. So much motion and color."

Her companion stepped forward. He pointed to an area splotched with red and blue streaked with a thick yellow overlay. "It's inspired, actually. Don't you love the textures?"

"The prices aren't outrageous, either." The second man stared at the brochure, located the title of the painting, and matched it to the price listed.

"I have a blank wall that's just crying out for something like this to fill it," the first woman said.

Kiki bit back a smile and enjoyed a wave of relief. More and more guests were arriving, gawking at the interior of the house as much as the paintings. If Suzi was lucky, she might just get a serious buyer out of the affair.

With a glass of white wine in hand, Kiki began to circulate the huge room where paintings were displayed. The house filled up in no time, and soon the guests were chatting with each other about the wonderful, inspired works of Alphonse Cappucchino.

When some of the comments she heard made her want to burst out laughing, Kiki took sips of wine. She was about to pop a rumaki into her mouth when she spotted Roland entering the room. He stood head and shoulders above most of the crowd. Em was at his side.

"Aloha, you two." Kiki looked them up and down. "You both look great all gussied up."

Em tugged on the hem of her short knit black dress. "I'm sure out of the habit of dressing for a formal cocktail event."

"It suits you, though. Looks like it's easy to get out of, too." Kiki turned to the detective. "Roland, you look like a male model."

"Glad I don't look like a female model." He didn't crack a smile.

"I can't thank you enough for being here. Just in case, that is." Kiki looked around. "Hard to imagine any of these folks are art thieves."

"You never know about people." He stared at a couple across the room then turned his attention back to her. Kiki couldn't help but notice how he kept his hand riding protectively on Em's waist.

"Were you able to get any other undercover officers assigned tonight?"

"No, sorry. I'm it. We're always short-handed as it is, and with a suspect in jail I had a hard time arguing for backup." He looked down at Em. "Technically I'm off duty on a date."

"Buzzy's the only suspect in custody, right?"

"I had no reason to hold Jasmine Bishop after I questioned her."

"Still, it *could* be her," Kiki said. "She could have been involved."

"Hard to imagine her acting alone." Em snagged a napkin and a wonton from a passing waiter's tray.

"We better circulate." Roland's gaze never stopped moving. For that Kiki was glad. She and the others had no plan other than to run the thieves down and sit on them if and when something happened.

Roland and Em walked off together. Kiki had to admit they made a good-looking pair.

Big Estelle was crossing the room, staring at her cell phone with a worried expression on her face. Kiki hurried over.

"What? What's happening?" Kiki tightened her grip on her wine glass.

"Nothing, I hope. I just called Mother's cell, and she's not answering."

Knowing how unpredictable the ninety-two-year-old could be, the Maidens had all agreed Little Estelle should not attend the event. Even Little Estelle claimed she'd be happier staying home with Alphonse as long as Big Estelle promised to keep her in the loop and let her know how things were progressing.

"I'm not going to panic," Big Estelle said. "When I left she was sitting next to a pitcher of martinis in the TV room with a couple of Netflix movies. Ever since she saw *Fifty Shades of Grey* she's been hooked on bondage flicks."

Kiki almost felt sorry for Alphonse until she noticed Trish on the other side of the room beside one of the largest canvases. She was waving frantically, trying to get Kiki's attention.

"If you don't get a hold of your mother in half an hour then maybe someone should check on her," she told Big Estelle before she hurried over to join Trish. She didn't trust Little Estelle any farther than she could toss her and her Gadabout.

Trish was standing beside a young, handsome couple in their forties she'd never seen before. They were both dressed for the occasion. Kiki was impressed the man even had on long pants.

"Kiki, this is David and Deborah Kane," Trish said. "I've been telling them all about Alphonse and his work and about Buzzy, too. They'd like to purchase this painting."

Kiki's gaze darted to the small card on a corner of the painting. There was a price written there in calligraphy. Two thousand. She almost felt bad taking their money. Almost. But Buzzy needed it, and so she didn't blink an eye when she said, "That is a spectacular piece."

"No doubt about it," David Kane said. "I haven't seen work this dramatic that speaks to me the way these Cappucchinos do. I'm willing to bet an Alphonse Cappucchino will be one of the best investments I've ever made."

Kiki checked out the young woman's jewelry. Gold Hawaiian heirloom bracelets were stacked on one arm. The size of her wedding ring assured Kiki they could well afford the painting whether Alphonse's work turned out to be a good investment or not.

"Cash, check, or credit card?" Kane asked.

Kiki pointed out Flora Carillo seated discretely behind a small table near the entrance to the large living room. "That fine-looking Hawaiian lady over there will be more than happy to take anything you'd like to give her."

As the Kanes bid Kiki goodbye and walked across the room, Kiki reached into her ample cleavage, pulled a Sharpie pen out of her strapless bra, and wrote SOLD in bold letters across the card on Alphonse's largest piece entitled *It's a Jungle Out There*.

# 39

EM COULDN'T remember the last time she'd put on her best little black dress and pearl necklace to attend a cocktail party, or any party for that matter, that she hadn't been catering. As she and Roland walked into the Maidens' fundraiser, she realized she hadn't been on a date to a party like this since she'd lived in Southern California.

Inside the luxurious Anini home with its atmospheric low lighting, plush area rugs, and gleaming teak and *koa* wood furnishings, she could have been at a mainland party. Until she heard the roar of the waves against the outer reef and inhaled the scent of white ginger emanating from one of the huge floral arrangements.

As she took in the classic elegance of the home and all of the extra touches the Hula Maidens had added to make the event so special, she realized the old gals could pull off anything they set their minds to. The waiters she'd hired were doing a great job of moving through the room in silence, making certain everyone had pupus. Even Pat seemed subdued by the upscale atmosphere as she manned the wine bar and also served Louie's hastily concocted chocolate banana martini named the Alphonse Cappucchino.

The most startling revelation was how fantastic the capuchin's art looked displayed in the fabulous setting. If she hadn't known the great Alphonse was a monkey, she would have never guessed.

She was pleased and surprised when Roland held on to her hand. They were rarely together as a couple, and when they were, he never seemed into public displays of affection.

An attractive woman with long waist-length blond hair dressed in a broomstick skirt and flowing tie-dyed gauze blouse floated by with a starry-eyed look on her face.

Roland leaned down and whispered, "Who's that?"

Em pursed her lips and studied the woman with an otherwordly quality about her. "I'm pretty sure that's Andromeda Galaxy."

Roland's gaze followed the other woman across the room.

Em said, "Need some full moon therapy? She worked wonders on

Kiki. Maybe she'll give you a private session."

Andromeda paused on the edge of the wide open to the *lanai* and stared out toward the ocean.

"I never suspected you'd be the jealous type."

After her ex's betrayal, Em told herself she'd never let herself be hurt by a cheating man again.

"Nope. Not jealous at all. You're free to move on."

Roland laughed. "She's not my type. Believe me."

"You checked her out pretty thoroughly."

"You think? I was just trying to figure out where I'd seen her before."

"She has rack cards all over the airports and tourist outlets."

"Speaking of jealous, there's your neighbor the writer." He nodded toward the other side of the room.

Em looked over as Nat Clark walked in, looking every bit the part of a screenwriter in a black T-shirt and blue jeans. His tortoiseshell glasses added to the look. He headed to the wine bar, and after Pat handed him a glass of wine, he perused the room.

When he saw her, Nat nodded and headed their way.

"Hi, Em. Detective." Nate and Roland shook hands. Bookended by the tall men, Em looked back and forth as they made small talk about the weather.

"How's your gig on Oahu?" Roland asked Nat.

"Going great. The new series is off and running, and my agent has an interview for me which involves my heading to New York." He turned to Em. "I wanted to run something by you whenever you get a chance." He glanced over at Roland and added, "Not tonight, of course."

"Sure. I'll be at the Goddess tomorrow to open up for the lunch crowd around eleven," she said.

"Great. I'll stop in then." He nodded toward a painting not far from where they stood. "These are very interesting."

Em hated to let him go on about the art pieces since she hadn't clued him or Roland in on the hoax. Luckily, Andromeda Galaxy caught his eye, and Nat dropped the subject of the paintings.

"Do you know who she is?" Nat indicated Andromeda with a lift of his wine glass.

"Andromeda Galaxy. She's into alternative healing and apparently here by herself," Em said.

"Then if you two will excuse me, I'm going to introduce myself. She looks interesting." Nat was always eager to meet characters who would enrich his writing. "I'll see you tomorrow before the tourists start pouring in for lunch," he added.

Em watched him walk toward Andromeda.

"You think he's going to ask you to go to New York with him?"

She turned to Roland, certain he was kidding, but his expression was completely serious.

"Why on earth would Nat ask me to go to New York with him?"

Roland shrugged. *"He's in love with you."*

When her cheeks flamed she was thankful for the low lighting in the room. "He is not. Why on earth would you say that?"

"He knows you're going out with me, but I'll bet he keeps asking you out. Besides, I see the way he looks at you." Roland shrugged. "It's a possibility, the New York thing."

"Now *you're* jealous." She smiled.

"So you admit it. You were, too."

She was blushing again. "Maybe for a nanosecond."

"Em!" Kiki was bearing down on them. "Things are going so great, I almost can't believe it."

"I'm so happy for you ladies. What a success."

Kiki giggled like a schoolgirl. "I know. Isn't it fantastic? Not only did tickets sell out, but I just checked in with Flora, and we've sold nine of Alphonse's pieces. Only nineteen to go."

"You're selling the paintings?" Em fingered her pearls and wondered what the ramifications were for not divulging the truth about Alphonse Cappucchino's identity to buyers.

"Of course. Is there a problem with that? People are clamoring to buy them. I have a feeling we'll sell out by the end of the evening." Kiki finished off her wine, handed the glass to a passing waiter, and winked. "Bring me another one of those when you have a chance, honey."

Em wished she'd told Nat about the hoax, not that he couldn't afford one of the paintings, nor did she think he'd be too upset about it when he found out the truth, but still. She turned and saw him laughing at something Andromeda was saying.

Kiki accepted another glass of wine from the returning waiter. "Have you met Andromeda Galaxy yet?"

"No, but I'm sure we will," she said.

Just then Precious appeared beside Kiki. She smiled up at Em and Roland and then told Kiki she was needed in the kitchen. Kiki told them to have a great time and hurried off again.

"What's up? You look worried." Roland glanced over at Nat and Andromeda. "Afraid you might lose one of your admirers?"

"Keep it up, and you might be the one." She squeezed his hand to let him know she was kidding. She looked around, made sure no one was close enough to hear. "Remember the Maidens' trip to support Louie at the Shake-Off competition in Oahu?"

"Of course. I'll never forget it." Not only had he flown over to help Em out when Nat had called to tell Roland she'd been suspected of her ex-husband's murder, but they'd spent the night together for the first time.

"Remember Alphonse?"

"The artist? I don't remember meeting him."

"*Alphonse*, Roland."

His brow wrinkled in a deep frown. "Wait. The monkey that was running wild at the Hilton Hawaiian Village?"

"*Shh.*" She nodded. "Keep your voice down."

"Alphonse the capuchin monkey." She took a long sip of wine.

"So I'm here to protect paintings by a monkey?"

"You're staked out to prevent an art heist. To catch the art thieves who stole Delacruz's paintings."

"His fake paintings."

"Maybe they stole the real paintings and replaced them. Whatever. You're here because Kiki and the girls came up with this plan to raise money for Buzzy and maybe, just maybe, lure the thieves out."

"They're selling monkey paintings, Em. They're making thousands of dollars selling paintings by a monkey."

She sighed. "What can I say?"

"Once in a while you should maybe tell them they're going too far."

Em let go of his hand. "Hey, Kiki's their leader. The Goddess is just their venue. I'm not a Hula Maiden. I don't have much to say about any of their decisions."

"You're close to them. You care about them. I think they'd listen to you if you ever tried to talk sense to them. Some of them, anyway." He wasn't kidding. He actually thought she could step in and stop the Hula Maidens from carrying out their crazy schemes. "Maybe you could threaten to stop their dancing at the Goddess."

She tried to imagine evenings at the Goddess without the Hula Maidens on stage. Suddenly their date had gone flat faster than an open bottle of champagne.

"Right," she mumbled. "And maybe someday pigs will fly." She started to walk away.

"Where are you going?"

"Outside to meet Andromeda Galaxy." She wasn't surprised when he followed her out to the *lanai*.

# 40

KIKI FOUND SUZI at Flora's table. "How much money have we made?" she asked.

"Plenty," Flora said. "We just sold four more paintings. We're up to six thousand dollars."

"Wow. That's great," Suzi said. "But Buzzy won't need defending if they prove Jasmine is the thief."

"I heard she was released already. Even if Buzzy is let go, he's missed a lot of work, and he's got bills to pay," Kiki reminded them.

"For sure," Flora said. "Don't we all?"

"It's time for our performance." Kiki turned to Suzi. "Round up everyone and have them all go out on the front *lanai*." She told Flora, "Hide the money box and your credit card machine before you join us."

"For sure," she said.

Suzi asked, "The party's going so well. You sure you want to break things up?"

"What? I can't believe what I'm hearing, Suzi. We have a new dance to present, and we're going to perform. Now get the others and meet me out there in two minutes."

Kiki picked up a pen off Flora's table and clinked it against her wine glass.

"Attention, everyone," she announced. "Please head out to the *lanai* on the *makai* side. As a thank-you for your overwhelming support, the Hula Maidens are going to perform a *mahalo* number for you. So, if your glass is empty, grab a refill, and we'll meet you on the *lanai* in two minutes."

Kiki wandered through the spacious living area, out to the beach-side *lanai*, gathering people as she went. When she returned to the main room she was pleased to see folks had cleared out quickly. The spacious outdoor garden area was bordered by flaming tiki torches and expansive enough to hold all the guests. Without even a sliver of moonlight yet tonight, thousands of stars glittered brilliantly in the midnight sky.

All of the Maidens lined up, looking classic in their black *pareaus* and white adornments. Kiki was more than proud of herself for thinking up what she dubbed their new black tie hula style.

Pat appeared in the wide open doorway. She signaled Kiki that the boom box was all set up and ready. Kiki nodded, and within a few seconds recorded Hawaiian music filled the air. Their new song, "Kauai Beauty," was slow. Kiki hoped the dance was moving enough to express their gratitude through their love of the island. They made it through two and a half verses when suddenly everything went black, and the music stopped.

A crowd let out a collective, "Aww."

Flora stepped on Precious's foot.

"Ow! What the heck?" the little woman yelped.

People reached for their cell phones and activated flashlight apps.

Kiki quickly looked up and down the beach. There wasn't a single light on at any house in Anini. She stepped onto a stone planter that bordered the *lanai* and clapped her hands for attention again.

"Looks like the power is out again. Hang tight, folks. There's still plenty of food and wine. The waiters will be out here in a second."

"Please, don't anyone move," Suzi requested. "We don't want anyone to trip and fall in the dark. I'm sure the power will be back on in a few minutes."

"Yeah, right," a man called out. "Remember the time a chicken got stuck in the main transformer, and the power was out on half the island?"

"Fried chicken!" somebody else hollered. Laughter rippled through the crowd.

"Hey, look!" Pat was on the *lanai* pointing north. "Is that a fire?"

Kiki turned around. Sure enough, flames were shooting up a power pole further down Anini Road near the park. It was far enough away that it wouldn't reach the house, but there were campers on that end of the beach.

"Roland?" Kiki called. "Where are you?"

"He's already calling it in." Em was edging her way through the crowd toward Kiki. "He's calling 911."

"Great. Maybe someone drove into that power pole and knocked out the lights," Suzi said.

"I hope not." Kiki, still on the planter, could see over all the others. She scanned the road and then the interior of the house. It looked even darker inside than when they'd all walked out. Then the reason suddenly hit her.

"Suzi, who blew out the candles in the living room?" Kiki started climbing off the planter.

Suzi hopped up and down on tiptoe, trying to see. "Are they out?"

Flora and Big Estelle were both tall enough to see into the house.

"They sure are," Big Estelle said.

"Oh, no." Kiki headed inside, shoving her way through the crowd, running into the living room. The first thing she noticed was an easel lying on the floor. The painting that had been on it was missing. She made a three-sixty-degree turn and saw an empty, broken stretcher bar. The canvas missing.

She screamed at the top of her lungs then yelled, "Call 911! Call 911!"

Pat came running in. "Another fire?"

"Worse!" Kiki put her wine glass down and balled up her fists. "Someone's broken in and taken two paintings! They got in right under our noses and swiped the ones closest to the open door."

David Kane was the next one into the room with his wife on his heels.

"For the love of Pete! They took our painting!"

"What in the heck was that?" Pat squinted out the open doors to the side garden.

Kiki ran up beside her. "What? What was what?"

"I thought I saw something outside." Pat pointed. "There. There it is. See that?" She darted across the *lanai* and jumped on the planter then leapt into the yard. Party guests surged off the oceanfront *lanai* into the living room. Kiki took off after Pat and didn't look back.

She reached the edge of the lawn where the thick hedge started and almost barreled right into Pat, who had come to a dead stop.

"I lost 'em," Pat said.

Kiki was gasping from the jog. She grabbed hold of Pat's shoulder and leaned on her for support. Voices from the living room filtered out but not loudly enough to drown out the sound of a splash.

"Did you hear that?" Pat whipped around like a hunting dog tracking a pig. She started running toward the stream that ran alongside the property and emptied into the ocean.

Kiki hiked up her *pareau*, tucked the hem into her underwear, and took off running again. Miniature ironwood pinecones no bigger than cranberries dug into the soles of her bare feet, but she kept running, determined to catch the art thief.

Pat was right on her heels. As she passed Kiki she yelled, "Well, I'll be battered and fried twice!" Then she took a flying leap off the stream bank. Kiki heard a cry, then sloshing and splashing and an occasional, "*Oof!* Ouch!"

A fire truck and rescue vehicles went screaming down Anini Road headed for the fire. Yelling at the top of her lungs, Kiki plunged down the bank after Pat and found her grappling with someone in a shiny black wetsuit. Pat was nearly submerged and getting the worst of it, so Kiki waded in swinging. She tried to grab hold of the dark figure encased in slippery latex but couldn't get a tight hold. Pat was beating the thief around the head and neck with closed fists, yelling at the top of her lungs.

"You might think you can steal from other folks, but don't nobody steal from us Hula Maidens!" Pat's fist finally connected with flesh. The thief let out a high-pitched yelp.

Kiki realized the perpetrator was a woman and lunged. She wrapped her arms around the thief's midsection. They both went down, dragging Pat along into the shallow stream with them. Kiki's hand connected with a rock. She hated to do it, but if she had to, she was going to bash the bitch's face in.

Suddenly Roland was behind Kiki. He caught her wrist in his hand and yelled, "Drop the rock. I've got this."

Pat was desperately trying to straddle the thief in the water. They rolled around like dogs on dead fish. Kiki managed to get a hold of one of the perp's arms and hung on tight. Roland grabbed the thief by the neck of the wet suit.

"You can let go, ladies," he said.

Pat said, "You sure?"

"I'm sure."

Kiki let go and pushed herself up and out of the muddy stream. Her *pareau* was soaking wet, plastered to her skin. Most of her shell necklaces had been broken and strands were missing. Her abundant hair adornments were destroyed. Gardenias and orchids floated downstream headed for the ocean.

"Can't I just get a lick in, just so's later I can brag that I did?" Pat had her fist balled up, aimed at the woman's head.

"Don't!" the thief yelled. "Don't hit me in the nose. Not my mouth either. I paid a fortune for cosmetic work."

Roland pulled handcuffs out of his back pocket. He had one of the perp's wrists securely behind her back already. There was no doubt he meant it when he said, "Let go, Pat."

"Aw, shoots. I really wanted to say I punched out Cat Woman," she groused.

Pat let go, and Roland hauled Alanna Grant to her feet. A round of applause and shouts of approval rolled over them from the crowd gathered on the stream bank. Kiki saw everyone from the party gathered on the lawn watching. Most of them still had drink glasses in their hands.

"Kiki, that was way better than a hula," one of the men called out.

"Do we know how to throw a party, or what?" Kiki shouted back. Everyone cheered again.

Roland led Alanna Grant out of the water and up the slippery bank. Pat climbed up and out easily. Kiki had to grab hold of a huge tree root sticking out of the bank and use it to hoist herself up the muddy slope.

When folks on the bank realized the thief Roland was leading toward the house was none other than Alanna Grant, a.k.a. Cat Woman, they parted like the Red Sea. Kiki and Pat dripped in his wake.

Precious had nudged her way to the edge of the crowd. "Looks like your career is over, Cat Woman," she chuckled.

"Where's my painting?" David Kane stepped in front of Roland, halting their progress.

Alanna remained silent. Kiki moved around Roland. More sirens wailed in the distance. Help was on the way.

"Where are they?" Kiki asked the producer's ex. "Where are Alphonse's paintings?"

"What paintings?" Defiant, Alanna lifted her chin. "I have no idea what you're talking about."

"Then what the heck are you doing here in that getup?"

"I was going to make an appearance in costume, make a plea for donations for your friend Buzzy."

"Yeah, right," Pat said. "Then why were you runnin'? Why fight us?"

Big Estelle trained her cell flashlight on Alanna. "How does she get her makeup to stay on like that?"

"Hollywood secrets," Kiki shot back. "Has to be totally water-proof."

"Too bad you aren't wearing that," Big Estelle said. Kiki knew without looking in a mirror that her makeup hadn't passed the wres-tling-in-a-stream test. She'd never find her eyelashes.

"Let us through," Roland said to Kane.

"Make her tell you where she hid the stolen paintings first," David Kane said.

"*Allegedly* stole." Alanna wiped her cheek on her shoulder.

"Back up, ever'body, and let Roland escort Ms. Grant to the house," Pat yelled. Once again the crowd parted. Suddenly the house lit up. Power was back on up and down the road.

Suzi trotted behind Kiki and Pat, hot on their heels.

"Whatever you do," the realtor warned, "don't anyone drip on the floors!"

# 41

EM SEPARATED HERSELF from Nat and Andromeda and fell in beside Roland. She'd been chatting with her neighbor and the full moon therapist on the *lanai* before all hell broke loose. The whole time she'd warned herself not to flare up over Roland's flirting with the airy-fairy blonde, but it wasn't working.

First the power outage, then Roland spotted the fire. Kiki went inside and let out a scream. When Kiki took off running across the side yard, the entire party ran after her. Now the show was over, and everyone was content to wander back inside and partake of more pupus and drinks while babbling about what happened.

Em followed Roland and Alanna Grant through the house to the wide open foyer off the kitchen. Kiki and Pat left a trail of water behind. When they reached the foyer Roland turned to Pat.

"Can you keep everyone out?"

"You betcha."

"You two can stay," he told Em and Kiki.

Em noticed Alanna's head was encased in a hood of the same black material as her bodysuit. It looked almost like liquid, but unlike the neoprene hoods surfers wore in freezing waters, Alanna's was topped with cat ears.

Kiki flicked one of the ears and said, "Meow."

A KPD officer in blue walked in the open front door. Roland took him aside and left Alanna cuffed and standing between Kiki and Em.

"You have fame, money, everything," Kiki said to Alanna. "Why did you do it? Why did you steal the Pollocks?"

"I didn't steal the Pollocks. I didn't steal those paintings tonight, either."

"Right. You just stopped by and ran past the house so you could jump into the stream and beat the pulp out of Pat."

"She jumped on me." Alanna remained defiant.

A second officer came in the front door, carrying a paint-spattered canvas that had been rolled and another that was half off its stretcher frame.

"These what you're looking for?" he asked Roland.

Roland nodded. "Where were they?"

"Next to the stream, under a *hau* bush."

Roland warned Alanna, "This will go a lot smoother if you'd just tell the truth."

Alanna stared at the paintings, and her eyes welled with tears. Slowly her shoulders sagged in defeat. "I did it for Cameron," she mumbled. "All of it was for Cameron."

"He put you up to this?" Roland asked.

"No, no. He didn't know anything about it. I worked alone. I wanted him to get the insurance money from the stolen Pollocks. He's more broke than anyone knows, so I stole his paintings. I rented the condo through Happy Hawaiian Days Vacation Rentals and stashed the paintings there for safekeeping. When the heat died down I was going to sell them on the black market."

"When did you exchange the real pieces with imitations?"

"I didn't. Like I said, as soon as things cooled off, I planned to sneak the real paintings off the island. In the meantime, Cameron could have claimed the insurance money, and I'd still have the real Pollocks to sell. But I have no idea where those fakes came from. We certainly thought they were real when we bought them. But I guess we were duped."

Tears were streaming down her face. With her hands cuffed behind her back she couldn't wipe them off. She tried using her shoulder.

"What about the Po'ipu painting? Why steal that one? And don't try to tell me you didn't."

She shrugged. "That was a test run. I broke into the gallery to see if I could get away with it. I was in and out of there without tripping an alarm or anyone seeing me. I needed to know exactly how long it would actually take for me to get a large painting out of a frame and off stretcher bars without causing too much damage. Turned out to be a piece of cake."

"So breaking into the gallery was no big deal?" Em was amazed.

"If you'd made as many Cat Woman movies as I have, you'd know all the ins and outs of being a cat burglar, too."

"Maybe you can cut your jail time by giving seminars to security companies. Teach them how to keep thieves from bypassing the systems." Kiki tried ringing water out of her hair.

"The gallery was a piece of cake. So was breaking into Cameron's system. The only code he uses for everything is the date of our anniversary, so I used that, and bingo, I was in. The problem was getting out."

Em wondered if anyone else had noticed how much Alanna apparently still cared for her ex.

Roland signaled the uniformed officer to take the cat burglar's arm. He said, "Alanna Grant, you're being arrested for three burglaries, assault, and the murder of Sebastian Kekina."

Panicked, Alanna tried to twist away from the officer. "I didn't kill him. I didn't kill anyone!"

"Then you want to tell me what happened?" Roland asked.

"The old man saw me slip around the corner of the house and started running down the driveway after me. I knew I could outrun him, and I did. I didn't know he died until I read it in the paper on Maui."

"Maui?"

"After I stashed the paintings at the condo, I flew out that same night on a private jet. When I came back to Kauai, I said I'd just landed. No one knew I'd been on island earlier."

"No one recognized you at all that first trip?" Em doubted that was possible.

"I'm great at disguises."

Roland added, "Sebastian Kekina suffered a heart attack because of your actions committing a felony. That's a crime punishable by law here."

"But . . ."

"You have the right to remain silent," Roland started reading Alanna her rights until he was interrupted by the frantic tooting of Little Estelle's Gadabout horn.

"Oh, no," Kiki groaned. "She's here."

"Do you think she rode that thing all the way down from Princeville?" Em couldn't believe the old gal had made it.

"It's only a handful of miles as the crow flies." Kiki's eyes widened. Her right hand slipped up to her hair.

"A handful maybe if she'd driven straight down the cliff."

"You don't think she brought *him* with her, do you?"

There was only one *him* Kiki could be referring too.

"Go wait out of sight in the kitchen," Em told her. "I'll go see."

"I'll hide in the pantry."

Little Estelle kept tooting. Roland raised his voice to be heard over the obnoxious sound. Em hurried outside, waved, and gestured to Little

Estelle to stop honking. Thankfully, there was no sign of Alphonse.

Em hurried down the entry steps and walked over to Little Estelle, who'd stuck lime-green florescent tape strips all over her clothes. Even with all the reflective tape Em tried not to think about what might have happened to the nonagenarian as she drove her scooter six miles on the highway and around the sharp curve on the Anini point in the dark.

"Hi, Em." Little Estelle sounded as perky as ever. "How's the party going?"

"Oh, the usual. The Maidens made a lot of money for Buzzy. They even sold most of Alphonse's paintings."

"Whoohoo!" Little Estelle did a high fist pump. "I knew my boy would be a hit."

"But then the power went out, and the house was broken into. Two of the largest paintings were stolen," Em added.

"Stolen? Cripes. I missed all that?"

"Right. But Kiki and Pat ran down the thief, and the police recovered the canvases."

Little Estelle slapped her knees and cackled with glee. "This is better than a movie. Sorry I missed it."

"Roland's arrested the thief who turned out to be Alanna Grant."

"Cat Woman?"

"Yes. He's reading her her rights and would appreciate you not honking the horn right now."

"For sure. Could you tell Big Estelle I'm out here, so we can load the Gadabout in our handicap van? I'm not looking forward to driving back again. I already had too many near misses in the dark. I know she's gonna be pissed that I drove myself over, but I got so bored. Alphonse polished off my pitcher of martinis and then he went ape and pulled the cords out of the cable box, so I wasn't able to watch my movies. After he passed out I thought to myself, why just sit around? So here I am. Looks like I missed all the action."

"I have a feeling that if you wait long enough, something else is bound to happen."

Little Estelle nodded sagely. "That's the truth. Something crazy is always happening on this rock."

# 42

WELCOME BACK BUZZY

Live Music & Hula

Happy Hour Prices All Night Long

A HUGE WHITE sign made of painted plywood hung from the *lanai* railing in front of the Goddess welcoming the community and any tourists lucky enough to walk into the celebration for Buzzy, a.k.a. Buford Burney the Third.

Not only had Buzzy's charges been dismissed after Alanna Grant's arrest, but the FBI was no longer interested in him and also cut him loose. Apparently the long arm of the law did not extend as far as Buford Burney the Third's military industrial family's clout. Their contributions to militarizing the country's war efforts around the globe made up for any crimes Buzzy may have committed as a protesting activist in the seventies.

Em reserved a seat for the guest of honor near the stage, but upon his arrival the hippie rejected it, preferring his usual small table in a back corner. He was there now, trying to avoid any fuss while he sipped on one of Tiko's nutritious smoothies. Since his stint in the slammer he'd come out dry and had forsaken beer, supposedly preferring the blended health drinks. Em had a feeling the petite, lovely Tiko had more to do with his reformation than the taste of the smoothies. Doing waitress duties tonight, Tiko buzzed around the room, pleasing customers as well as checking on Buzzy whenever she had a minute to spare.

"We're running out of Captain Morgan Spiced," Sophie called over her shoulder to Em. They were both behind the bar filling orders as fast as possible.

"Got it. Looks like Louie's latest is a hit," Em shouted over the din. She finished up washing and rinsing tumblers and lined them up on the bar where Sophie could grab them.

"You bet. Everyone's loving the Jailhouse Rocks," Sophie said.

"That's Jailhouse-On-The-Rocks," Louie corrected as he sauntered over to join them. He was all smiles. "What a great crowd!"

"I hope you're here to help," Em said.

"Of course." He was decked out in a red Aloha shirt. A strand of black *kukui* nuts dangled from his neck. He'd even donned his best white Panama hat for the occasion. Louie glanced toward the front door and saw a couple standing there looking uncertain.

"Aloha, friends!" he shouted. "*E komo mai!* Come on in and join the party!"

"I'll go get the rum." Em dried her hands, sidestepped Louie and Sophie, and headed for the pantry. The errand would give her a chance to see Roland, who was there with the Kekina family and the entire *Mahalo* Security clan. When he arrived he told her he'd stay until her shift ended, though right now it looked like that was not going to happen until the wee hours of the morning.

She paused beside Roland's chair, suddenly aware of how she must look. Her ponytail was coming out of its scrunchie; her Goddess tank top was spattered with cocktail mix. She'd passed glowing and graduated to sweaty an hour ago.

"Howzit?" She shoved a stray lock of hair out of her eyes. "Anyone need anything?"

Kekina family members held up their glasses in a toast. "We're good. *Mahalo*," Leo said.

Roland spoke loud enough for her ears only, "I need something, but it's not on the menu."

Em couldn't resist smiling down into his eyes. "Special orders take longer."

"I need another fork." Leo's wife broke the spell.

Mo Makanai was wearing a ginormous *Mahalo* Security T-shirt. "How 'bout another order of calamari? It's so *ono*."

"You got it." Em spotted Tiko across the room, waited until she caught her eye, and signaled her over. "Your waitress will be right with you," she said.

She went into the kitchen and made sure Kimo wasn't over-whelmed. He was handling the copious orders with the same kick-back calm he always possessed. Em figured his chill factor was how he'd managed to survive life with Kiki over the years.

After grabbing a bottle of spiced rum and some backup tequila from the pantry cabinet, she headed back to the bar. Passing the ladies' room she saw Kiki and the Hula Maidens inside pinning the last few floral touches to their hair adornments. They were all there, all dressed in their formal black *pareaus* again, the same outfits they'd worn the night of the fundraiser. Even Little Estelle, sitting in the back of the main room parked on her scooter, had worn a black *pareau*.

"You all look fantastic," Em called out. They did all look glamorous, much better than when they wore any of Kiki's over-the-top costume creations. "Almost too upscale for this place," she added.

Kiki came to the doorway. "We didn't get to finish our new number at the fundraiser, so we're going to dance it for you tonight."

"Great idea. I'm sure it's wonderful." They were here in full force. All Em could hope was that none of them fell off the stage. She started to walk away and then did a double take. "Is that Andromeda Galaxy?"

The woman was in the ladies' room pinning flowers in Precious's hair. Em must have been too busy to notice when she walked in.

"It is. She's turned into our groupie. Said we are one powerful bunch."

"Well, don't break a leg," Em said.

"For sure. No falling down." Kiki ducked back inside.

Em dropped the liquor off behind the bar, picked up a tray, and was about to bus tables when she noticed Jasmine Bishop in the front doorway scanning the room.

Em left the bar and walked over to greet the young woman personally. Jasmine looked like an *Elle Magazine* summer edition cover model in a floral print sundress with a fitted waist and full skirt. She had on vintage red earrings and red platform sandals. Her long brunette hair hung past her shoulders in a sleek, wavy style. Her lipstick was as crimson as her shoes.

As soon as she saw Em she smiled.

Em greeted her with aloha. "Are you looking for a table? If you don't mind sharing, I can seat you right away." She doubted the starlet would want to rub shoulders with the locals, but if not, it was going to be a long wait.

Jasmine's smile dimmed. "Actually, I'm wondering if your friend the detective is here. Detective Sharpe?"

Em blinked. "You want to see Roland Sharpe?"

Jasmine nodded. Em tried to smack down a spike of jealousy. She was really going to have to watch it, but where Roland was concerned, it was getting hard to keep her emotions under control.

"He's here with some friends," Em said.

"Is there anywhere I can talk to him privately? It's important."

"Of course. Follow me." Em led her through the bar to Louie's office and motioned her inside. "I'll get the detective."

Jasmine balked. "Do you think Kiki can join us? I'd rather not talk to him alone," she said.

"The Hula Maidens are about to go on stage. I can take a couple of minutes if you'd like."

"Oh, that would be great." Jasmine's relief was immediate.

Em left her and went back to Roland's table. She arrived just as Tiko delivered a platter piled high with deep-fried calamari.

"Roland, I hate to interrupt, but someone wants to see you in Louie's office," Em said.

He smiled, excused himself, and stood up.

"Great idea." He jumped up and followed her to the office. "I was hoping you'd take a break." He reached for her hip just as she was about to open the office door. Em turned to him. He was inches away. She gently removed his hand.

"There really is someone to see you. Jasmine Bishop wants to talk to you. She seems very hesitant. She asked me to be there, too."

In the blink of an eye his demeanor switched to professional mode. His smile faded. He opened the door, and they went inside. Jasmine was sitting on the edge of the desk. As they entered she stood up, smoothed her already perfectly-styled hair, then held out her hand to shake first Roland's and then Em's. Em noticed a leopard and chartreuse clutch box in her other hand.

Em recognized the small purse from her days as a Newport Beach housewife and was certain the Bottega Veneta's thirty-eight-hundred-dollar price tag was lost on ninety-nine point nine percent of the crowd in the bar.

"Thank you so much for meeting with me," Jasmine told Roland. "I hate to bother you while you're busy celebrating." The woman appeared so nervous Em wondered why she was there. She didn't have to wonder long.

Jasmine took a deep breath and said, "I had time to think about a lot of things while I was sitting in the police station. I knew Cameron didn't steal his own paintings. That is, I don't think he had anything to do with having Alanna or anyone else steal them for him."

"Why not?" Roland asked.

"He was too shocked the night they disappeared. Genuinely beside himself. He couldn't have faked it that well." She opened the clutch and pulled out a piece of paper. "I found this in his office today."

Roland opened the small thin paper. He looked at it a second, then read it aloud for Em's benefit. "It's an invoice made out to Cameron Delacruz from a Gary Springer for services rendered in the amount of twenty thousand dollars. It's marked paid in full." Roland looked up at Jasmine. "So who is Gary Springer? Why bring this to me?"

"I googled him. He's an artist and apparently quite a good one. He's a member of ISTAE, the union for motion picture set painters and sign writers. Cameron probably met him on a movie shoot."

Em was curious. "How did you get that receipt? I thought you'd moved to the St. Lexis?"

"I'm still staying there," Jasmine said. "At least I will be for a day or two. I know the key code to Cameron's house."

"He never changed it after the break-in?"

"Oh, he did, but it was easy enough to pick up his cell phone when he was in the shower and find it. He stored it under Kauai House, if you can believe it. All I had to do to get into the system was hit the contact number, and I saw the code."

Roland glanced down at the receipt. "So if Springer is a professional artist . . ."

"He could have copied the Pollocks," Em said.

Jasmine nodded. "Since Cameron had the receipt, and if Gary Springer did the forgery, then Cameron knew the Pollocks were fake all along."

"Which might be the real reason he was so upset the night they were stolen," Em said. "He was afraid someone might eventually find out they were fakes."

Roland said to Jasmine, "You realize I'll have to question him, possibly arrest him for insurance fraud at the very least."

"Cameron would have let me sit in jail and never admitted the only things he lost were a couple of fake paintings. Let's face it, the man can be a real ass. He let Alanna think the paintings she stole were real until the insurance adjuster showed up. He could have let her in on the forgeries, and she might have given them back to him. Or not even stolen them in the first place. Somehow they could have gotten out of this mess, but he said nothing. If she'd known the forgeries were his idea, maybe she'd have never crashed the fundraiser still trying to help him out."

"Then again," Roland said, "she may get a thrill out of being a cat burglar."

"Why would Delacruz have copies of the originals made in the first place?" Em was still confused.

Roland said, "He wouldn't have to stage a robbery. He could have slipped the originals out on the black market and sold them for millions. Maybe he already has. With the fakes on the wall, no one would be the wiser. Alanna admitted he was more broke than anyone knows. When the forged paintings were stolen, he went with it. He didn't cop to the forgeries so he could at least collect on the insurance. He must be as broke as Alanna claimed."

"Broke and desperate," Em said.

Jasmine said, "He has connections and friends in all the high places in Hollywood. Handing that receipt over to you has probably ruined my chances in the business, but that's okay. From what I've seen I've no desire for that world anymore. I have a law degree. Maybe not as glamorous, but it's lucrative."

Outside the office door a roar went up from the crowd accompanied by thunderous applause that went on and on. Shouts of *hana hou* rang out over the ruckus. The audience was calling for an encore. It was so loud Em peeked out to see what was going on.

The Hula Maidens were lined up on stage in their formal hula attire and were taking bows. The audience clapped nonstop, screaming for more. Kiki took the mic off the stand and shushed them.

"*Mahalo*, everyone! Before we do another number we're going to celebrate the success of this one while the band takes a break. We'll be back in ten minutes."

Em looked over at the bar and caught Sophie's eye. Sophie gave her a thumbs-up and mouthed, "They were great!"

Em smiled, happy for the old gals. The Hula Maidens were really on a roll. She was about to close the office door again when she noticed Cameron Delacruz sitting on a barstool sipping a drink. He appeared to be as far down in the dumps as a man could get as he stared at the top of the bar.

She closed the door and shut out the sounds of raucous voices, silverware clattering on ceramic dishes, and traffic backed up on the highway.

"I'll be headed out to Delacruz's compound," Roland was saying.

"You won't have to. Guess who is sitting at the bar," Em said.

"Convenient. That'll save me some gas." He headed for the door.

"You can wait in here if you like," Em told Jasmine.

"No way. He doesn't scare me."

Em and Jasmine followed Roland out. When Delacruz saw Jasmine his sour expression brightened.

"Hey, babe," Cameron greeted Jasmine before he turned to the man on the chair beside him and said, "You mind, buddy? This is my girlfriend."

The man didn't look happy, but he grabbed his beer and started to get up until Jasmine waved him back into the seat.

"Please, that's not necessary," Jasmine said.

Delacruz completely ignored Roland and Em and focused on Jasmine. "Listen, hon, I want to apologize for what happened. If I'd known it was Alanna all along . . ."

Jasmine cut him off. "You'd have warned me that I was going to be hauled in for questioning?"

Delacruz pointed at Roland. "He took my phone. I couldn't call and let you know what was happening."

Roland added, "To his credit, that's true."

"But you knew the Pollocks were forged before the insurance adjuster told you so." Jasmine wasn't asking Delacruz, she was telling him.

He turned bright red before all the color quickly rushed from his face. "You're crazy."

Roland held up the receipt. "Not according to Gary Springer."

Delacruz glanced around the room as if looking for an escape route. "You talked to Springer?"

"No," Roland admitted. "Not yet. But I'm having LAPD pick him up for questioning as we speak. If he thinks he's looking at prison time for forgery, he'll confirm you hired him."

Cameron turned on Jasmine. "You did this."

She shrugged. "Oops."

"I'll ruin you, bitch. You'll never work in Hollywood again." His harsh tone was absorbed by the noise in the room.

"I'm all over that anyway." She smiled at the younger man on the stool beside Delacruz. He'd been watching the exchange, eavesdropping, and trying unsuccessfully to act as if he wasn't.

"Mr. Delacruz, I'll need you to come with me," Roland said.

The producer didn't budge. "So I had the Pollocks copied. So what? I did it to keep the originals safe and sound. They're locked in a storage container in the Valley. That's not illegal."

"When the originals were believed stolen, you didn't tell anyone the missing pieces were copies. You tried to claim the insurance on them," Roland said.

"Your ex-wife stole them thinking you'd get a big payout because you never let her in on the truth," Jasmine added. "She did it for you. She's still in love with you, and you're too blind to see it. Either that or you're too wrapped up in yourself to notice. Even I could tell she's still in love with you. You're both crooks. You deserve each other."

Roland moved closer to Delacruz. "I won't humiliate you by cuffing you in here if you get up and come peacefully. Otherwise I'm afraid your photo will be all over the Internet if people see me cuff you and start pulling out their cell phones."

Delacruz drained his glass and stood up.

The guy on the stool next to him asked Jasmine, "Buy you a drink?"

"That would be nice." She slid onto Cameron's empty barstool.

Roland turned to Em. "Tell Leo and his family I had to leave. I doubt I'll be back before you close."

"That's okay." Em tried not to sound disappointed. "By the time this crowd is gone we'll be wiped out."

"I'd still like to come by later," Roland said.

"I'll be here."

# 43

AFTER ROLAND discretely walked Delacruz out, Em went behind the bar.

"You need a break," she told Sophie. It wasn't a question.

"Boy, do I." Sophie handed Em the order ticket Tiko had just put in, poured a huge glass of water, and headed toward the kitchen.

Em was pouring a round of Jailhouse Rocks when she heard a loud altercation near the stage. Her stomach knotted at the sound of a man's irate tone.

"My lawyer is all over this like stink on . . . on . . . poop!"

Em tried to see what was going on but couldn't until someone near the bar stepped away, and she recognized David Kane standing in front of Kiki. He was waving papers around and wasn't happy. His wife was right behind him.

"It was all in fun for the *fun*draiser," Kiki said. One by one the Maidens gathered around her.

Kane shouted, "I paid two thousand for a piece of art thinking it was going to go up in value. Do you think I'd have considered that for one minute had I known it was *monkey* art?"

His face was purple. His wife was hanging on his arm, trying to hold him back.

Kiki pulled herself up to her full height and yanked up the top of her black *pareau*. "Monkey art. The very idea is brilliant. What makes you think the paintings won't become more valuable anyway?"

"The very idea is insane!" Kane waved one of the papers he'd been holding in one hand.

"How do you know it's monkey art?" She pursed her lips and shook her head.

He waved the paper in her face again. "*This* is how I know." He held up a page with writing on it. "This came in the mail today. It's a certificate of authentication. It came with *this*." He held up a photograph. "That's a photo of the artist Alphonse Cappucchino, and it's signed.

Signed with a *handprint*. A monkey's handprint. Alphonse Cappucchino is a monkey!"

Big Estelle slapped herself on the forehead and yelled, "Mother!"

Outside the front door came the toot, toot, toot of Little Estelle's Gadabout and a second later Little Estelle rolled through the door. Em found herself regretting the refurbished handicapped ramp they'd recently installed.

Sometime in the past hour, Little Estelle must had slipped out, and now she was back with an oversized canvas tote bag balanced on the basket attached to her steering bar.

"Oh, no," Em mumbled. "Oh, friggin' no."

"What? What's going on?" Louie had been regaling patrons at the bar with one of his many stories. He had no idea what was going on.

Little Estelle kept tooting until the crowd parted as she wove around tables and made her way slowly to the stage area where Kiki and the Kanes were going at it toe-to-toe. A pall of silence fell over the bar. Folks at the back tables were on their feet. Everyone was watching the scene unfold as if it were an episode of *Trouble in Paradise*.

"Mother, what have you done?" Big Estelle stared at the wizened senior in horror.

"Alphonse worked his furry little butt off, and what thanks does he get? Flora gave me the names of all the people who bought paintings, so I made up certificates of authentication and sent them out with autographed photos of Alphonse. He'll finally get the credit he deserves."

Kane shouted, "See? See? She admits it. Alphonse Cappucchino *is* a chimp!"

"Technically he's no chimp. He's a capuchin monkey," Little Estelle said. "I'd be willing to bet he has more talent in his little paw than you or your lawyer put together."

Kane leaned over Little Estelle. "I don't care if he can fart nickels. I want my money back. So will all the other buyers when they find out about this."

Louie leaned closer to Em. "Am I drunk, or did the bag on Little Estelle's handlebars just move on its own?"

"Oh, no." Em ran around the end of the bar.

"What?" Louie said. "What's happening?"

"Pray there's nothing in that bag." She headed for the stage area where the Maidens had Kiki's back.

Kiki was focused on Kane and had no idea what was going on. "You said you'd never seen a piece of art so inspired. So dramatic. You said no piece of art ever spoke to you the way the Cappucchinos do. That's a quote."

"I was duped. It was all a big hoax."

Suddenly the top of the canvas tote flew open. A loud demonic sound, something between chatter, laughter, and a howl came from inside. A red fez slowly rose out of the top of the tote followed by the cream-colored fur on Alphonse's head, neck, and shoulders. His mouth was wide open, forming something between a smile and a grimace.

Kiki opened her mouth to scream, but nothing came out. The phalanx of Hula Maidens closed around her. Em couldn't get there fast enough to be of any help unless she ran across tabletops. It turned out she didn't have to worry.

Alphonse leapt onto a table then from one to another until he ended up on the bar. He grabbed a martini glass in his paw and did a tap dance for a minute. He rolled his lips under and bared his teeth in a terrifying imitation of a smile. The crowd started clapping in time to his steps. The Tiki Tones's drummer picked up the beat, and the rest of the band started playing "Hey, Hey We're the Monkees." Those old enough to remember the song sang along.

Em spotted Kiki in the middle of the circle of Maidens. She was pale but still on her feet watching Alphonse cavort on the bar. Kiki's gaze scanned the crowd. Then she snapped her fingers. Pat grabbed the mic from the singer's microphone stand. The Tiki Tones stopped playing.

"Isn't that about the cutest thing you've ever seen?" Kiki stared right into David Kane's face. "Owning one of his paintings would be pretty darn incredible, wouldn't it, folks? We have a few left, but they're going fast. If anyone is interested, let me know."

By now the entire crowd was in love with Alphonse. They were chanting his name.

Without musical accompaniment he danced a minute or two longer and then stopped. Holding his martini glass up to Louie, Alphonse chattered away until Louie filled it with a splash of gold rum. Then the capuchin climbed to the top shelf of the bar without spilling a drop, sat down, crossed his legs, and sipped his martini.

"Isn't that about the most precious thing ever?" Little Estelle waved at Alphonse, and he threw her a kiss.

Kiki handed the mic back to Danny, leader of the Tiki Tones. Her color was slowly coming back, but she carefully kept one eye on Alphonse. Em finally made her way over to Kiki.

"He didn't attack me." Kiki looked a little stunned, but at least she could still string a sentence together. "He didn't attack."

"Hell no," Little Estelle said. "All those anger management classes and all that art therapy is paying off. My Alphonse Cappucchino's as close to a national treasure as you can get."

Atop the bar, the national treasure let out a couple of ear-splitting screams, waved his martini glass, and toasted the crowd.

# 44

IT WAS MIDNIGHT before the bar was empty except for Uncle Louie, the Goddess staff, and Kiki, who was waiting for Kimo. No one seemed to have the energy to get up and go home. Em explained Delacruz's involvement in his own art hoax as briefly as she could, which also explained why Roland had disappeared from the party early.

"I thought we'd never get that monkey off the bar." Uncle Louie was the only one who still had any energy left. Em was convinced he siphoned all his get-up-and-go from a crowd.

"No one was going to budge until Alphonse came down, either," Tiko said.

Buzzy smiled at Tiko. "He didn't even go for the banana mango smoothie you fixed him."

"He might have if I'd put rum in it," Louie said. "But he wasn't coming down for love or money."

Em yawned. "Every time someone reached for him, he bared his teeth. It was a good idea to wait until he passed out and rolled off."

"Thank gosh he didn't hurt himself when he hit the ice bin," Tiko said.

"He's a great draw." Louie's focus was always entertainment. "Who woulda ever thought we'd have a dancing monkey in here?"

"Don't think he's a permanent fixture. I told Little Estelle never again," Em said.

"Waste of breath." Sophie had her feet up on the long banquette across from her. Her hair was tipped with neon purple, but the spiked ends had wilted hours ago.

"I think we should add him to the show." Louie wasn't giving up.

Kiki had been leaning back with her eyes closed, but she quickly sat up. "Let's not go that far, Louie. He and I may have had a truce tonight, but I'd prefer not to be around him. Besides, I think Andromeda is interested in joining the Hula Maidens. Isn't a dancing hippie enough?"

"Yeah." Kimo drained a beer bottle. "And don't forget there's the dancing midget."

Kiki slapped his arm. "How many times do I have to tell you that's not politically correct? Precious is a Little Person."

"I know. That's what I said. You ready to go?" Kimo stood up and pulled his truck keys out of his shorts.

"Before you go, like, I'd like to say somethin' to Kiki and all of you," Buzzy said.

He surprised Em by speaking up again. She'd never seen him so animated. Then again, she'd never seen him so sober.

Kimo sat back down. Everyone appeared to be as shocked as Em by Buzzy addressing what he probably considered a crowd.

"I want to thank you all for everything. You're my family, ya know? You raised money for me and threw this great party. Now that you know my real name, I'm hoping that won't change anything."

"We know your family disowned you," Kiki admitted.

"No biggie," he said. Then he said directly to Kiki, "I heard what that guy said about suing you over the monkey paintings. No worries. I'm gonna give you the money to pay back all the people who bought them. You sold them for my benefit, so I can't let you and the Hula Maidens get sued."

"Don't you worry," Kiki said. "I'm hoping after tonight when word gets out about Alphonse's appearance they'll want to keep the paintings. Everyone sure loved him."

"The show didn't cost them a dime," Louie said. "But people react differently when they think they got ripped off."

"Besides, it's a lot of money, Buzzy," Em said.

"No worries." Buzzy smiled. Em found herself thinking he actually had a couple really nice teeth. "I've got plenty. I can pay them back."

"Plenty of what?" Tiko stared as if she'd never seen him before.

"Plenty of money I don't need. Nobody in the family knows my little sister's still in contact with me. She inherited my share of Granddad's trust and never felt right keeping it. So every once in a while she sends me money. I had enough to pay for a lawyer if I needed one. I want to give it to you, Kiki, to pay off the monkey business."

"You have money?" Uncle Louie looked stunned.

"Lots of it," Buzzy said.

"Where?" Sophie wanted to know.

"In Ziploc bags stuffed in my tree."

Kimo held up his empty beer bottle. "How 'bout a toast. To Buford!"

Buzzy's smile faded.

"What's wrong?" Tiko asked. "You got the shakes? You need a smoothie?"

"I'll pay off any angry art patrons on one condition," he said.

"What's that?" Kiki leaned on the table.

"Like, you gotta never, ever call me Buford again."

Everyone agreed not to. There were a few more toasts: one to Kiki for the fundraiser and the Hula Maidens' first flawless performance, one to Kimo for keeping up with the dinner orders. Sophie toasted Tiko for pitching in so well. Louie hailed Sophie for breaking their all-time record for most drinks served in one night.

One by one they all filtered out. Em was so exhausted she could barely hold her head up. Finally she and Buzzy were the only ones left.

"I'd appreciate it if you let me keep my job bussing tables," Buzzy said to Em.

"I've been thinking I might have you paint a few signs if you're ever up for art work."

"Maybe." He got up to walk to the door and paused, looking back. "You remember he said he hated cats?"

Em wondered about the extent of his possible brain cell damage for a second. Or maybe it was a casualty of living on Kauai, and her own were diminishing.

"I'm sorry," she said. "Who hates cats?"

"The old guy, the one who died in the driveway that night. His spirit was hanging around, and he said he hated cats."

Em rubbed her forehead above the bridge of her nose. "Uncle Bass?"

"Yeah. The dead guy."

"I remember now. You did say that. I thought he meant *feral* cats."

"Right, but he was really talking about . . ."

"Cat Woman," Em said.

"Yep. Cat Woman, get it? It was her all along." Buzzy nodded and walked out the door into the night. Amazed, she watched him for a couple of minutes. Maybe he did have psychic powers.

*You've already lived on Kauai too long.*

She tried not to let the idea terrify her.

She exited through the office and had just locked the door on the parking lot side of the building. She was headed to the beach house when Roland drove up. An immediate jolt of adrenaline woke her up a bit, but her steps were still dragging. She watched him park and cross the lot to her.

"You look like you've had it." He draped an arm around her waist.

"What a night." Em sagged against him. "The place has never been so crowded."

"Everybody loves a party."

"Everyone loves all-night happy hour prices. Not to mention a dancing monkey."

"Don't tell me," he said.

"Yep. Alphonse made a surprise appearance thanks to Little Estelle."

"Did Kiki survive?"

"She did. Not only that, but the Hula Maidens actually performed a new song, and it went off without a hitch. No one fell off the stage; no one set their hair on fire. It was amazing."

"Sounds like everything worked out. Couldn't have asked for more, eh?"

"I should have paid closer attention to what Buzzy said the night of the Delacruz robbery. He wouldn't have had to sit in jail, and the case would have been solved sooner."

"How?"

"Buzzy's psychic connections. The night Uncle Bass died, Buzzy said the old man spoke to him. He said Sebastian's spirit was still hanging around, and he told Buzzy that he hated cats. I'll admit it's cryptic, but it was a heavy clue."

"Cat Woman."

"Right. Cat Woman. Uncle Bass tried to tell Buzzy who robbed the house and who he chased down the driveway. Who knew that *I hate cats* translates in psychic afterlife chatter to Alanna in her cat suit."

"You really believe that?"

She shrugged. "Unfortunately, it kinda makes sense."

"You really want to believe in a guy who communes with dolphins and lives in a tree?"

"People believe in stuff that makes about as much sense." They'd reached the front door. "I'm dead on my feet, or I'd ask you in," she said.

"Your uncle home?"

"He's home. Since his fiancée drove her car over the edge of the road and drowned he hasn't dated much. He's home every night."

Roland brushed a wayward lock of her hair back over her ear. Her ponytail had died hours ago. "No worries, I just came by to say goodnight."

"You live in Kapa'a. Kind of out of the way, isn't it?"

"You're not happy to see me?" He looped his arms around her waist, drew her closer.

"I'm always happy to see you."

"So, did you talk to your neighbor this morning? About New York?"

Em laughed. "Is that why you're here? That's been bugging you?"

"As a matter of fact, it has. What did he want?"

"As a matter of fact, I did talk to him. Are you still afraid I'm moving to New York with Nat?"

"Should I be?"

"I am moving, actually."

Roland went dead silent and stared down at her.

Em smiled. "I'm moving into his house next door. He asked if I'd like to housesit for six months, keep the place open, fight off the geckos and the mildew, and stay there until he gets back. Seeing as how it's right next door to the Goddess and my uncle, I said yes."

When Roland didn't respond she added, "Naturally, I'll move out when the movie wraps and Nat comes back."

It was a little too dark to see his expression clearly. She couldn't tell what he was thinking. "So, why are you so quiet?"

"I'm just trying to wrap my mind around you having your own place," he said.

"Maybe you should wrap your mind around figuring out where to park that undercover cop car so no one will know when you're spending the night."

# Tropical Libations from Uncle Louie's Legendary Booze Bible

## Alphonse Cappucchino

*A drink worthy of the famous yet reclusive fez wearing artist, Alphonse Cappucchino, who not only paints but has been known to entertain a crowd for hours with his monkeyshines. It's a drink more than a monkey will love.*

½ large frozen banana or one small banana
1 oz. golden rum
1 oz. dark rum
½ tsp. instant coffee crystals
Chocolate syrup
Ice

Mix all ingredients except the chocolate in a blender and blend on high until frothy.

Drizzle Chocolate syrup around the inside of a martini glass.

Pour in the drink mix and enjoy!

## Thriller

*Uncle Louie traveled to Korowai, Southeast of Java where he photographed the tree houses of the Paupuan tribe, until he discovered they lived high off the jungle floor because they feared their headhunting neighbors. Needless to say, Louie was outta there fast.* Thriller *was such a hit Uncle Louie makes a cocktail shaker full at a time and just stirs the ingredients.*

20 oz. (5 tall jiggers) Tequila
20 oz. (5 tall jiggers) Triple sec
4 oz. (1 tall jigger) of Chili Pepper Water (see recipe below)
Juice of 1 Lime
Lime slice for garnish

Pour all into a shaker. Stir. Pour over ice in a margarita or cocktail glass. Garnish with lime slice.


## Chili Pepper Water

*Kimo says this is a great addition to soups, stews, beverages or whatever you'd like to spice up.*

1 garlic glove, peeled and diced
2 fresh red Hawaiian chili peppers, stems removed and halved
1 teaspoon Hawaiian salt
1 tablespoon white vinegar
1 3/4 cup water

Place and garlic, peppers and salt into a bowl and mash together. Place chili pepper mixture into a bottle or jar. Next, boil water and vinegar together, turn off heat. Cool about 10-15 minutes and add to pepper mixture in the jar. Seal tightly and keep refrigerated. Makes about 2 cups.


## Jailhouse on the Rocks

*A sweet concoction created to celebrate Buzzy's release from the slammer. When Louie discovered Buzzy was on the wagon, he figured the aging hippie would still enjoy the sugar, lime and pineapple mixture over ice.*

1 tsp. granulated sugar
¼ oz. lime juice
¼ oz. pineapple juice
1 and ¼ oz. white rum

Shake with cracked ice. Pour ingredients from shaker without straining over more ice. Decorate with lime round.


## Kimo's Easy Rum Soaked Tropical Upside-Down Yum Cake

*Kimo's go-to dessert for any special (or not so special) occasion.*

1 Box Yellow Cake Mix (and whatever ingredients called for on the box)
2 Sliced Bananas
1 20 oz. can pineapple slices (drain and reserve juice)
Shredded coconut (much as you like)
1 6 oz. jar Maraschino cherries

½ cup or more chopped Macadamia nuts (or pecan halves) to taste
¼ C. Butter
1 Cup Brown Sugar
Golden rum (optional)

Heat oven to 350 degrees.

Melt the butter in a 9x13 pan. Evenly sprinkle brown sugar over it.

Lay the sliced bananas, pineapple slices, and any other small chunks of tropical fruit you like (mango, papaya) on the brown sugar and butter mixture. Arrange Maraschino cherries and sprinkle on nuts and coconut. Gently press down a bit.

Mix the cake as directed on the box but add reserved pineapple juice to liquid required on box for whatever amount box calls for. Mix batter and pour gently over the fruit and nut mix. Bake according to package directions.

Have a tray ready to turn the cake onto when it's done baking, flip it over so that it's upside down and all the delicious fruit and buttery brown sugar topping drizzles down over cake.

Optional: Poke thin holes in the cake with toothpicks and drizzle rum over cake. Let it absorb the flavor before serving. Cool 30 minutes. Serve warm or cool with some whipped cream if desired. YUM. Garnish with orchids or other flowers.

## Kimo's "Retro" Rumaki Pupu

*Kimo has been serving Rumaki (sometimes known as rumake) for as long as he can remember. It was a hit at Trader Vic's and other Tiki restaurants in the 50's and 60's and never goes out of style. Be sure to make plenty because these ono (yummy) pupus will be gone wikiwiki!*

For 24 servings you will need:

8 slices Bacon (cut into thirds)
12 whole Water Chestnuts
12 whole pitted dates
(OR 12 each of either liver, pineapple, shrimp or scallops to wrap in bacon strips)
24 Toothpicks
Your favorite teriyaki sauce or barbeque sauce.

Soak water chestnuts or whatever you are using in marinade for at least 30 minutes.

Wrap in bacon and secure with toothpick. Brush with marinade. Broil for 10 to 15 minutes until bacon is crisp or you can bake 20 -25 minutes at 375 degrees. Half way through you can roll them over.

**Note:** Some cooks like to use ½ pieces of bacon per rumaki but Kimo thinks that's too much bacon so he cuts the bacon into thirds.

# About the Author

JILL MARIE LANDIS has written nearly thirty novels which have earned distinguished awards and slots on such national bestseller lists as the USA TODAY Top 50 and the New York Times Best Sellers Plus. She is a seven-time finalist for Romance Writers of America's RITA Award in both Single Title and Contemporary Romance as well as a Golden Heart and RITA Award winner. She's written historical and contemporary romance, inspirational historical romance, and she is now penning the Tiki Goddess Mysteries.

Visit her at thetikigoddess.com

CPSIA information can be obtained at www.ICGtesting.com
Printed in the USA
LVOW11s1817140416

483632LV00002B/473/P